Hudson Lake

By Laura Mazzuca Toops

Twilight Times Books
Kingsport, Tennessee

Hudson Lake

This is a work of fiction, although inspired by actual events. All concepts, characters and events portrayed in this book are used fictitiously and any resemblance to real people or events is purely coincidental.

Paladin Timeless Books, an imprint of
Twilight Times Books
Kingsport, TN 37664
www.twilighttimesbooks.com/

First paperback printing, February 2007

Library of Congress Cataloging-in-Publication Data

Toops, Laura Mazzuca, 1955-
  Hudson Lake / by Laura Mazzuca Toops.
      p. cm.
   ISBN-13: 978-1-933353-57-9 (pbk. : alk. paper)
   ISBN-10: 1-933353-57-0 (pbk. : alk. paper)
  1. Chicago (Ill.)--Fiction. I. Title.
  PS3620.O586H83 2006
  813'.6--dc22
                2006009270

Cover art by Bryan Shackelford

Printed in the United States of America

To Banjo

Acknowledgments

I'd like to thank everyone who assisted in the research, writing and general midwifery of this novel:

Phil Pospychala, who started it all; Rich Johnson, a gentleman and a scholar; Fred Shafer of Northwestern University, for his literary and editorial expertise; Kevin Baker, for encouragement, wisdom and martinis; Nancy Hertz, for the novel's essential re-vision; Mike and Leah Bezin, for bringing me to Hudson Lake in the first place; Bill Saunders, for his seminal 1999 article on Bix at Hudson Lake; Sue Fischer, a crack troubleshooter of historical inaccuracy; Dana Groves at the New Carlisle Historical Society and Jim Rodgers at the La Porte County Historical Society, for photo reproductions; Kristen Sanders, archivist at Indiana University, for information on Harriet's freshman coursework; Kristi Corlett, my untiring reader and friend, *namaste*; the microfilm departments at the Chicago Public Library and St. Joseph County Public Library; the Michigan City Library and its terrific Web site; Alma, who personally introduced me to the ghosts at the Blue Lantern; Gus, Liz, Joe, Eric and the old Friday night gang at Nevin's; Emily, Doug and John, who lived and breathed Bix along with me; and to everyone else who finds inspiration, joy and comfort in the life and music of Bix Beiderbecke. Thanks!

Tram: Say now, how come there ain't no singin' on this here record?
Bing: Mr. Tram, there's gonna be singin' presently, of a sort.
Tram: Well, you know I ain't heard no singin' yet.
Bing: You just get a load of this song—(he scats)
Tram: Is that it?
Bing: Well now, that's part of it, that's the prelude...

— *Patter between Frank Trumbauer and Bing Crosby, "Mississippi Mud"*
(Okeh, Jan. 20, 1928)

Prelude

June 1926
Hudson Lake Resort
New Carlisle, Indiana

Her name was Joy. It was an assumed name and an assumed attitude, because joy wasn't something she always felt, or at least something she hadn't felt in years.

Once she was called it, she lived it—with her brassy bobbed red hair, wide rouged mouth and raucous laugh, the laugh that echoed all the way across the lake from her room on the third floor of the Hotel Hudson. You could hear her all hours of the day, with her wind-up portable phonograph and that laugh.

Every day that June, in the heat of the late morning, Joy would come downstairs in a bathing suit and robe and high-heeled slippers. She'd cross the road to the lake, go down to the pebbly shallows at the edge and stick her feet in, splaying her toes with their crimson-painted nails so the distorted image of her foot beneath the clear water looked like a squat, white starfish. She'd ease in up to her waist, squealing at the cold, the water dyeing the bottom half of her red wool bathing suit a dark maroon. And then she'd wade back to shore, light a cigarette, and crunch back along the gravel path to the little yellow cottage in the field behind the hotel, the one where the single musicians lived.

At twilight, when the dwindling sun dyed the lake the color of Joy's bathing suit, the little yellow cottage and the cottages along the shore began to stir. Lights came on; swatches of music, muffled conversation and laughter floated out across the water; screen doors squeaked open and closed on rusty hinges like a badly tuned violin section. Once it was dusk, Joy would emerge from the little yellow cottage, crooning some hot jazz song in a mournful contralto, cigarette tip glowing in the darkness, and stagger back to the hotel.

Back in Chicago, some seventy miles away, streets intersected at uncompromising right angles, a glowing grid outlined by rows of streetlights connected like a string of pearls. Lines of autos headed down the lakefront in a serpentine dance from the north to the south, from the east at the beaches and the frenetic glow of State Street to the darkened bungalows to the west. People went to sleep or came awake in hordes. They headed to the Loop, Boul Mich and Uptown cafes and hotels for a dose of the businessman's bounce, the sweet stuff, all oozing saxes and formal arrangements, played by respectable white men reading music from charts—Vincent Lopez at the College Inn, Fred Travers and His Orchestra at the bepalmed Terrace Garden in the Morrison Hotel, Ralph Williams and the Rainbo Gardens Orchestra on the North Side.

Or they'd pass the Loop and keep going south to the black-and-tans, joints with peeling paint and mismatched chairs, where the music ran from hot cornet to low-down gutbucket as purveyed by King Oliver, Louis Armstrong, Johnny Dodds, all sleek and citified in shiny black tuxedos and stiff wing collars.

All over town, from the swanky hotels to the lowest dives, dance floors were a crush of sweating and scented men and women, pressed against each other under layers of blue serge and beaded chiffon, spurred on and on by music and bootleg gin until the joints closed at two, at three, at dawn, or when the dancers dropped.

But at Hudson Lake, with frogs thrumming along the shore and a solitary duck on its black, glassy surface, it was usually quiet enough to hear Joy singing her sad song in the twilight—at least until eight every night except Mondays, when the Jean Goldkette Orchestra, led by Frankie Trumbauer and featuring Bix Beiderbecke on cornet, hit the bandstand of the dance hall.

And the music they played wasn't the businessman's bounce, wasn't the gutbucket of the South Side, but something else. It was something that drew all those Chicago musicians to hear them every Saturday and Sunday, something that made the most tone-deaf local Hoosiers cock their heads for an instant and listen as if a lover with the sweetest voice was calling them from a long distance away. It was something that made Joy smile, thinking how the notes oozed from the bell of a horn, viscous and golden as honey, tickling into her ears as she lay on the saggy mattress in her room at the Hotel Hudson, singing her own sweet songs.

Chapter 1

The Blue Lantern sprawled along the lake, ready to ooze music from its bank of windows facing the water. Clumps of loud, laughing people disembarked from the South Shore train stop across Chicago Road and meandered over.

Harriet Braun stared at the slick young men in flashy suits, some wearing tuxedos and toting instrument cases, as if coming from gigs of their own. Women in frocks that probably cost more than Harriet would make all summer were talking to each other in languid drawls, blowing cigarette smoke through aristocratic nostrils and looking around at the other clientele from under kohled eyes.

"Harriet!" She turned. Charlie Horvath, the manager who worked for Jean Goldkette, was sweating with excitement, slapping shoulders and steering groups of revelers through the balmy evening air toward the dance hall. He grinned at her. "So you finally decided to come out and hear the band. Is this your first show?"

Harriet smiled and fell into step with Horvath and the rest of the crowd. "Funny, isn't it? I mainly took the job because of the music, and this is the first chance I've gotten to see the band, although I can hear it loud and clear from across the road. Mrs. Smith keeps me so busy at the hotel I don't have much of a chance to have any fun."

Horvath rolled his eyes dramatically. "Oh, Mrs. Smith runs that little hotel like a prison. Why couldn't a smart, pretty college girl like you find a better place to work over the summer?"

"Oh, it's not so bad. Anyhow, I'm going to have fun tonight."

"Good for you!" Horvath barked. "But watch yourself. Sometimes there's trouble." And then he was gone, busy ushering people into the Blue Lantern.

Funny Horvath should say that, Harried mused. It was just what Mrs. Smith was always saying, how the citified musicians from the Jean Goldkette band didn't belong here and were going to cause trouble. They didn't look like much trouble to Harriet. Although she hadn't seen them play yet, she'd caught glimpses of the musicians, mostly when they were lined up in the hotel hallway in their bathrobes, spindly white legs exposed, towels over arms, waiting to get a 25-cent bath before the big Saturday night show.

True, they didn't look like the Hotel Hudson's usual clientele—families from Michigan City and South Bend, with peeling sunburned skin and bland faces, alike as a herd of Hereford cows. The musicians were alike in a different way—fast-talking, cigarette smoking, with rapid-fire city slang and flashy clothes, smelling of hair pomade and bootleg alcohol.

But they seemed harmless. Half of them were married, their wives smiling and complacent in beacon robes and pincurls, chatting among themselves on the cottage porches during the day. And the single ones didn't look much different from the boys Harriet dated at Indiana U.

As she pushed through the crowd into the brightly-lit soda fountain up front, Harriet noticed that Ray Reynolds, the soda jerk, and his teenaged assistant were doing a booming business. People were jammed in shoulder to shoulder at the counter, and Ray's hands were a blur as he wielded dripping metal scoopers of strawberry and vanilla, fizzled seltzer into long, tall glasses, sluiced syrup over mounds of whipped cream and minted fragrant golden coins of banana slices.

Harriet eased her way through the crowd, inhaling the crush of sweat, smoke, powder and perfume, all underlined by the sharp odor of shellac that Horvath had administered to the wooden surfaces just last week. And another odor, faint but noticeable, emanating from the soda fountain—the smell of bootleg liquor. It was an open secret that Ray dispensed shots of local moonshine into the bottles of Blue Bird cola and Orange Squeeze soda pop he sold. There had been a lot of big police raids in South Bend lately, with speakeasies getting chopped up and people thrown in jail. Harriet hoped Ray was discreet enough to avoid something like that at the Blue Lantern. Maybe that's what Horvath meant by trouble.

"Li'l sister! There ya are!" Joy was resplendent in a splash of glittering red silk, clutching the arm of a swarthy, bespectacled boy with a ribbon of dance tickets in his hand. He was chewing his bottom lip and gazing at Joy's breasts with an expression of undisguised lust.

"You look adorable, honey! Okay, the dress is a little on the Mary Pickford side, but what the hell, you're so cute it don't even matter. Harriet, meet Benny. He's here to see the band. This kid can play the clarinet like nobody's business, right, honey? Now, come on. I got us the best seats in the house, right in front of the bandstand, and I hadda fight Horvath tooth an' nail to keep 'em. Benny, go grab us our table, okay?" As Benny walked away, Joy linked arms with Harriet and immediately began whispering into her ear, her breath moist and urgent.

"Ohmygod, honey, I'm so glad you're here. I can handle Benny, he's just a sweet little puppy dog, but this greenhorn I danced with before has been followin' me around all goddamn night. He's as big as a house and I think he wants me to bear his children, for God's sake. And say, I got a load of how old Charlie Horvath was givin' *you* the eye. Honest to God, kiddo, men, you can't live with 'em and you can't shoot 'em..." She led Harriet through a set of French doors and into the dance hall.

The room was long and arch-ceilinged. Two aisles, open to banks of windows and arranged with tables and chairs, ran on both sides of the long dance floor. The end of the room overlooked Hudson Lake from a porch at the back. Amber bulbs flickered in bronze sconces on the walls between the windows, and the newly waxed and varnished dance floor reflected lights off its surface like the lake reflected stars.

Joy hustled them to their table and settled into a chair, glancing around the room like a fluttering homing pigeon finally at rest. "Benny, be a doll and run get mama a bottle of Blue Bird *with*, will ya? Here's some dough. Get one for you and li'l sister, too." The boy walked through the crowd and Joy leaned across the table confidentially. "I tell ya, that kid can play. He just landed a job with a big orchestra, and him only seventeen. In a couple years he'll be givin' a lot of these fellas a run for their money."

"How do you know all these musicians?" Harriet asked, glancing around the room at the well-dressed crowd that clearly wasn't local. I'm local, she thought, fingering the folds of her Mary Pickford number. She wished she'd let Joy talk her into borrowing her arsenic-green satin dress, the one cut far down the back that would have showed her shoulder blades.

"Why, from Chicago, toots. I told you that's where I'm from, didn't I?" Joy clacked her beaded handbag onto the table and dug for cigarettes. "Well, maybe I didn't. I seen little Benny play at the Hull House on the West Side, years ago, strictly yokel dances for the wops and the hebes. But I knew right away he had something." She lit up, her smile turning Cheshire-like. "Bickie took me."

"You mean the trumpet player in the band?"

"*Cornet*. Just like Louie Armstrong. I seen him, too. Oh yeah, we went *everywhere.* The Friar's Inn, Valentino's, the Rendez-Vous where Bickie played, even the Sunset and the other nigger joints on the South Side. We heard all the hottest bands in the city."

"I've seen a lot of bands, too," Harriet said, trying to sound worldly. "Rudy loves jazz. Last winter and spring we went to hear every band that came on campus, and we even went to Kansas City with Rudy's brother once to hear Coon-Sanders' Nighthawks."

Joy gave her a smile that Harriet interpreted as pitying. She puffed her cigarette, grinning, and leaned toward Harriet again. "These guys tonight are better than any of 'em. And you'll see why."

Benny headed back toward their table, carrying three pop bottles. Joy air-kissed him a thanks, and Harriet swallowed a mouthful, practically spitting it out on the table.

"God, what *is* this...."

"Aw, damn it, did Ray put in too much pop again? Benny, you know you have to watch him." Joy sipped at her straw. "No, it's fine. What's wrong, li'l sister?"

Harriet sniffed the bottle. "It's...."

"Not the best stuff in LaPorte County, but at least it'll get ya happy. What's wrong, don't you like gin?"

Harriet put down the bottle and laughed, pushing it toward Joy. "I don't drink much, that's all."

Joy lifted her bottle toward Harriet. "Your funeral, kiddo. Oh, here comes Itzy. That means they'll be startin' any time."

Harriet watched as a lanky man in a tuxedo with a long, lugubrious face and a nose to match mounted the bandstand and began playing notes on the piano, his ear inclined toward the keyboard to hear over the crowd. One by one, other tuxedoed band members followed him onstage, setting up music racks, tootling on saxophones and clarinets, tapping cymbals and drumheads and wooden percussion blocks.

Horvath stepped onstage and murmured something to a serious-looking young man holding a saxophone. They both looked over the crowd, as if searching for someone. And then Horvath pointed and grinned and the sax man turned to the other musicians, giving them a cue. Harriet turned to see the last musician stride across the floor and step up on the stage. She started laughing.

"So *that's* Bickie?" she asked Joy, who was pointing and laughing at the man in the rumpled tuxedo and crooked bow tie. "Bix? The guy you've been talking about all this time?"

"Hey, Beiderbecke, fix your soup and fish!" Benny called.

Horvath clapped for attention. "Ladies and gentlemen, welcome to the beautiful Blue Lantern Inn. I'm Charlie Horvath, general manager of the Jean Goldkette organization, and it is with great pleasure that I'd like to introduce tonight's entertainment—direct from Detroit, the fabulous Jean Goldkette Orchestra, under the direction of the renowned Frank Trumbauer on saxophone..." the wooden-faced man took a bow, "...and on cornet, the incomparable Mr. Bix Beiderbecke!"

The man Joy called Bickie had his back to the crowd, arranging a chair for himself by the piano and the drum kit, not out in front the way you'd think a horn player should be. He turned and waved, more in dismissal than acknowledgement.

Harriet looked around, surprised to see that more than half the crowd was on its feet, whistling and stomping in recognition of this man with the incongruous features of a baby doll—small red mouth, snub nose, and eyes that seemed to be laughing at something. He was medium height and solidly built, and Harriet was reminded of Rudy and his fraternity brothers, the ones who played football. He sat in the chair between the piano and the drum kit and crossed one knee over the other, wiped his mouth with the back of his hand, and put the horn to his lips. And then Trumbauer counted to four and the band started to play.

They kicked off with "Nobody's Sweetheart," opening with the cornet player and his startlingly clean tones, then shifting to the sax man, who played out front with all the seriousness of a monk. It was a tricky part, replete with arpeggios and trills, and the band thumped along behind him, nobody stealing his thunder. But halfway through the tune, the saxophone and the cornet began exchanging licks in an intuitive call-and-response way that had the savvy crowd on its feet, some dancing, others at tables and up by the bandstand, just listening.

She sat there, mouth open, half-smiling, listening to the two instruments playing tag with each other. The sax would play a figure and coyly wait, and the cornet would follow suit, answering with an echoing phrase, twisted just enough to make it different. And then both instruments hooked up in harmony, like a couple of buddies out on the town with arms around each other's shoulders, escorting the tune to its end.

Joy slapped Harriet on the arm as the crowd hollered its approval. "Well?" she shouted over the noise. "Whaddaya think?"

"They're great!" Harriet said and before she knew it Joy and Benny had carried her up to the bandstand, Joy elbowing her way through the crowd of "alligators" hanging around the stage, and directly to the patent-leather feet of Trumbauer himself. Joy reached up and tugged at his pants cuff.

"Hi, Frankie," she said, winking. The dour-faced man glanced down, rolled his eyes and signaled the band, which kicked into a speeded-up version of "Dinah." This time the cornet player took the lead, driving the band like a getaway car. At the chorus he and the trumpet man were as tight as a matched pair of horses in harness and then the cornet took a solo turn, delivering an effortless arc of notes that had the crowd around the bandstand shouting for more.

When he was done, the cornet player just put his horn on his knee and sat there, lips pursed, as if pondering what he just said on his instrument and how he should have worded it differently. And then it was his turn for a solo again and instead of standing up to take it, he leaned over in his chair, the bell of the horn pointed at the floor, and let fly a whirl of sound, as easy as breathing.

Harriet felt a tap on the shoulder and before she knew it Benny had pulled her onto the dance floor, with Joy cheering them on. She let him lead her in an easy fox trot, one with the crowd, the music making every movement as fluid as swimming.

She stopped counting tunes and dance partners after that, only cried out song titles in pleased surprise as the music roared past and a stream of men from the stag line cut in on each other to dance with her. She never got a chance to try another sip of her doctored Blue Bird pop because she never got back to the table, until Trumbauer finally announced a break.

And then Joy shook herself out of the embrace of a raw-boned boy with the sunburned look of a farmer and dragged Harriet and Benny back to the darkened porch that was open to the breeze off the lake.

"That's him, the big rube," she whispered to Harriet, nodding toward the raw-boned boy. "I think I shook him. I told him Bickie's from Chicago, and a friend of Al Capone's. Think that'll hold him?" She laughed and pulled up a cane-backed chair. "The guys in the band always come out here on their breaks," she said, waving one of the Japanese paper fans that the dance hall passed out as party favors. Her red dress was dark with sweat under the arms, her wet hair sticking to forehead and cheeks in jagged spikes. She nodded. "Here he is now."

Bix had to stop about a dozen times between the bandstand and the porch to shake hands with people, but he eventually made it. A lanky, grinning young man who Harriet recognized as the band's clarinet player trailed behind him.

Bix slapped Benny on the back and sank down into a chair between him and Joy.

"How'd it sound?" he asked, pulling a flask from his breast pocket and offering it to Benny.

"Fuzzy's a little off tonight," Benny said, passing the flask to Joy.

"Yeah, and I am, too. That 'Suzie' solo was pretty rotten, I thought, right after I blew it."

"Aw, shut up, Beiderbecke," jeered the clarinet player. "We all know you really think you can walk on water."

"Here he goes, fishing for compliments," Joy laughed, tilting the gurgling flask to her mouth. "Sounded fine to me. What'd you think, li'l sister?"

Harriet felt her face burn as everyone turned to look at her. "Oh, I'm no expert. I just love good, hot dance music," she said. "I've heard a lot of bands at the university, and this orchestra is the best yet."

"Oh? Where d'ya go to school?" Bix asked. He had dark, intense eyes and a way of staring that made Harriet feel uncomfortable.

"Indiana U."

"Nice campus," he said, taking the flask from Joy and downing a deep swallow. "We played there with the Wolverines a couple years back, and for the junior prom just last month." He drank again and extended the flask to Harriet.

"Listen to Joe College," Joy hooted. "Here, she don't drink. Gimme."

The clarinet player cleared his throat. "*I* drink," he said.

"You sure?" Bix asked Harriet, shaking the flask. "Still half left. Good stuff, too."

"Oh, why not," Harriet said. "Thanks." She watched her hand reach for the flask, feeling a mild shock at her own daring. Not that she'd never had a drink before; she just didn't like it. But in the presence of this sophisticated group of musicians, refusing a drink just seemed too priggish, too *local*. She put the flask to her lips and allowed a shallow mouthful to trickle in, swallowing quickly so her eyes wouldn't water at the lingering burn.

"Hey, Beiderbecke, I said *I* drink!" the clarinet player called again.

"Yeah, yeah, Russell, that's a given. What's your name?" he asked, leaning forward, forearms on knees, eyes glittering up at Harriet in the half-light.

"Oh, I forgot!" Joy said, slapping Bix on the arm with her fan. "Guess I'll never make the social register. Harriet Braun, meet Bix Beiderbecke. Bix, Harriet Braun. And the stringbean who's so thirsty is Pee Wee Russell."

The clarinet player finally intercepted the hip flask as Bix leaned over to shake Harriet's hand. She felt a sudden tickle of sexual response between her legs. *Why?* she thought, resentful of her body's mindless reaction. He isn't anything to look at. *His tuxedo isn't pressed right, and his hand's all sweaty, his ears stick out like jug handles and his hair's coming loose from the pomade he glossed it back with.* She thought of Rudy's self-assured smile, wavy blond hair, athletic build. If Rudy played the cornet, he'd never ask anyone if it sounded all right, even if it didn't. It must be his eyes, she thought, that and the way he plays. It sure as heck isn't anything else.

Harriet reflexively jerked her hand away, then laughed to disguise the rudeness of the gesture, taking another shallow sip from the flask to cover her embarrassment.

"Excuse me."

They all looked up. The raw-boned boy in the wrinkled linen suit who had been dancing with Joy stood over them, weaving. Harriet could smell the fumes of bootleg hooch from where she sat. "I come to ask Joy if she wants a soda."

"No thanks, dearie, I'm already drinking," Joy trilled, white teeth gleaming. "Say, didn't I tell you I was with Bickie here?"

The boy's jaw worked under his sunburned cheek, as if he was grinding his teeth together. "That's not what you said before. We danced together three times and you let me buy you a soda. And walk out on the porch." The tone of his voice had changed from neutral to menacing, and Harriet was suddenly aware of his height and the width of his shoulders.

"Fade, you rube," Pee Wee said, standing, his fists coming up.

"You punks," the boy seethed, his hulking frame looking almost as if it was expanding with his anger. "Who the hell do you think you are? Think you own this place? Well, I got news. We live here, you don't."

"Hey, come on, nobody wants any trouble," Bix said, standing and putting a hand on the boy's shoulder. "We're all here to have a good time right? Relax, pal. Here, have a drink." He held out the flask to the boy, who knocked it out of Bix's hand.

"Get your hands off me, you goddamn fairy," he shouted, and suddenly Bix launched himself at the boy, grabbing him by the lapels of his jacket and yanking his face down to his.

"Look, you son of a bitch, I said we don't want any trouble, and what do you do? You try and pick a fight. Come on, Pee Wee, let's take him for a little walk down by the lake. And go get Dan."

"My pleasure." Pee Wee grabbed the boy under one elbow, Bix got him by the other and they half-dragged him toward the door.

"Oh, please stop it," Harriet blurted, surprised at herself for saying anything. Everything had been so fun up to now, the music and the talk. This wasn't the way anyone should be acting, not anyone halfway civilized, anyway.

Bix turned and looked right at her, his features bunched into a scowl, with a glare that said plainer than any words, *Mind your own goddamn business.* They continued dragging the struggling boy toward the exit.

"Now what's going on, fellows? More trouble with one of the customers?" It was Frank Trumbauer, with Ray Reynolds at his side, holding what looked like a length of pipe. He took a look at the boy and laughed.

"Oh, Mr. Trumbauer, it's just Howard Flaherty, he's a little addle-pated, always has been, everyone around here knows that, always has been," he chattered. "Now what the heck are these boys planning to do with him?"

"Bust his skull, what else?" Pee Wee mumbled.

"I told him to lay off, and he wouldn't," Bix said, his round face mottled with red. "He's harassing the women, and...."

Ray went up to the raw-boned boy and yanked him by the arm, smile fixed in place all the while. "Now, come on, Howard, look, you got all these people upset. Apologize to the ladies and let's get on home, all right?"

The boy stood staring at the pipe in Ray's hand and nodded, his face sullen. He mumbled something that could be construed as an apology before Ray led him to the door, gripping his arm all the way, the length of pipe waggling in his free hand.

Trumbauer stood staring at Bix and Pee Wee, his eyes fierce.

"He started it," Pee Wee blurted, breaking the silence.

Trumbauer pursed his lips. "All right, it's over now and we've got another set to play. Go on, Pee Wee. I want a word with Bix." With a withering look, Trumbauer glared the clarinet player back to the bandstand, then rounded on Bix in a hushed, furious tone. Harriet was close enough to hear every word.

"You want Jean to can you again?"

Harriet watched as Bix hung his head and jammed his fists into his pockets like a sullen schoolboy. Trumbauer went on.

"I hadda do a lot of fast talking last time to persuade him not to, and the sight reading's only part of it. It's the drinking and the hellraising. Don't you realize how many guys would sell their eye teeth to be in your shoes?" He stopped to take a deep breath and shot the cuffs on his shirt. "You better decide what's more important to you, drinking or playing. You can't do both. Come on, we're up again in ten." He and Bix walked to the bandstand, where they rearranged chairs and music stands for the next set.

Joy let out a low, impressed whistle. "Jeez, Tram really read Bickie the riot act."

Harriet turned to stare at Joy. "Does this sort of thing happen a lot? Fights like this?"

"Aw, that wasn't anything," Joy said, picking up Bix's flask from the floor and shaking it to see if there was anything left. "Bickie and Pee Wee are still sober. Otherwise it woulda been a real dust-up. Anyhow, the rube had it comin'."

And your friend Bickie has a little problem with his temper, Harriet thought, recalling how quickly his boyish face had gone from placid good humor to contorted anger, his fists knotted and ready to pummel the raw-boned boy. She thought of the wave of sexual feeling that had washed over her when he touched her hand and was suddenly embarrassed.

The band started playing again and Harriet and Joy went back to the bandstand. All through the set, Harriet felt Bix's eyes on her, but she refused to look at him. But after two choruses of "Royal Garden Blues," she looked up and saw him mouthing, "Sorry!" Then he grinned and pointed the cornet right at her before blasting his solo, and she knew she wasn't mad anymore.

The sound of the band was still echoing in her ears as Harriet and Mr. Traub and the rusty Ford jounced along the rutted road back to the farmhouse on John Emery Road, where Harriet rented an attic room with the Traubs. A full moon turned the mist rising over the fields a glowing silver, and the air smelled like cut grass and wildly growing weeds and the faint, lingering order of a miscreant skunk.

She leaned her head out the window and breathed it all in, pushing back her mass of curls, which had gone frizzy with the humidity. Bix Beiderbecke, she thought. Bix is a nickname, short for what? I should have asked him where he went to college. Anybody who played like he did probably had lots of experience, maybe even majored in music. *And that kid should have never tried to bother Joy.* Strange, how easygoing Bix seemed up until then. The thought of his temper, juxtaposed against his horn playing and his pleasant demeanor, had made her nervous, made her want to stand between him and the farm boy, to protect both of them. Strange.

"Had a good time, then?" Mr. Traub asked.

"Wonderful," she said, eyes closed. "How was your Grange meeting?"

"Can't complain. Won almost five dollars in the last pot."

They were silent the rest of the way, and she thought of how the musicians were just getting started on their Saturday night, according to Joy. Trumbauer and Doc Ryker and their wives were driving out to the Riverside Resort. Pee Wee and Sonny and Dan and Benny were going into South Bend to the Terrace Garden for Chinese, and then to some speakeasy on Indiana Avenue they'd heard about, where Joy and Bix would meet them later. When Harriet left, Bix had been sitting at the piano onstage, noodling around with some dreamy chords while the janitor stacked upended chairs on tables and swept streamers and confetti from the glistening floor. The piano echoed in the empty hall, sounding lonesome and eerie.

"You're not goin' home now, are ya?" Joy had hollered from her perch on the bench next to Bix. "We're just warmin' up. Wanna go to the Terrace Garden for some egg foo yung?"

"Yeah, your buddy Howard might show," Bix deadpanned as Joy messed up his hair. He shot a glance at Harriet and grinned, all temper forgotten.

"I can't, my ride's here," Harriet said, wishing she could stay with them.

"Next time Frank'll give you a ride home," Bix said, watching her with big, dark eyes as his fingers automatically moved on the keyboard. "Or Pee Wee, if we ever get the Buick running again. Thing's been sitting next to the cottage ever since the last time it died on us."

Harriet had left them there, Joy with an elbow on Bix's shoulder, humming along with his playing.

When they got back to the farmhouse, Mrs. Traub was waiting up for them, standing on the front porch with the light on.

"Harriet, a phone call," she said, frowning. She handed Harriet a piece of paper with a phone number written in heavy, meticulous pencil. "From Indianapolis!"

"Was it a young man?" Harriet asked, grinning.

"Oh, *ja*," Mrs. Traub said, nodding her meaty head. "Very serious young man. Nice, deep voice. You call him now, *ja*? It sounded so important."

Harriet stood at the crank phone in the hallway, rang up the operator in South Bend and gave her Rudy's phone number. The phone rang while the South Bend operator breathed on the other end. Finally, a click and a hello.

"Rudy? It's Harriet. Can you hear me?"

"Harry, baby, it's past two in the morning. Where the hell were you?"

She laughed. "I thought I'd finally make a night of it and see the band. They're really good, too, a Jean Goldkette outfit from St. Louis."

"Huh. Suppose the place is full of cake-eaters from Notre Dame and Purdue. They advertise that place all over the Midwest. Hey, stay away from those college sheiks, you hear?" He laughed, and Harriet pictured him at his aunt's house in Indianapolis, lounged on a sofa or leaning his long frame against a doorjamb. Good old Rudy.

"It's wonderful to hear your voice," she said. "Did you get my letters?"

"Sure did. How about mine? Get that clipping I sent you?"

"Yes. I'm so proud of you, Rudy. So they're really going to hire you after graduation?"

"It's a cinch. Salary's nothing to write home about, but it's the biggest architectural firm in the state. I'm learning a lot here. Say, it's an awful quiet town without you. I miss you, baby."

Harriet felt her face burn red. Mrs. Traub cleared her throat from where she was standing, right behind her.

"Oh, leave the girl alone, Ingrid," Mr. Traub muttered as he clomped upstairs to bed.

"Me, too," Harriet said into the mouthpiece. She could hear the faint breathing of the party-line operator. "So! When are you coming to visit?"

"That's what I called about. Fourth of July weekend. I get three days off. Think the hotel can put me up?"

"I'll talk to Mrs. Smith first thing Monday morning," Harriet said, beaming. "Oh, Rudy, I miss you," she blurted, ignoring Mrs. Traub, the party line and everything else. "It'll be wonderful to see you here. And we'll have fun, too. We can go swimming, go into town to see the movies, and there's this wonderful band here...."

"They hot?"

"The hottest! Even better than Red Nichols that time we saw them. In fact, the cornet player...."

"Say, how's your cousin? She showing you the sights? I'm telling you, stay away from those Notre Dame guys." He chuckled and his voice changed to the one she knew so well, the one he used in the darkness of his car, and on their long walks at twilight on campus at Indiana University, or when they were pressed against each other at his fraternity house dances. "Baby, I can't wait to see you again. Two more weeks. You know what I mean? Harry?"

A sudden tidal wave of homesickness crashed over her—for Rudy, for the Indiana U. campus, for her mother and sisters and their rickety old house on the outskirts of Indianapolis. She glanced out the front door at the black country night outside, a darkness that could have just as easily been on a distant, airless planet as in this little rural town.

The night that had been so fragrant and innocuous on the ride home now seemed like it was smothering her, as if it wanted to crush her into nothingness, the massive darkness and the depthless, burning layers of stars obliterating her as easily as pressing a flower into a book until there was nothing left except a pale, dry husk.

She clenched her eyes shut and laughed, trying to shake off the morbid thought. "Come soon, Rudy," she whispered, clutching the phone's earpiece hard enough to hurt her fingers. "And write, okay? Please write?"

"Every damn day, baby. I'll be there on Saturday. Be waiting."

"I will. Good night, Rudy."

"'Night, baby. Love you. You hear?"

"Me, too." She hung up and looked outside again. The foreboding mood had evaporated as quickly as it came, leaving nothing behind but the familiar Indiana night. Mrs. Traub was pretending to be busy rearranging umbrellas in the hall tree rack.

"Everything all right?" she asked, her smile turning sly.

"Wonderful, just wonderful," Harriet said, then laughed to hear what sounded like Joy's voice coming out of her mouth. "Just jake."

Chapter 2

Joy

Afternoons at the little yellow cottage, I like to sleep. I hear the screen door slam as Bickie heads to the front porch and riffles a few notes, warming up. Dan comes by, he's heading into New Carlisle, and Bickie asks him to pick him up a bottle. He plays some more, stops to shake the spit out of his horn, plays again, and the afternoon is hot, the window shades glow orange, the sun shifts outside. He plays and plays, all the songs they'll play tonight and some he just makes up. I can sleep all day in my kimono under twisted sheets, and the horn sound gets twisted around the dreams I have, too.

Then he comes back in, leans over me and asks if I want him to get me a sandwich or something to eat from the hotel. Smiling, smooth-haired, his cute little squashed face snuggling against mine, smelling like sun-warmed skin.

I never do get that sandwich because right then he usually wants it and so do I, because he isn't drinking yet and there aren't many times when there's nobody here but us. But now everybody is either in town or swimming or fishing down by the lake and I always want it from him after being asleep all afternoon and waking up feeling warm and heavy from the sun beating down on the tarpaper roof, like my arms and legs and everything else are made of soft, melting wax.

He gets up to put the hook-and-eye latch on the screen door, holding up his trousers with one hand. Not that that'll stop those goofs if they really want to get in. Itzy knocked out the window screen once, climbed through and practically fell on the bed, and Pee Wee will just stand on the porch and kick at the door until somebody lets him in.

But nobody bothers us today, and when he comes back to bed we take our time for once and I wrap my melty wax limbs around him until he's all melty too. Bickie is so cute and so sweet and I can't get enough of it with him, I love everything about him. It's been this way ever since they came here last month and I was already waiting for him. Well, I guess I really been waiting for him for something like four years.

Later on when the fellas get back they'll all rag at me so much about it and get me mad, even though they make me laugh, too, until Bickie tells them to lay off and then we start passing the bottle Dan brought and then the instruments come out, horn and sax and drum traps, and I sing a little bit with them and then it's time for me to go back to the hotel and take a bath before the show, being careful not to scrub too hard down there where it's still tender from this afternoon.

Sometimes I wonder what Harriet makes of all this. She's probably shocked, especially since that old bitch Mrs. Smith who owns the hotel and the dance hall is constantly harping on how bad the musicians are, and here I am, sleeping with one of 'em practically under her nose. I know the old lady'd like to throw me out but what the hell, my money spends as good as anyone's, and she ain't about to give that up.

But Harriet's a good kid, like the kid sister I never had. I even call her Little Sister. It's fun to have another girl around to talk to, especially one who's so smart, smart enough to go to school to become a doctor. I never knew anyone as smart as Harriet, but she's so sweet she never acts stuck-up about it, though I know sure as hell how much smarter she is than a dumbbell like me. We never talk about anything fancy—just clothes, and how she ought to wear her hair, and music, and men. She never says a word about me and Bickie.

I lay in the bathtub and try and ignore the old bitch banging on the door for me to hurry up and I think about the first time I saw him. Not last year, but back four years ago March in that basement joint on Wabash, the Friar's Inn, when I first went to Chicago and was feeling so blue. I never wanted to go home so after my shift at the Blackhawk I'd go different places in the Loop, order a drink and just sit 'til they threw me out. I saw a lot of places that way and heard a lot of music—at Friar's and at Bert Kelly's Stables, oh, lots of places.

He came in out of the snow that night like a wet dog, in a belted overcoat and a pushed-in hat, and the snow was caked all over him and sliding off in gloppy wet sheets that landed in a puddle on the floor. There was something under his arm in a wet brown paper bag.

I heard him trying to sweet-talk the doorman into letting him in but I didn't think much of it again until he went and sat up by the band, nodding at the boys like he knew them. And then he took off the overcoat and let it drip over a chair and underneath he was wearing a moth-eaten old blue sweater tucked into a pair of baggy pants, like a real rube, I could recognize them right away, and he was one, straight from the sticks, right off the farm, no question.

Then he peeled away wet shreds of that brown paper bag and there was a horn. I laughed to myself thinking he was gonna have the nerve to ask to play with these guys, the New Orleans Rhythm Kings, who could cut you up with their licks, and they would, too, if you dared to get up there and couldn't make the grade. I seen it happen plenty. But this kid just looked at the fellas and asked them to play "Angry," and the sax player just shook his head and laughed and said okay, like it was a big joke between them.

Some guys in some clubs are all right, especially the relief band when it's late enough and there's hardly any customers, they'll let a kid sit in. Over at the Stables they'd let me sing with them sometimes, and at the Friar's, too, if they were in the right mood, which usually meant they had just enough gin or muggles and not too much so where they got to feeling mean.

But this kid came up on the stand and started to play and he fit right in like a wheel in a clock, like he'd been working with the band six nights a week instead of just walking in off the street in his goofy school kid outfit.

He had a funny kind of way about him, the way he sat in the back and crossed his legs like a girl, pointing his horn down at the floor, no grandstanding like the rest of the band. They played "Angry" just like he asked, and when he was done, taking a nice little eight-bar solo in the middle and the applause died down because he was pretty damn good, he just walked off the stage, put that soggy coat back on and headed for the door, and nobody going to stop him.

I caught up with him on the stairway and he turned to look at me with that funny, squashed little face of his, his mouth still red from playing, and I leaned against the wall and laughed so hard I almost peed myself. Because he was a kid, a little boy, hadda still be in high school, no matter how hot he played and how much he smelled of beer, which he did, now that I was close enough to get a whiff.

We went to a Thompson's cafeteria where it was late enough that the place was loaded with nances who looked at us and laughed when we came in, wrists flappin to beat the band. I didn't blame 'em, laughin at a couple of rubes like us, 'cause that's what we were—him a punk kid sneaked off from some prep school up north, me barely six months off the goddamn sheep ranch in Montana.

We drank lots of black coffee and he ate donuts like he was starved, and I let him cadge cigarettes off me. He didn't talk much, just looked around at all the homos and rummies coming in and out of the place, his big brown eyes over the rim of the coffee cup taking everything in. He told me his name, which sounded like a Dutch vaudeville act, and told me he's from Iowa, a rube just like I guessed, and asked where I'm from and looked right at me the whole time, smiling, really listening, not like everybody in the city who says yeah and uh-huh and look around at everything else while you're talking except you. He listened like a rube, all eyes and ears. I told him just enough so he knew I was new here, too, and like him, goddamn glad to be in Chicago.

Well, the kid was a baby, turned out, just had his nineteenth birthday, and still in high school because he'd flunked out a year. Lonely as I was in a big new city, I was over twenty-one and legal and not crazy enough to rob the cradle and try to make him. So for laughs I walked him to the North Shore station on Wabash and put him on the train back to Lake Forest, where he'd get in around four in the morning and classes starting at eight. I laughed every time I thought about it.

He was a funny kid and I'd see him now and then at the Friar's, once when I was singing and heard him and his schoolboy buddies hooting and hollering for me, a regular claque all my own, made me feel like Bee Palmer the Shimmy Queen herself. And I'd hear him play there, too, getting better every time, so good that the band didn't laugh anymore when he came up, but stood there listening when he pulled his solos, their feet tapping, heads nodding, respecting him, even though he was still just a kid.

But then I didn't see him anymore, and forgot all about him except for sometimes when I'd be somewhere and think I'd hear the cornet the way he played it, which was really not like anyone else I'd ever heard before or since.

We didn't meet up again until last April, the day before Easter, when I was working at the Green Mill Café way up north, waiting tables and singing now and then with the band when they let me. But that night I was just waiting tables, my feet hurting already from four hours on the shift, and I had the two-top tables near the doors and the guy at one of the tables had his head stuck behind the big red menu and when he put it down it was him, the kid with the funny name, Bix, Bickie, I called him. He looked better than he did back in the days at the Friar's Inn, older now and all decked out in a tux since he was playing in the relief band at the Rendez-Vous Café on Diversey. That's a big place, too, with Charlie Straight's orchestra and a floor show they just added, so it seemed like the kid was doing all right. Anyhow, he was twenty-two by then, all grown up and living in a third-floor room at the Diversey Arms, right upstairs from the café where he worked. I slipped him a sandwich and coffee on the house and he told me he'd come back to get me later after my shift ended, and he did. He brought me back to the Rendez-Vous and we stayed there 'til the joint closed, and then we went to a little speak around the corner and talked over coffee cups filled with gin, and a little dinge band was playing that he just had to sit in with, and by the time he was done, those boys were treating him like a brother.

When we finally stumbled out of there at five in the morning it was too late for me to get back to my flat on Wilson, so he offered to let me stay at his place and I did. I'll never forget the way the sun came through the window and the sound of the church bells in the neighborhood—I forgot all about it being Easter. He put some funny opera music on the phonograph and I fell asleep on the couch, watching him as he sat on the floor with his ear next to the speaker, his eyes closed, his fingers moving with the music like he was playing the piano.

You're probably thinking I went the limit with him then, but I didn't, surprise! He never even kissed me. I woke up next day with a blanket tucked around me and him practicing his cornet in the bedroom, a mute in his horn so he wouldn't bother me. It being Easter and me being off work, he treated me to an early dinner at the Blackhawk downtown where I used to work, and then he went off to play in the holiday show at the Rendez-Vous.

He was there til the end of June, and we did everything together. When he wasn't dragging me to after-hours joints all over town to listen to him sit in with the house bands, we were going to the movies, or Cubs Park, or Riverview. That crazy kid loved the Bobs, that big, fast roller coaster they have there. We'd just get off, our legs still wobbly from the ride, and he'd be back in line to get on again.

And no, we didn't go the limit. Didn't even come close. And that was just fine with me. Sometimes we necked, and sometimes I stayed at his place, but we never did it. We were too busy having fun, like I never did back when I was a kid, with the whole damn city of Chicago as our grown-up playground.

One night I came close to telling him everything. We were eating sandwiches at two in the morning at Skooglund's Cafeteria on Wilson and I asked him about his family, and he told me he they were mad at him because he never graduated from that prep school and ran off to be a musician instead because he was too old to be in school, anyway. It made him blue to talk about it, and that got me riled. I could see where the life he was living wasn't exactly the answer to a mother's prayer, but hell, he was earning a halfway decent, legit living and more important, he was a sweet-natured guy who everybody loved 'cause he was so generous and easygoing, the very best kind of friend.

And so I told him a little—about the sheep ranch and Montana and how you could go for days not talking to anyone, 'til the sheep started to look human. Of how you could get up in the morning and look out the window and see nothing but land, and more land, and some mountains in the distance. How all those miles of nothing and no one could make you nuts after awhile, and how cozy and nice it was to be in a big, crowded city, in a flat with someone always home above or below you, riding packed in a streetcar, sashaying down State Street in a new outfit with a million other folks, and best of all, being able to get out and have some fun and never be alone unless you wanted to.

He listened the way he always did and then he nodded and said, "So you're running away, too."

I still didn't tell him about what I left and why—about my husband Vern, and my sister-in-law Millie, and Michael, my baby, the one they made me give up. I was going to, but then in June he got a telegram, one he'd been waiting for from Frankie Trumbauer to come join him in St. Louis to play at the big Arcadia Ballroom in the Jean Goldkette Orchestra, and it was all over pretty fast after that. I went downtown with him to the Musicians Local 10 to get his union card back and then we were saying goodbye at Dearborn Street station and he was getting on the Wabash to St. Louis.

He wrote to me a lot at first, but then the letters slowed down and I knew he'd found a steady girl. It didn't really bother me since after all, I had no claim on him. He wrote about maybe marrying her, and I wrote back congratulations, but even then I couldn't see it working. He traveled too much and drank too much and needed music too much to be the kind of husband this girl wanted. She was a home girl, from the way he described her, and those types need their men on a leash and by the balls, if you'll excuse my French.

I guess that sounds catty, but it turns out I was right, because something happened and the girl broke his heart. I could tell because his letters turned strange and sad and by the start of this year you could tell it was mostly over between them, even if he didn't say so. I figured I knew what happened, and as it turned out, I figured right, but I didn't know for sure 'til later, when I came and waited for him here at the Hotel Hudson.

He wrote me in May saying he was coming to Indiana with Frankie and some of the Goldkette band for the summer, but I wasn't planning on seeing him. I figured maybe I'd go over one Saturday on the South Shore just to say my hellos and then leave. But then I had to get out of Chicago because I found out they were looking for me there. And Hudson Lake, Indiana seemed like a good place to go.

I was already living at the Hotel Hudson when the Goldkette band came on the South Shore that afternoon. I watched from my window as Jean Goldkette, a mousy little fella with Harold Lloyd glasses, stood around bossing the fellows and I saw Bickie get off the train, smoking a cigarette and carrying his cornet.

Boy, was he surprised when I knocked on the cottage door. Mostly glad surprised, but you could tell I was the last person he expected to see here. So we went and got a couple of pops at the soda fountain and sat out by the lake and then I finally told him everything, because by then I had to. And he let me cry a little, and put his arms around me, and then he told me what happened between him and the home girl in St. Louis, and why he was damn glad to be at Hudson Lake, too.

And then he took out a handkerchief and wiped my eyes and somehow it was like a beginning, like that Easter morning we'd heard the church bells ring. He kissed me and we went back to the cottage while Pee Wee and Itzy and Dan and Sonny were hollering and splashing in the lake, and we did it, and then we did it again, and we been doing it ever since.

I know it can't last forever, and I don't want it to. I spent too much of my life trying to hold stuff together when the best thing would have been to let it fall apart. I know when the summer is over Bickie and the band will be gone, and I'll have to find somewhere else to go, too.

But right now, while the sun is so nice and warms up the lake just right, and the music is flowing, and Bickie is loving me, I don't care. I don't want one single other thing. I'm just going to keep going to the cottage and singing whenever I can, and let tomorrow take care of itself.

Chapter 3

Mrs. Smith kept harping about how the Fourth of July weekend was going to be a disaster, and in spite of her excitement over Rudy's impending visit, Harriet was beginning to believe she might be right. Saturday morning dawned hot enough to peel paint, and while Harriet was chopping up a pot of hard-boiled eggs for salad, she heard the beginnings of the usual goings-on at the little yellow cottage behind the Hotel Hudson, where the single musicians lived.

"Buddy! Get over here *right now!*" Mrs. Smith yelled.

Harriet broke off from her work to glance out the kitchen window. Fifteen-year-old Buddy was trying to peer into the windows of the little yellow cottage. He looked around at the sound of his mother's voice and loped back through the weedy yard to the hotel, lips moving in silent objection the whole way.

"What, Ma?" he asked, pushing open the screen door.

"How many times have I told you to stay away from those people? It's bad enough they have to be right next door. I don't want you talking to them, do you understand me? Mark my words, there's going to be trouble here because of them."

"Jeez, Ma, they ain't bad guys. One of 'em lent me a mouthpiece for my bugle, and...."

"And God knows what kind of diseases you'll get from it!" she yelped, waddling over to the sink and shaking in a blizzard of Old Dutch cleansing powder. "Big hot-shot band from St. Louis," Mrs. Smith muttered as she scrubbed out the sink, the wattles on her upper arms jiggling. "When we ran the place, we never charged admission, me and the Mister, God rest his soul. Back when it was the Casino, folks could come and dance for free. Now just because Goldkette leases the place and calls it the Blue Lantern, he thinks he can charge a dollar fifty." She snorted. "For what? To hear *those* bums? Why aren't our local boys like Joe Dockstader and his Indianans good enough anymore?"

"Jeez, Ma, keep it down, wontcha? They'll hear ya," Buddy mumbled, still standing at the screen door.

"What do I care? Now get yourself over to Ellwood's and get us some ice, and don't be dawdling out by that cottage, you understand?"

Buddy shrugged and slammed out the screen door. Harriet watched out the window as he walked down Chicago Road, ice tongs in hand, kicking gravel as he went. A panting yellow dog slouched at an angle from the Blue Lantern to the hotel side of the road. Harriet glanced at her watch. Four hours until Rudy got here. She felt her stomach clench like it always did when she was about to see Rudy after a long separation, filling with the same sort of nervousness she felt around him the first time they'd met—a combination of anticipation, excitement, and fear. Just like high school again. She thought of the awkward dances where she'd sat, a perfect wallflower, wearing a dress she'd sewed herself from a Butterick pattern and a nervous smile, sweaty fingers twining and untwining in her lap. Running to the girls' cloak room if any boy even looked in her direction. Only wanting to hear the music and go home.

"Harriet?" Mrs. Smith snapped. "Seeing as you don't have anything better to do 'cept look out the window and stare at your watch, go on upstairs and strip the bedding."

On her way back down, Harriet hesitated on the landing as she heard Mrs. Smith muttering her name. She stood there, holding her breath, listening to the woman in the kitchen talking to herself under her breath. "That girl will be absolutely no help to me once her boyfriend comes tonight. And him tying up Room 7 for three whole days at peak season, when I could put a family of four in there and charge them twice what he's paying. Now, where is that boy? I swear if I had the strength I'd tan his britches. How long does it take him to get down there and back?"

Harriet exhaled softly as Mrs. Smith's monologue turned to her errant son. She fixed what she hoped was a pleasant smile on her face and came back into the kitchen just in time to see Charlie Horvath saunter in the back door, all smiles, rubbing his hands together like a housefly at a picnic.

"Well, good morning, everyone! Looks like we're all set for a busy day, eh?"

"Don't I know it," Mrs. Smith muttered. "I've got guests in every room and had to turn people away on the phone, right through this morning, and me short-handed." She shot Harriet an accusing glance.

Horvath patted her on the shoulder and grinned. "Now, Mrs. Smith, you're doing a fine job. You just keep up the good work here at the hotel, and we'll handle everything else." He turned to walk away.

"Really? Well, maybe you should start with that gang out there," Mrs. Smith said, jerking a thumb toward the yard.

By this time the musicians were up and pitching empty bottles into a garbage can outside the window and making a lot of noise. Fuzzy was singing off key, Pee Wee setting off firecrackers, and Frank Trumbauer was parading around in some sort of moth-eaten cowboy outfit. The sight was so ridiculous it made Harriet laugh out loud, which earned her another scathing glance from Mrs. Smith.

"This sort of thing goes on day after day with no let-up, till early morning when they finally go to sleep," Mrs. Smith said to Horvath. "*If* they finally go to sleep. There are women in there, and bootleg alcohol, and God knows what-all."

Harriet peered out the door and stifled a laugh at the sight of Pee Wee tossing a smoking string of Black Cat firecrackers toward the outhouse, trying to scare whoever was in there. Musicians in various states of dress and undress were swarming in and out, all loud, most already drunk, she guessed. For some reason, she didn't see Bix among them.

"Just some high spirits, Mrs. Smith, that's all," Horvath said. "These boys like to let off steam after work, just like anybody else. But if it'll make you happy, I'll go have a word with them, all right?"

Mrs. Smith wiped her hands on her apron and sighed. "This must all seem pretty silly to you, I suppose, being as you're from a big city and all. But it isn't funny to us." She handed a mixing bowl of chopped eggs to Harriet, who dusted some paprika over the eggs, added a dollop of mayonnaise, and started stirring. "We take the law seriously here in Indiana. Especially Prohibition. I don't know if you read the papers, but there was a big arrest just last month in Indianapolis, the biggest bootlegging ring in the state. We don't think the law is a laughing matter."

Yes, except for Ray Reynolds and the lucrative little sideline he's operating out of your soda fountain, Harriet thought. Mrs. Smith was always worried about trouble, but it seemed to Harriet the main source of any trouble at Hudson Lake would come from Ray and the bad quality bootleg hootch he sold.

"Ma'am, I don't think the police are going to bother with some out-of-town boys carrying a couple pints of gin...."

"I'm not just talking about the police, Mr. Horvath," Mrs. Smith said, slamming the wooden spoon on the cutting board. "I'm talking about our own people. Men from LaPorte and South Bend and Mishawaka. Men who take the law into their own hands." She folded her arms across her bosom. "Do I have to draw you a picture?"

Horvath patted her arm again. "I'll talk to the boys, tell them to settle down a little. But I can't promise anything, it being the Fourth and all. They're sure in a holiday mood." He walked out the door and toward the cottage, where the musicians greeted him with a barrage of wolf whistles and kissing noises.

"Holiday mood," Mrs. Smith muttered, and began slicing up pickles. "More like a Roman orgy, you ask me."

The back door banged open. Buddy stood in the doorway, looking surly. "They're outta ice. And they don't know when they're gonna get more." He turned to leave.

"Wait one minute, Mr. High-and-Mighty. What exactly did *they* say I'm supposed to do, with a full hotel and twenty plucked chickens I need to keep from turning? Don't give me that look, young man. You're going to have to go all the way to LaPorte and bring back as much ice as you can get. Pack the back of the truck with sawdust and hurry up, before everything melts in this God-awful heat. And then go back and pick up Auntie Bertha because God knows I'll need all the help I can get. Wait. Who's that driving up the road?"

Mrs. Smith craned her neck to see around Buddy, and Harriet joined her at the screen door. There was a Ford chugging and rattling down Chicago Road, raising a cloud of dust. The rusty car pulled right past the hotel, bumped over the grass and into the field, coming to a stop in front of the little yellow cottage. The musicians out there began hollering and gathered around the Ford.

Mrs. Smith gasped. She turned to Harriet. "Didn't I tell you this weekend was doomed beyond redemption?"

Harriet stared as a teenage girl with a painted face and a head of stringy hair beneath a horsehair cloche slithered out from behind the wheel of the Ford, hitching up the skirt of her yellow satin dress high enough to show the lacy edge of her bloomers. She stood there as the musicians gathered around, poking into the back seat of the car, and emerging with gallon jugs of what Harriet could only assume was moonshine.

The girl raised her voice over the babble of the musicians. "Where's Pee Wee? I want to talk to Pee Wee."

The man in question stuck his head out the front door of the cottage. "Who the hell's that?"

She waved. "Crystal Hawkins, 'member me? You told me to come have a party. Well, here I am."

∞∞

Harriet watched as people started coming in on the South Shore excursion cars. Because it was a holiday show, the Goldkette band was alternating with Joe Dockstader and his Indianans. The band had brought back Lola Trowbridge for the occasion, a local girl with a voice like Vaughn DeLeath and a face like a long, hard winter.

She hurried to finish her chores and then walked down to the lake, where families with picnic baskets were spending the day. Colorful kites fluttered over Bluebird Beach, children squealed and splashed in the water, and the music played on in the dance hall.

Ray, at the soda fountain, was scooping up ice cream cones for a pack of sand-coated kids in bathing suits as Mrs. Smith stood there haranguing him.

"Don't think I don't know what's going on here," Mrs. Smith said, shoving Ray aside and rummaging behind the counter among the cardboard cartons of Horlich's Malted Milk mix and stacks of soda and sundae dishes. "Don't you realize they could come and close the whole place down and throw us all in jail? And why? Just so you could make some money on the side selling doctored pop!"

"Don't know what you're talking about, Loretta," Ray said, helping her to poke around. "See? Nothin here but seltzer water and syrup."

"Don't lie to me. I've seen you do it with my own two eyes."

Ray winked. "Business is good. What do you care why?"

Harriet decided to interrupt while she could still get a word in. "Do you need anything else, Mrs. Smith?"

Mrs. Smith turned to her, gray hair flying around her face like a dandelion gone to seed. "You tell him, Harriet. You're from Indianapolis. Oh, they may not be the big shots they were back in '24, but they did get the governor elected, and don't you forget it."

Harriet thought a moment before it connected. "Oh, you mean the Klan? Things have died down a lot with them since Stephenson was convicted." She glanced at her watch. What did she care about the Klan? She'd been glad when the Grand Dragon was sent to prison for kidnapping and killing a woman, and the Klan ranks in Indianapolis began to dwindle. The Klan had given everybody in the state a bad name with their ignorant ravings against Catholics and foreigners and Negroes. Anyhow, she still had to get back to the Traubs, take a bath and change before Rudy arrived.

"Well, Ray seems to forget that riot right in downtown South Bend happened a couple years ago. Klanners and those kids from Notre Dame." Mrs. Smith shuddered. "Blood in the streets. Crosses burning in the Mishawaka hills. Terrible!"

"Aw, banana oil," Ray muttered, clashing his ice cream dishes back into place. "I was there, Lor. Couple of Hundred-Percenters got their bathrobes tore, is all. Served 'em right for tryin' to have a rally against Catholics right next door to Notre Dame."

"Well, Cyrus Walker's heading up the South Bend chapter now. Don't you know they're planning a big picnic and rally at Island Park on Monday? And Cyrus is just itching for a project to get new members? Well, I don't want my hotel to be a Klan project, just because some bum musicians from St. Louis can't keep their flies buttoned."

Harriet gasped involuntarily, shocked that Mrs. Smith would talk that way.

"Now, Lor, that's a little raw, don't you think?" Ray said, leaning heavily on the soda-fountain counter. "They're just kids, after all."

Harriet hurried away, not wanting to hear anything else. As she crossed Chicago Road, she noticed there was some sort of commotion down by the little yellow cottage, but she didn't really want to know what was going on. Rudy was coming, and that was all that mattered.

On her way back to the hotel, she saw Buddy carrying a crate of oranges out of the kitchen. She followed a few paces behind him, watching as he walked through the weeds, past the tethered cow, and up the steps of the cottage. She heard a lot of shouting and laugher and smiled to herself. Joy was probably there, hanging on Bix's neck, having a ball. Well, Joy wasn't the only one who'd be having a ball tonight, she thought. There would be the band, and dancing, and fireworks at midnight over the lake, and she'd be enjoying every minute of it with Rudy. And nothing was going to put her into a bad mood, especially not some pointless discussion about the Ku Klux Klan.

Buddy came out of the cottage, darted a glance around, then skulked back toward the kitchen, avoiding Harriet's eyes.

"What's up over there, a big party?" Harriet asked, lengthening her stride to keep up with him.

He shook his head, watching his feet swish through the overgrown weeds. "You don't want to know."

"Why? What's going on?"

Buddy stopped walking and gave her a surprisingly adult stare. "When's your boyfriend coming? Tonight? I'd head over to Playland Park, I was you. They got a band and fireworks, too. That's what I'm gonna do. I don't care what the old lady says." He started walking away, faster now.

"Wait, Buddy. Stop. What are you talking about?"

"Take my word for it, there's gonna be trouble, that's all." And then he sprinted back toward the house.

Harriet yelled after him, "Buddy Smith, now you sound *just like your mother!*"

ଚ୍ଚେ

By the time Rudy arrived at Hudson Lake, Harriet and half the clientele at the Blue Lantern knew exactly what was going on at the little yellow cottage. She watched through the kitchen door as the band members swelled in and out of the place on breaks, topping off their pop bottles, swigging down bolts of the Hawkins sisters' finest, straight up or mixed with Mrs. Smith's orange juice.

Throughout the day, between cutting up chicken and mixing biscuit dough, Harriet watched as Mrs. Smith fretted over the situation, alternately begging Ray to go in and break up the party, and trying to ignore what was going on in the futile hope things would run their course and end quickly.

But they didn't. Instead, as the daylight dwindled and night came on, the family groups packed up their picnic baskets and left, and more people came to see the bands, including a huge crowd from Chicago on the South Shore train. By the time midnight rolled around, the dance hall was packed to capacity, and when the Goldkette band took its breaks to give Dockstader a chance, Harriet saw more people going into the little yellow cottage—men with citified clothing and musical instruments, women wearing light frocks and heavy makeup.

And then after the special holiday fireworks exploded over the lake, trailing streamers of red and green and yellow flame into the night while the band played "It's Three O'clock in the Morning," the trains loaded up with tired and crumpled humanity for their return trip to the city, and the party started in earnest.

೮ಾ೦೫

Harriet and Rudy were sitting on the beach the next morning when Martha and Mary Hawkins came to collect their niece. All they could hear from their vantage point were some heated tones of voice and a blur of invective as the sisters stood arguing with Mrs. Smith on the boardwalk in front of the Blue Lantern.

They watched as Martha turned away from Mrs. Smith and stalked toward the little yellow cottage, her long stride pulling her ankle-length skirt tight around her legs. Then she hammered on the door, yanked it open and went right in. No one came out for the next half-hour, but the sound of screaming and breaking glass went on for quite some time.

Finally, Martha emerged, tugging Crystal along by a hank of her mousy hair. The girl wore an Indian blanket wrapped around her naked shoulders like some white woman unwillingly recaptured from a friendly tribe, her face puffy and slick with tears, carrying her high-heeled shoes in one hand and the remains of her dress balled up in the other.

Mary ran up to them and flanked the girl on the other side, and the two sisters marched Crystal back to their Ford, stuffed her into the back seat, and drove away.

Harriet heard the story as it came out over the next few days in dribs and drabs, growing in magnitude as it was whispered over sundaes at the Blue Lantern's soda fountain, out on the streets of LaPorte by matrons gossiping with market baskets on their arms, and across the tables of food at the big Ku Klux Klan picnic lunch and rally Monday at Island Park. The talk was how that addled Hawkins girl, barely sixteen years old, had gussied herself up like a Chicago Levee floozy and gone up to that cottage, brought all her aunts' best moonshine, and given herself repeatedly, in an interesting variety of ways, to each and every one of those out-of-town musicians.

It went around about how Martha Hawkins had dragged her niece out of there without a stitch of clothes on, and the place had five men living in it, and, well, you can imagine the rest. Five men! And how Crystal had screamed and howled like some wild animal, throwing bottles like she was possessed by a demon, and how some of the talk went that she might have been drugged, just like Aimee Semple McPherson, the poor woman, drugged kidnapped and God only knew what else.

Except other versions of the story claimed Crystal Hawkins had just laughed at her aunt when she came to get her, that she'd been lying stark naked in bed between a Jew from New York and a boy who looked like he might have had some nigger blood in him, and that she'd spit in her aunt's face and hollered at her that the Jew promised he was going to take her away to New York with him, and that she was going, she didn't care if he was a Jew, a nigger, or a cannibal with a bone through his nose, anything to get the hell away from here.

But in spite of all the embellishments and exaggerations, Harriet knew the straightforward truth of what happened: that Crystal Hawkins had not only willingly let herself be passed around like a hip flask for consumption by most of the members of the Jean Goldkette band, but had thoughtfully provided the refreshments.

And that no matter which version you believed, it wasn't likely that the local chapter of the Ku Klux Klan would let it lie.

Chapter 4

Bix swung into the Blue Lantern clutching a bottle of Orange Squeeze pop half-filled with gin. He liked to sit up front and drink his doctored Orange Squeeze and stare at Joe Dockstader to see how long it would take to get him nervous enough to start blowing clams. It usually didn't take long.

He slid into a seat near the bandstand and caught Joe's eye, tossing him a quick salute of acknowledgement. Joe gave him a wall-eyed look, like a horse just about to bolt, and kept plugging at his strictly corn-fed interpretation of "Ain't She Sweet." Bix glanced at his watch. Another five minutes should do it.

God, this place was dead during the week, when the Goldkette band alternated with Joe Dockstader's Indianans, he thought. Truth be told, the Indianans were more to the liking of the scattering of locals who bothered showing up.

Things were particularly bad on Tuesday, and today was Tuesday—a truly dead-dog day when the only clientele, according to Horvath, were a bunch of high school kids who drove in from Pinhook, and a table of painfully dressed-up young farmers and their wives who were killing time before the late showing of a Harry Langdon movie in South Bend.

Bix knew the farmers weren't interested in the hot stuff the Goldkette band was playing. They wanted to hear chestnuts like "Whispering" and "Japanese Sandman," so Joe's band was in its glory. Joe played his trumpet with a metal derby mute, stepping out in front of the band for his warbly solos and fanning the mute dramatically over the bell of the horn as he played.

The Goldkette band had just finished a set, ripping through a hot-assed version of "My Pretty Girl" stomp to close, and the harmonies were so tight, and Bix was blowing so hard, that he'd seen sparks explode behind his eyelids, and he leaned over when he finished, dizzy with the music and the gin he'd drunk before going on. The farmers had never gotten off their hands.

Now, with Joe diddling his trumpet front and center, the handful of spectators were finally dancing and enjoying themselves instead of exchanging confused glances or getting up to visit the soda fountain or the can. Funny how the

Saturday and Sunday crowds couldn't get enough of the Goldkette band, and how they died with the locals during the week, Bix thought.

Tram came in, adjusting his tie. "What a hayseed," he muttered, pulling up a chair and settling in next to Bix. "Next thing you know he'll be leading them in a quadrille. Hey, why are you staring at him like that?"

Bix put a finger to his lips. "Sssh. Three minutes and counting."

The band segued into "Hot Lips," with Joe reproducing the Henry Busse solo note for note from the Whiteman record. The locals ate it up, even when Joe started hitting clinkers toward the end of the solo. Bix glanced down at his watch again. "Four minutes," he grinned. "A new record."

The locals stood and clapped when the Indianans wrapped up their set and headed outside for a smoke.

"Great playing, Joe," Bix called as Dockstader hurried past, chewing the inside of his lip and avoiding Bix's eye. He nodded in curt acknowledgement and left.

"Could be worse," Tram murmured, leaning back in his chair and picking at the handkerchief in his breast pocket. "Could be Verne Ricketts and his Dance Compelling Orchestra over at Playland Park." He winced as if in pain.

"I don't know, the locals seem to like these hokey bands," Bix said. "And we're dying during the week."

Tram grunted. "Yeah, and Horvath told me he's worried about the take. Weekends can't carry this place." He jerked his chin at the sparse crowd. "Sure ain't like the Arcadia Ballroom in St. Louis."

The Arcadia. Bix remembered the crowds that came out to dance there, night after night, even during the week. This place was nothing like the Arcadia, with its Moorish arches and balconies, colored bandstand lights, cushioned ballroom floor, sophisticated city crowds. And girls. For an instant Ruth's image flicked into his mind, smiling in her white satin dress, frail shoulders bare, powdered, fragrant. Sitting at a table with her sisters, or dancing with someone else, her eyes always on him, then waiting for him after the crowds were gone, riding with him in a taxicab through the streets of St. Louis. In his mind, she turned to him in the darkness of the cab, smile strangely tight, ready to speak. *Stop now.*

Tram looked down at his shoes and coughed. "Say, Bix, how're things working out with Fuzzy? He any help readin' the charts?"

Bix blinked up at Tram, his mind still somewhere in St. Louis with Ruth. He forced a smile. "Fuzzy's been great. All we need to do is leave the section lead stuff to him. Sometimes he gives me an elbow in the ribs when I need to solo, and...."

"Nobody can beat you when it comes to hot solos, but you're a section man, too. You need to get your reading down pat." Tram pretended to wipe a speck of dust off his shiny patent leather shoe.

"I been working at it, really hard," Bix said, wiping his mouth with the back of his hand and looking around the almost-empty dance hall. "Every day. Ask the boys, you don't believe me. I'm always out on the porch, playing...."

"But you can't just play. You gotta read. And I can tell at rehearsals it ain't easy for you."

Bix drummed his fingers again on the table, two-three-four, over and over, like he was fingering the valves on the cornet, like he was back at school at his desk and failing again. *Time to explain.* He took a breath and faced Tram with what he hoped was a friendly smile. "Look, Tram. I know you stuck your neck out for me with Jean, getting him to take me back. You know how much I appreciate it. Hey, ask Fuzzy, he'll tell you how much better I am now. Why, just the other day...."

Tram's face went Indian hard. "Yeah, just the other day you practically pounded on a local kid because he looked at your girl cross-eyed, and on the Fourth—well, all I can say is you boys are lucky the police weren't called in on that."

Bix took a deep breath to try and loosen the knot that was forming in his gut. "What's that got to do with reading music?" he said, trying to keep his voice calm.

"Jean's heard you're nothing but trouble because of the drinking. Hell, last time he was here checking up on things, you and Pee Wee were off on a bender. And I had to cover up for you. Again."

"I know, Tram, and don't think I don't appreciate...."

"Never mind appreciate. Just shape up, all right? Now come on, we're on again after this set." He got up and walked away.

Bix checked the level on the Orange Squeeze bottle. More than half gone, which meant he'd have to top it off before they started playing again. He stood and headed outside, where he emptied the contents of his flask into the bottle of warm pop, swirled it around to mix it, and started walking down to the pier.

Christ, thank God that was over, he thought, inhaling the smell of algae and water and wet wood under the pier. It made him feel like a chump when Tram gave him the Dutch uncle lecture. It wasn't like he didn't practice. Fuzzy was working with him at every rehearsal, coaching him on technique, fingering and reading. But sometimes the notes on the charts all seemed to blur together, or looked completely foreign to Bix, like the Jewish letters he saw on the street signs once when they went to New York. It was so much easier to just keep still, and listen to Fuzzy play the section, and then just play it back at him. In fact, most of the time when Fuzzy praised him on his improved reading, that's what Bix was really doing—playing back what he'd absorbed and stored in his brain.

And why did Tram have to go and bring up booze? Just because Tram was a teetotaler didn't mean the rest of the band had to follow his lead. Anyhow, what the hell else was there to do out here in the middle of nowhere except drink? Bix didn't know why it always ended up this way, with someone lecturing him, and with him standing there, trying to explain himself—to Tram or Jean Goldkette or—or anyone else. He was keeping up, he was trying his damndest. There was no reason for Tram to lecture him. Tram was only a couple years older than Bix, and Tram was his friend, but sometimes he acted like his goddamn old man. And God knows Bix didn't need another one of those.

Two shadowy shapes came toward him, laughing, one long and lanky, the other shorter. Pee Wee and Doc Ryker, cigarettes glowing in the darkness.

"Hey, if it ain't Bixie. How's the crowd?" Ryker asked.

"Strictly corn-fed, what there is of them. Joe's givin' 'em 'Hot Lips,'" Bix said, miming the band leader's hammy playing style.

"Got any of that stuff left?" Pee Wee asked, peeking into Bix's breast pocket for the flask. "Oh, here it is. Goddamn! Empty."

"We gotta go see the sisters tomorrow, if we can get the car running," Bix said. "You want any, Doc?" He tilted the pop bottle to his lips, draining it.

Ryker shook his bald head. "That shellac those old broads sell is gonna put you guys away," he said. "And after what you did to their niece on the Fourth, I'd stay away from them, I was you. Me, I'm making the trip to Chicago next Monday and getting some of the real stuff. Hey, why didn't you guys bring some back from Joe's when you were in St. Louis last time?"

Pee Wee glowered at Bix so venomously that he started laughing. "We did, but goddamn Bix drank it all on the train ride back. You son of a bitch."

"Hey, you weren't doing too bad a job of putting it away yourself, pal," Bix said, leaning over the edge of the pier and dropping the now-empty Orange Squeeze bottle into the lake. It made an interesting *glub-glub* sound as it went down. "And I didn't do nothing to their niece. I was passed out. Anyhow, I tried to get Pee Wee to go and apologize, but...."

"Hey, I'll be goddamned if I'll apologize for giving that skunky Crystal what she deserved, especially after what she gave me," Pee Wee grumbled. "Crabs! The goddamn skunky bitch...."

"Yeah, and we all had to go to the drugstore in LaPorte and ask the pharmacist for ointment to get rid of it," Bix said. "Even me, and I was too drunk to do anything with her. Come on, there's nothing doing here. Let's go see the sisters."

"Christ, Bix, we still gotta play another set. And we were just there last week. Are you out already?"

"This is Bix you're talking to, Doc," Pee Wee said, ducking as Bix aimed an open-handed slap at his head. "The man with the iron stomach." His long face pulled into a sarcastic grin that made him look like a human jack-o-lantern.

"Yeah, and the cheesecloth liver," Ryker said. "Look, Norma's on the warpath and I gotta make nice and go right home after the show. I'm not driving ten miles out on those washboard roads just so you bottle babies can wet your whistles. But I'll borrow you the car, ya want."

"Good deal!" Bix perked up, pulling out his wallet and thumbing through the greenbacks to see how many gallons of corn liquor he could afford until next payday. At three bucks a gallon jug, he could afford plenty.

Ryker squinted into the darkness across the road at the figure advancing on them.

"Hey, who's that coming over?"

Bix glanced up. "Aw, that's Mrs. Smith the hotel's kid."

"That pain in the ass," Pee Wee said. "Tell him to go chase himself."

"No, leave him. He ain't a bad kid. Anyhow, he'll take his bike into town and go get cigarettes for you if you treat him human." Bix watched as Buddy Smith waved and walked out onto the pier.

"Hey, Bix. Hey, Pee Wee."

"Hey yourself, Skeezix," Pee Wee said. "What are you doing out after dark? Mama'll spank."

"Hey, Bix, I been practicing every day, just like you told me," Buddy said, taking a trumpet mouthpiece from the pocket of his khaki shirt and putting it to his lips. "See? And you're right, it don't hurt my mouth to play now."

"That's the ticket," Bix said, taking out his own mouthpiece and blowing a few sounds that sounded like syncopated duck calls. "Ya gotta practice every day, otherwise you lose your lip."

"That the line you use on Joy, Bix?" Pee Wee laughed, dodging another head slap.

"Ignore this punk with the dirty mouth. Reed men don't know anything about it. And another good way to practice is to take a feather, lay on the bed, and see how long you can keep it in the air by blowing."

"That's another line he uses on Joy," Pee Wee cracked, then shrieked in a loud falsetto, "'Oh, that's it, Bickie, right there! Oh, yes, Bickie! Yes!'"

"That's it, Russell, you asked for it!" Bix leaped on Pee Wee and wrestled him to the pier as Ryker stood there laughing and Buddy fidgeted. He pinned Pee Wee to the planking, holding down his gangly arms, his own arms trembling with the effort. It felt good to use his muscles again, even for something as stupid as this. But Pee Wee wasn't about to give up. They came close to rolling off the edge twice before coming up panting and sweaty, with Bix getting a last headlock on Pee Wee.

He looked up and saw Tram's silhouette walking toward them. "What's up, Frankie?" he called, adjusting his rumpled clothes.

"Last set's cancelled," Tram said, pulling off his tie. "The kids are gone, the farmers left for the movies, and there's nobody here."

"That settles it. We're gonna go see the sisters," Bix said. "Doc, gimme the keys."

"Can I come, too?" Buddy asked.

"Aw, get lost, squirt," Pee Wee said.

"Sure," Bix said, holding the car keys near his ear and making them jingle. "You're driving."

ଚ୍ଚଓଷ

Back roads, night-heavy smell of weeds and vegetation. There were no streetlights and Ryker's Dodge convertible was making it along the dirt road by feel, inching over ruts and rocks. Buddy's hands shuddered on the steering wheel as they negotiated a particularly hard bump.

"How much farther?" he asked, voice cracking.

"Hey, you live here, punk. You tell us," Pee Wee said.

Bix knew the terrain like the back of his hand. "The road curves up ahead," he said. "And yeah, see? Lights."

The farmhouse was down at the end of the road, awash in fields of rustling corn. They bumped into the front yard. Buddy killed the engine and they sat for a moment and listened to it tick, as if the Dodge was catching its breath from a long, exhausting run.

"You guys better stay out here a minute while I try and smooth things over with the old ladies," Bix said. He got out and headed up creaky steps to the front porch, where a kerosene lamp burned behind the lace curtains at the parlor window. He could smell rotting wood and the sick-sweet aroma of corn mash.

It was already almost two in the morning, but from previous visits he knew the sisters stayed up all night, listening to wax cylinder recordings of Fred Van Eps and the Sousa Band and playing endless hands of canasta.

As he stood on the front porch, Bix quickly ran over in his mind what he'd say to try and smooth things over. *Explain. And make it right, so we can forget it.* "Look, what we did was wrong," he muttered under his breath as he stood on the porch waiting for someone to come to the door. "And we're all really sorry. We'll do anything to make up for it. What we did was wrong. We're all really sorry. We'll do anything...."

He knocked and leaned his ear against the door, listening. Inside he could hear Martha muttering under her breath all down the hall, the slap of her slippers against the floor, and then the slide of the chain lock and the door opening. She stood there in a flowered cotton wrapper, gray hair pulled back, wrinkled face grim.

"Hey, hello there, Martha. Can I come in for a minute?"

She opened the door, still not speaking.

Bix stepped in and looked past Martha and the stacks of twine-tied newspapers and *National Geographics* that lined the hallway. Mary sat at the kitchen table under a pull-down kerosene lamp, a cup of coffee and a deck of cards in front of her, faded blond hair flowing over her shoulders.

Bix looked at his feet. "Well, what I came over here to say is that what we did was wrong. And we're all really sorry. We'll do anything to make up for it. We even...."

Her face went slack and Bix felt the tension in the air evaporate a little. "You might as well come into the kitchen and sit down, after coming all this way," she said, gesturing to a chair across from Mary, who sat staring at him, smiling faintly. He sat and immediately started drumming his fingers on the table.

"Like I said, we're..."

"That niece of ours is far from blameless in this. She admitted as much."

"Really, Martha, Pee Wee or nobody told her to come bring that moon...."

"We know." Martha sighed. "Our brother sent her here to stay with us because he wanted to get her away from bad companions and some trouble she'd gotten into back home." She looked at Bix, face grim. "She's a wild one, Bix. A bad girl, no two ways about it. There's one in every family."

Bix looked at Martha, jarred by her choice of words. *One in every family*—where had he heard that before? He almost laughed out loud when it clicked. The old man. Naturally. It was one of his favorite sayings. "There's one in every family," he'd say every time Bix did something wrong, "and you're the one in ours."

"Well, what's done is done," Martha said. "She's back home now, and I've told my brother I won't have her back. Not for all the tea in China." Her wrinkled face softened and she smiled at Bix. "You're not a bad boy," she said, reaching out to pat his hand. "And you've got a wonderful way with music about you. Why do you drink so much, honey? It really isn't good for you."

He flushed, fingers drumming. *Not again.* "Heck, Martha, all the boys like a drink now and then. What else is there to do around here?"

She snorted. "You'd be better off with a steady girlfriend, someone other than that hussy out at the lake. A nice, steady girl who'll look after you."

Bix slouched down in the chair. "No ball and chain for me," he muttered.

"You know, you remind me of a fellow I knew, many years ago. He had a way with music, too, and never wanted to be tied down to any woman." She looked at a spot over Bix's head and smiled. "Another wild boy. Willful. Brazen! Didn't care a fig for what people thought about him—didn't want to be like everybody else. Was bound and determined to make it in the city, playing piano. He went off and moved to New York City."

"What happened to him?"

Her smile fell away into a web of creases. "We never heard from him again. Years later, somebody from out East told us that he'd ended up playing for drinks wherever he could get the work. He never even lived to see forty."

There's one in every family.

Nice story, he thought, the sort of story the old man would tell him in one of their little talks in the parlor in the house on Grand Avenue. He would drone on as Bix stared at the mantelpiece with its brown ceramic frieze of two birds huddled on a flowering branch, willing one of them to flutter its wings and fly the hell away from here, soar over the rooftops of Grand Avenue, high up into the clouds until the house was a distant dot, until Davenport was nothing but a sprawl of distant dots along the gleaming ribbon of the Mississippi, and follow that ribbon away, as far as it could go...

And what's she trying to say, that I'm going to end up like that, just because I'm not married and working in the old man's coal yard? I'm only twenty-three. I swim and play baseball and tennis, I'm in great health. And I got my whole life ahead of me, with plenty of time to do everything I want to do. What I want to do, not what everybody else thinks I should do.

As if reading his mind, Martha sighed and patted Bix's hand again. "Well, I suppose you're right. A little drink now and then never hurt anyone." She sat upright, her face turning hard again. "But there's some others in this town might not look at things that way."

"What do you mean? It's all over and done with now, right? Can't we just forget about it?"

She pursed her lips and stared at the wall. "I've been hearing talk. You boys better keep your noses clean now to the end of the summer. Or there might be trouble, if not with the police, then with the Ku Klux Klan."

Bix laughed. "You mean those goofy guys in bed sheets?"

"Out here they take them seriously. Don't say I didn't warn you. Bix, you're looking so thin. Would you care for a sandwich while you're here? And I know the boys are out in the car. Go ahead, call them in."

"How about a slice of seed cake, Bixie?" Mary said, permitted to speak at last now that peace was established. "Sister made it just this morning."

Pee Wee and Buddy came in and the sisters covered the table with jars of glowing red preserves, fresh butter and thick wedges of cake. Mary set a plate with a ham sandwich in front of Bix while Martha went out to the barn and brought in the gallon jugs of corn liquor. *Finally.* "Here, give it a try," Martha said, brimming a clutch of mismatched jelly jars with the clear liquid and passing them around.

Bix shot it back, feeling the liquid trace a burning trail down his throat and into his stomach, where it proceeded to glow like a well-banked fire.

Martha patted him on the shoulder and poured him another shot while Pee Wee and Buddy downed theirs.

Mary scurried to the phonograph into the parlor, which was filled a moment later with the crackly sounds of the John Philip Sousa band playing "Stars and Stripes Forever." Pee Wee started shuffling and dealing the cards between the sisters, Buddy and himself. Bix, suddenly remembering something, picked up a kerosene lamp from the sideboard and carried it and his freshly replenished jelly jar into the parlor.

The keys of the pump organ were cracked and yellowed and he wasn't much on pump organs, but hell, a keyboard was a keyboard. He experimentally formed some chords, fingers spread wide. When the John Philip Sousa cylinder ended, he pumped the foot pedals and gasped out the opening bars of "Nearer My God to Thee," in the back of his mind listening to Pee Wee and Buddy in the kitchen arguing about the rules of canasta, and Mary crooning the words of the hymn as she cleared up the dishes. He paused to finish off the shot of moonshine and wiped his mouth on the sleeve of his shirt. His lips were starting to feel numb.

Then he launched into "Onward Christian Soldiers," feeling the familiar warmth of the booze and the music blend into a soothing haze that gradually enveloped him, making the other voices and sounds fade away. Sometimes it took awhile to get to that point, but the sisters' moonshine was first-rate stuff, and playing these hymns put him right back to his boyhood in Davenport, took him completely away from the moment.

He played, comparing in his mind this sad wheezing with the sounds his mother coaxed from the massive pipe organ at the First Presbyterian Church back home—sonorous, rolling sounds, ranging from deep bass notes that shuddered up through the soles of his shoes and vibrated in his stomach, to the peeps of the smallest pipes, chittering like crickets between his ears. As he played he was back in his hard seat at the end of the Beiderbecke pew, staring at the stained-glass window depicting Christ recruiting the disciples and feeling Burnie's elbow jabbing into his ribs whenever he started to doze off.

And then, after his mother played the recessional and everybody crowded out of the church, it would be time to go off to a Sunday pork roast dinner at Oma's big house on Seventh Street, high on the bluffs overlooking LeClaire

Park and the Mississippi River. And on Christmas his cousins would be there, and after the tree and the presents and two servings of dessert, there'd be endless hands of cards for the grownups and more music in Oma's parlor, Bix playing the piano, his cousin Gertrude singing, everybody laughing and happy, Mother clapping and singing along, and Dad, even Dad smiling and proud.

As he played, he thought about what Martha just said about finding a steady girl. It was the first time he'd thought about it with any seriousness since he and Ruth had called it quits. The truth of it was, he was having a hell of a lot more fun right now, getting drunk and playing around on the organ, than he'd be having with a girl—or at least a girl like Crystal Hawkins, who didn't know which end was up. Stupid girls were boring. The kind of girls Bix liked were hard to come by—girls with a brain, maybe even like that girl Harriet who worked at the Hotel Hudson, the girl who went to Indiana U. It might be nice getting to know a girl like that, even just to talk to, especially one as pretty as she was, he thought, remembering how her soft brown eyes lit up when they'd talked about music.

It was different with Joy. Joy was no genius, but she understood the music, and she understood him. He felt as comfortable with her as he did with the guys in the cottage. You didn't have to put on a show for Joy. You could be yourself, even drunk or hung over, she didn't care. She was the kind of girl you could share the bathroom with.

And anyhow, if it came down to a draw between women and music, Bix would always take music. The fact was, he'd never recovered from hearing an Original Dixieland Jazz Band record in the Beiderbecke's parlor when he was fourteen. After a childhood of genteel band music in the park, church music, light popular tunes, that stuff had reached through the slotted wooden speaker of the Victrola and assaulted him. It had been a blast of cacophonous sound, a braying like melodious barnyard animals, in double-time, triple-time, like a Ford with the throttle off and the engine racing. It hit Bix in the guts, the vitals, turned his knees weak, and shook him like a hard-on.

And hit him about the same age as his first hard-ons, and thus the two sensations became inextricably bound, the music and a physical sensuality, neither of which he could fully control at first. And even when he could control it, the residual feelings were still there, so now certain music sent him dizzy, made him moan, felt like hands, like mouths on him. After all, the word *jazz* originally meant *fucking*.

But women confused Bix. He liked them, they could be a hell of a lot of fun, but after the laughs were over, they always changed. Everything got serious. You started out dating, and going places, and sometimes you ended up in bed which was fine with Bix, although half the time he didn't even care whether that happened or not. He just liked going places and having some laughs. He almost hated when it got to the bed stage, because that's always when they got funny.

Like with Ruth. They'd had so much fun at first, hitting all the speaks, bowling, golfing, double-dating with her sisters and a couple of the other guys in the band. But then....

"Hey Bix, we better go." He looked up to see Buddy shaking his arm. "My mother'll skin me alive if she finds out where I am."

"Right you are, my good man," Bix muttered in an upper-crust English accent. He rose unsteadily and stumbled out into the kitchen. He always forgot just how strong the sisters' moonshine was until after he'd had a few shots under his belt.

He hooked up a gallon jug from the table, fumbled in his wallet for some money, handed it to Mary, and headed toward the hallway, bumping into the kitchen table on the way.

"Yeah, come on, let's beat it," Pee Wee said, putting an arm around Bix's shoulders to steady him.

"Goodbye, boys," Mary smiled, tousling Bix's hair as they staggered back through the kitchen. "See you soon."

Bix dug in his pockets for the keys to Ryker's Dodge and placed them ceremoniously into Buddy's hands. "Home, James," he said. And he passed out in the backseat on the way back to the cottage just as the first birds of the morning began singing in the trees around the lake.

Chapter 5

Ray Reynolds had a rattletrap old Ford truck that he used on the backroads of LaPorte County to visit and collect from the area bootleggers. It had such a distinctive rattle and grind when shifting gears that there was no mistaking the sound of it, even from a half-mile away. Farmers would come and stand in front of their barns when they heard Ray's truck, because Ray coming was like Santa Claus bringing Christmas. Practically everyone in the area had a bumper crop of corn this year, which meant there was plenty to spare to make corn liquor, both for illegal sale and personal consumption.

As Ray guided the Ford up the dirt road to Melvin Ross's farm, he thought of the signs of wealth around the county since Prohibition became the law of the land. Melvin had just bought a new John Deere tractor, shiny and green, stored under tarp in his freshly painted barn. Clyde Babbitt had bought his old lady a new gas stove, replacing a cast-iron monstrosity that had been in the family for generations. Other folks had bought new automobiles, gussied up their farmhouses, even taken their wives and kids on vacation to places like New York and Chicago. For most of them, Prohibition was the best thing to happen since they chased the Indians off the land, and a hell of a lot easier— easier than falling out of bed, as Ray always described it.

After all, making corn liquor was nothing new in LaPorte County. Ray's daddy and granddaddy had done it, as had most everyone else's daddy and granddaddy, for their own consumption. Even those addle-pated old Hawkins sisters, whose niece had started such a ruckus at Hudson Lake on the Fourth, cooked their own brew, using their granddaddy's recipe. Doing it for profit was just a matter of volume, as he'd explained to the fellows, and buying some newer and bigger equipment to crank out the surplus.

And handling requisitions was nothing new to Ray. Hell, hadn't he done that in the U.S. Army, where he'd been a quartermaster with the First Infantry Division? Figures had been the only thing he was good at in school, and book-keeping came natural to Ray—especially the kind of bookkeeping where you're skimming a little off the top, selling a little on the side. Make sure to keep everybody happy, that was the trick.

Of course, there was an initial investment to pay for the equipment they needed—copper tubing, the big galvanized vats they used for fermenting, and the denatured alcohol itself. So Ray set up an account over at Malcolm Wilkie's hardware store in downtown South Bend, where Malcolm gave him a discount on whatever the leggers needed. And to keep Malcolm happy, Ray gave him a cut of the profit. Things worked out so well that Malcolm even had his delivery boy bring the equipment right out to the leggers—a funny touch, since the delivery boy was Trent Walker, whose old man Cyrus was on the highway patrol and the Ku Kluxers to boot.

As Ray steered the truck into the farmyard, he saw Melvin emerge from the barn, where he kept his alky cooking equipment. Knowing Melvin, though, he was probably polishing his damn tractor again instead of checking on the mash. Ray watched as Melvin walked over, pulling a red kerchief out of his coveralls and mopping his brow, as if he'd just got done plowing the back forty.

"You hear the news?" he called as he walked over to Ray's truck. "Police did another raid over to South Bend."

Ray shrugged and pulled out Melvin's envelope. "Ain't no skin off our noses. Police gotta justify their existence somehow, and most of that's for the newspapers. Hell, half the councilmen are cooking hooch. Think they're gonna jeopardize their investment?"

Melvin grunted. "Even so, fella runs the joint on Indiana says there've been some out-of-towners nosin' around the place, askin' questions."

"I'm telling you, Melvin, the cops ain't gonna...."

"Oh, not cops, Ray, no sir," Melvin said, eyes wide. "No sir. More like the sorta tough customers you see over to that dance hall on Saturday nights. City fellas, all dressed up, with big automobiles. You suppose we got some competition?"

Before he could wave it away, Ray got to thinking that maybe Melvin was right. After all, their sales and production were up considerable from last year, mostly because of the business out at the Hudson Lake dance hall. Not only the buck-a-shot stuff that Ray dispensed at the soda fountain, but gallon goods, sold to the musicians and the customers who came to hear them. Now who the hell was trying to nose into his business? It couldn't be the Indianapolis bootlegging ring—they had their own suppliers and their own territory, and there was an unspoken agreement that they'd steer clear of LaPorte County.

"What are you tryin to say, Melvin? That big-city gangsters are lookin' to cut into LaPorte County?" He laughed to show he didn't mean it, which managed to coax a smile from the stoic Melvin. But the idea was already growing in Ray's mind.

Why *shouldn't* a big bootleg operation want a piece of the action in LaPorte County? They were doing good business with the lowest of overhead, with manufacturing and distribution running like clockwork. The last thing they needed was some gorilla outfit from out of town coming in and taking over, squeezing them out of the equation.

No, the thing to do was to see it coming and go on the offensive—to show whoever wanted to take over that it was in their best interest to keep the system that was already working.

Melvin stood there counting the twenties from the envelope Ray had handed him. No, these old boys wouldn't like it if some citified outfit came in and started disrupting their source of income. They wouldn't stand for it. They may be a little rough around the edges, but they weren't the dumb galoots outsiders might take them for.

"Well, thanks for the information, Melvin," Ray said, starting up the truck in a spew of exhaust smoke. "I'll be on the lookout for any strangers askin' questions. Can I count on you to take a stand if it comes to that?"

Melvin's grin grew broader. "Got a double-ought shotgun I'd be more than happy to oil up and use, if I needed to," he said.

"Well, keep her oiled, Melvin," Ray grinned, "keep her oiled."

Chapter 6

Harriet didn't became obsessed with Bix; that wasn't the way she approached things. Instead, in the weeks since she first met him at the Blue Lantern, she blocked out the sound of Mrs. Smith's incessant tirade against Buddy—on indefinite probation and wood-chopping patrol since his unauthorized visit to the Hawkins spinsters—and watched.

She kept her eyes on the little yellow cottage through the screen of the kitchen door while her hands automatically went about folding towels, stirring oatmeal, pouring water, mopping floors. She watched Bix with the same detached interest she used when tracking the activity of a lab rat, or an amoeba twitching in the spotlit platform of a microscope.

Although she hadn't forgotten the hair-trigger temper he'd displayed the first night she'd met him, it wasn't something she'd seen from him again. Rather, there was something she couldn't put her finger on that set him apart from the other musicians, something peculiar and not of a type, like the one inoculated rat in a trial group that's acting different from the other rats but doesn't know why.

While the fellows she now knew as Pee Wee, Dan and Itzy went horsing around in the lake, Bix would swim laps, then hoist himself onto the pier, woolen bathing suit streaming water, and sit watching them. On Mondays, when they'd take the South Shore into Chicago, all dressed in tailored suits, colorful ties and shirts the color of sherbet, he'd hook onto the departing train car just as it was pulling out of the station, wearing a worn brown suit, a too-tight vest, and a tie with a knot that was always just slightly askew. Sometimes she'd hear music from the little yellow cottage, phonograph records of what sounded like a symphonic orchestra instead of the usual hot jazz. And some mornings when she got to work, while the rest of the musicians were just getting to bed, she'd see him sitting alone at the end of the pier reading a book, or walking under the trees along the lake. Even when he was part of the crowd, he seemed to be alone, encased in some bubble of solitude that included only him and his thoughts.

Harriet wondered what he thought about out there—whether it was the music, or Joy, or maybe a girl he'd left back home. It was impossible to tell.

Bix was proving difficult to categorize, which was frustrating to someone as organized as Harriet. There was a solitary aura about him, a trait she could hear in his music, times when he'd take a solo so tangential to the melody that even the other musicians would look at him in confusion until they understood how perfectly it fit in. She theorized there were depths to him that were neither college boy nor traveling musician.

She found herself constantly finding things to do up in Joy's room, where she'd drop an innocuously worded question and wait for Joy to run with the conversational ball.

Most times she did, with her rattled accounts of her and Bickie and last spring in Chicago—a frantic narrative that ratcheted on like a stripped-down jalopy, full of speakeasies, amusement parks and late-night music sessions. Along the way she finally gave Joy permission to henna her hair, although the color blended into her natural brown and the results were less than dramatic. But although she learned the names of all the nightclubs they'd visited, Joy's narrative didn't tell Harriet a thing about what Bix was really like.

One afternoon, after delivering the crates to Ray at the soda fountain and getting a splinter for her trouble, Harriet walked down to the pier, finger stuck in her mouth, and stood there waiting for a breeze, her thin cotton dress plastered to her sweaty body.

It was already mid-July, and the real Midwest heat was starting to congeal over the compound huddled around Hudson Lake. All sorts of flying creatures were zooming or fluttering over the water, most in pairs, some coupled in flight, like the damselflies that hovered like animated knitting needles.

She was watching two yellow sulphur butterflies pirouette around each other and trying to remember their exact Latin genus name from high school biology when she heard a creak and a cough behind her.

Bix stood there in a crumpled white shirt, blotched tie, baggy belted trousers. He held something cupped loosely in his hand. After observing him for the last several weeks, Harriet found his sudden appearance almost like an apparition she'd conjured up herself. *Doesn't he own any decent clothes that fit?*, she thought before the smile automatically took over.

"Hello, Bix," she said. "Remember me? Harriet Braun, from the...."

"Indiana U.," he said in his inflectionless voice, eyes squinted against the sun so she couldn't tell if he was laughing or scowling. He walked past her and sat down at the end of the pier, opening his hand and dropping a pile of stones.

"Sure, I remember you." He picked up a stone and flung it into the lake, watching the ripples it left spread, then disappear.

"Boy, sure is hot, isn't it?" she asked, pushing her hair back from her face, acutely aware of her body and the smell it must be exuding. "Whoever said Indiana is a temperate climate lied."

He selected another stone from the pile, not looking at her. "Where do you keep yourself? I know you work at the hotel, but I never see you. Does Mrs. Smith keep you locked up in there like what's-her-name? You know. The girl with the hair in that fairy tale." He tossed the stone into the lake.

"Rapunzel." She laughed at the analogy, surprised he had made a connection like that. "We're not supposed to fraternize," she said. "Especially after you and your friends took Buddy out on a joyride and didn't bring him back until five in the morning. His mother barely lets him out of the house now." Harriet sat next to him, tucking her skirt around her legs, briefly wondering if she was being too forward and hoping she didn't smell too bad, but too curious about him to leave.

He sighed. "There goes my chauffeur. Hey, watch it," he said, inching over to make room for her. "You're fraternizing."

"No, I'm waiting for Buddy to come pick me up and take me back to my boardinghouse. That's about all she'll let him do now. And I'm off duty, so it's all nice and legal."

Bix glanced at her, eyes squinted. "Hey, you did something to your hair. It looks different."

Harriet laughed, feeling her face flush. "Oh, yes. Your friend Joy talked me into a henna. How do you like it?" Rudy probably would have never even noticed it, she thought.

He looked down again and hefted another stone. "Looks nice. It's got red in it. But not too much."

She picked a smooth, flat stone from the pile and skipped it across the lake, bouncing it five times, wondering what he was thinking.

Bix whistled softly. "Hot stuff. Hey, how come you never come around and hear the band that much? Saw you and your boyfriend at the big show on the Fourth, but not much afterward."

She shrugged. "No use antagonizing Mrs. Smith. And I've been pretty busy. Oh, there's my ride." She looked up as she heard the rattle of the Smith's Ford truck pull up to the pier. Buddy was at the wheel, chewing his lips and looking nervous. Buddy wouldn't say anything to his mother about her talking to Bix, but she didn't care if he did. This was all completely harmless. Bix knew she had a boyfriend, and anyhow, he had Joy, he wasn't interested in her. And she was only interested in him because the way he played cornet made her want to find out what made him tick.

"Well, goodbye," Harriet said, extending a hand for Bix to shake. "It was nice talking to you." She got that sexual tingle again when their hands touched, the same as the first night she met him. *And now I really don't understand why,* she thought. *I thought he'd be interesting. But for someone who's traveled all over, who's so brilliant on the horn, he sure doesn't have much to say. But still*—There was something boyish and appealing about his round, frank face, and now that she was close enough in daylight, she saw his eyes were dark brown.

He wiped his hand on his shirt and jammed it suddenly into his pocket. "Hey, want to go fishing sometime?" he blurted. "I mean, when you're off work. They bite pretty good around sunset, and I could give you a ride back to your boardinghouse in Doc Ryker's car when we're done. How about it?"

She stood there for a second, not knowing what to say, the unexpectedness of his suggestion taking her completely by surprise. "I have to go now, but yes, that would be nice. I'd like that," she rattled, heedless of Mrs. Smith's admonitions and everything else, suddenly just wanting to see him again, to talk to him and find out once and for all what he was really like.

His whole face lit up when he smiled, like a schoolboy being told he has the day off.

"How about tomorrow?"

Buddy blew the horn.

"I've got to go now, but sure, I'd love to go fishing. I'll meet you after work tomorrow, right here. All right?"

"Jake. See ya then."

ട്രOCB

By the time Harriet was done with her work and changed into a clean dress, the sun had slid into a pocket of clouds low on the horizon. Bix was already down by the lake, throwing bamboo fishing poles and a tackle box into a red rowboat tied to the end of the pier. She noticed right away that he'd dressed for the occasion in a clean shirt and tie, white flannel pants and a pair of saddle shoes. His hair was glossy with pomade and a minuscule dab of toilet paper, tinged with red, stuck to his chin in testimony to a recent shave.

"Here," she said, walking to the end of the pier and holding up a wicker basket. "I brought us some dinner."

His face bunched into the smile that was already becoming familiar to her. "And I've got the libations. Home brew somebody's uncle put up. You ever fished before?"

"Years ago, with my dad. I can barely remember anything about it, except how much I screamed when he put the worms on the hooks."

Bix looked at her blankly, then slapped his forehead. "Jeez, the nightcrawlers! I forgot all about 'em." He stood there and rubbed his temples with his fingertips, staring into the boat. "I suppose I could run back to the hotel and...."

"What's in the tackle box? Don't you have any lures?"

"Lures? Yeah, I suppose Itzy has some in there." He opened the tackle box, clinking around several brown bottles and mumbling under his breath. "But maybe I took 'em out to make more room for the beer, I don't remember."

"Forget it. We can use pieces of bread. Come on, let's go."

"Oh. Bread. Okay, I suppose you're right. I'm not much of an outdoorsman, or can't you tell? Here, I'll help you in."

Harriet laughed. "I think you're missing something else."

"Huh?" He looked into the boat. "Besides the nightcrawlers?"

"Where are the oars?"

He slapped his forehead again. "Boy, am I a mental midget. Okay, back to the boathouse. Wait just a second, and I'll be right back, really. Right back. Just stay right here."

Harriet sat on the edge of the pier and laughed to herself as he hurried toward the boathouse, still mumbling to himself. She fluffed out the skirt of her freshly pressed cotton print dress and opened the wicker basket to take inventory. Four chicken salad sandwiches wrapped in wax paper, a small jar of pickles, a Mason jar of lemonade, and two slices of blueberry pie Mrs. Smith had just baked.

It was funny he was so nervous, she thought. But then, she was a little nervous herself, although she didn't know why. There was nothing threatening about him. He wasn't the type to get her out on the lake and try to put the make on her. But her stomach had seized into a tight knot of apprehension, and she wondered if she'd be able to hold down any of Mrs. Smith's chicken salad sandwiches. Stop it right now, she thought. This isn't high school. You're a big girl, or at least you know all the big-girl lines. Nobody would suspect that if she could split herself in two, the shadow-Harriet, the one who was scared, would run away and hide in the boathouse, leaving the Harriet who knew all the lines in the rowboat with this musician and his unreadable, dark eyes.

Bix came hurrying back down the pier, oars cradled in his arms. "Here we go. Now we're ready." He threw the oars into the boat and got in, then reached a hand up for her. Harriet felt a momentary unsettling as they sat down and Bix locked the oars into place. Then he unlooped the rope, took the oars and began pulling the boat out into the middle of the lake.

He rowed until they were well away from the cattails and seaweed that choked the shoreline, far enough away so that the splashing and shouting of the last of the swimmers on Bluebird Beach smoothed out into a ripple of background noise.

He opened the tackle box and she opened the picnic basket and they exchanged goods. There were some brightly painted metal lures nestled in the compartments on the bottom of the box, so they tied them to the lines on the fishing poles and dropped them into the water, watching as the lures sank into the darkness of the lake.

Bix sat with a chicken salad sandwich in one hand, the fishing pole in the other, and watched the water intently, not speaking. He was humming under his breath, a skein of notes that sounded familiar, like the variation on some melody she'd heard a million times. She leaned and listened closer and heard it was a syncopated version of "Row, Row, Row Your Boat."

"Where are you from, Bix?" she asked softly, almost afraid to disturb him.

He glanced up, chewing, and swallowed before he answered. "Davenport, Iowa. River town. Lots of music comin' in on the excursion riverboats, all up and down the Mississippi. You?"

"Oh, I'm from Indianapolis, just outside of town. We have a little farm there. Where did you go to school?"

He shrugged. "Davenport High School. Lake Forest Academy." He laughed. "Eight days at the University of Iowa as an unclassified student."

"Didn't you graduate?"

"Nope. Never even finished high school. Got kicked out of Lake Forest before I got done. And they wouldn't let me take more music classes at the U., and then I was involved in a little ruckus at some joint in town, so...." He broke off, rubbing the palms of his hands on his pants and continued staring at the fishing pole. "Shouldn't be long now. I caught a couple of big ones out here last week, right around this time."

Kicked out, Harriet thought. Not even a high school diploma. *Is he really that stupid? Or is it something else?*

"How did you start playing music?" she asked, sipping lemonade from the Mason jar.

The smile again, the one that compressed his pliant features and crinkled his eyes so he seemed to be laughing at a secret joke. "Used to play for nickels before I even started first grade. Piano. Then cornet later, in a kids' band, then on the riverboats. Then dance bands at Lake Forest, all over Chicago. The Cy-Bix Band, we played frat house dances and stuff. Then the Wolverines. We cut some sides for Gennett. Toured a lot, even New York, the Cinderella Ballroom. Then Chicago again with Charlie Straight's band, and then me and Tram hooked up in St. Louis at the Arcadia." He sighed. "This Goldkette gig is the biggest thing that's happened to me. Great bunch of guys, too. I'm learning a lot." He jiggled the fishing pole and tossed the crusts of his sandwich overboard.

No, he's not stupid, she thought. Unschooled, and inarticulate, but naturally talented. Gifted, with the potential to do so much more. "Do you think you'll ever go back to school?" she asked.

"Don't think so. But I do want to learn more about music." He looked up at her, straight into her eyes for the first time that day, and again she was struck by the intensity she saw there. "Have you ever heard of Ravel? How about Stravinsky? *The Rites of Spring? Afternoon of a Faun?* Wow. Now *that's* music." He reached for one of the bottles in the tackle box. "When I was living in St. Louis, we'd go to the symphony all the time, me and Hassler, the sax man with the band. Boy, we heard it all. Great sound in that hall. All the classics, although I'm not big on that romantic slush, or even the classical. That stuff's like listening to someone play scales, for Christ's sake. But the new stuff—wow."

Harriet continued looking at him, new thoughts turning in her mind. She still couldn't categorize him, but that was all right. Under the rumpled clothes and the itinerant musician's life, he was like her—he was passionate about something.

"It seems funny that a jazzman would like that kind of music," she said.

"Hell, it's the berries!" He leaned forward, excited. "Say, did you ever shake hands with a classical musician? Like a first violinist in a world-class symphony orchestra? Their hands—they're *hard*. You can feel the muscles under the skin. Their skin is soft. But from all the playing, the practice, the muscles in their hands are like iron." He held up his own hand, looking at it. "Especially a violinist. Not their bowing hand, but the hand they use to finger with. They got fingers like bands of iron." He laughed and ducked his head, as if suddenly self-conscious. "It's funny they call us musicians. We're just guys in a band. Now those symphony orchestra players, what they do up there—that's real musicianship. Makes us look like chumps."

He reached down into the tackle box for a bottle opener and popped the cap off the beer. Foam spilled out over his hands and dripped into the bottom of the boat. He handed her the bottle, then opened one for himself. They sat there sipping silently, Bix back staring at the fishing pole, Harriet staring at Bix.

"Would you like to play in a symphony orchestra?" she asked.

He looked at her again, and she saw the enthusiasm in his eyes die, like a light suddenly switched off. "Can't." He tipped the beer bottle to his mouth, throat working, then wiped foam from his lips with the back of his hand. "You gotta read music to play in any kind of symphony orchestra. And I'm about as good at reading music as I am at any other kind of schoolwork. Which is lousy."

"Oh, I don't believe that. You play so beautifully."

"By ear, most of it. Or improvisation. I hear it in my head, then I play it. That won't fly in the horn section of a symphony orchestra."

"Can't you work with someone who'll help you?"

"Aw, they all try. Tram, and Fuzzy Farrar, our trumpet man, lots of other guys. It's hard, though, because I learned to play all half-assed. Fingering all wrong, and it's hard for me to follow the notes. I even went to the head brass man at the St. Louis Symphony, practically begged him to take me on as a student. All he said is I got a gift for music and he can't teach me anything."

The part about having a gift for music is very true, Harriet thought. He just needs some help and encouragement, like she got in high school when her biology teacher recognized she had a talent. Someone who understands how special he is.

He looked up at her, smiling. "Enough jawing about me. What's your story? Joy says you're in pre-med. That true?"

She looked down and smoothed her skirt, uncomfortable now that he'd turned the tables on her. She didn't want to talk about herself. "Yes, I just finished up my freshman year."

"Bet it's pretty tough sledding, huh? All those science classes."

"It wasn't bad." She ticked the courses off on her fingers. "Two semesters of French and English composition and zoology, three hours of psychology, five hours of Chemistry 1. I did well enough to get my scholarship renewed, anyway."

"Chemistry," he groaned. "My downfall. So how did a farm girl from Indianapolis get interested in medicine, anyway?"

Harriet smiled to herself. "Blame it on having three little sisters. I went from fixing their broken dolls to fixing them whenever they got hurt. Lots of iodine and castor oil."

"Naw, anybody can do that. You must have been really smart in school." There was something wistful about the way he said it, not meeting her eyes.

"I just liked it, that's all. I was always interested in how the body works." She felt herself blushing as the words left her mouth. "I mean, how the body works from a scientific standpoint," she rattled. She briefly thought of dissecting frogs, pithing them first, then neatly incising them from sternum to anus, holding apart the flaps of flesh with long pins, and watching in amazement as the tiny seed-shaped heart kept on beating. Long after it needed to, long after its owner was beyond the reach of its rhythm.

"So you want to be a doctor and heal people."

She smiled. "No, a medical researcher. Anybody can be a country sawbones. That's what my high school biology teacher told me. He always said I was blessed with a 'calm and analytical mind.' Some blessing."

"Nothing wrong with a girl being smart," he said, opening another beer, offering it to her, then sipping it himself when she declined. He looked her in the eye. "Lonely, though, I bet."

She stared at him, surprised, feeling as if he'd somehow looked into her eyes and seen that shadow-Harriet, the one who had existed before she went off to college. The awkward girl walking down the halls with biology books pressed to her chest, avoiding everyone's eyes. The girl who only felt comfortable in front of the microscope, after class when everybody else was gone. Caring for her kid sisters, doing housework while her mother worked, or babysitting other people's kids, cleaning other people's houses, for the extra money they needed.

She'd forced herself to change once she got to college. The day she arrived on the Indiana U. campus, with its red-brick lecture halls and dorms nestled along avenues of arching old trees, she knew she had to make it her home, that she couldn't creep through the hallways of her life anymore. She used the music to open the windows and let in the fresh air. There were dances every weekend and music everywhere on campus, from parties at the fraternity houses to the gathering places like the Book Nook, the cramped little sandwich shop where students came to impress each other with their hot playing. Her only responsibility was to get good grades, which was a breeze for her. Best of all, at college she could get her fill of music.

And she had Rudy, who supported her in everything, who loved her, even offered to work and put her through medical school if she was really serious about it. Lonely? Why should she be? And then she remembered how she'd watched Bix all these days, not talking to him, just speculating about what was going on in his mind. That was something a lonely person like the shadow-Harriet would do.

And hadn't she always felt different from her family and the people she grew up with, as if she wasn't theirs at all, but some changeling stuck in the cradle by an evil imp? Sometimes she even felt that way with Rudy, those times when he assumed their being together forever was a given when he should know that nothing was a given. But how could Bix know that?

"Well, but you have your boyfriend," Bix said, as if reading her mind. "What's he like?"

Harriet paused and took a breath, trying to shake off the morbid chain of thought Bix's innocuous comment had started. "Oh, he's another kid from Indy, a junior on a scholarship for architecture."

"Wait, don't tell me. Smart. Good-looking. A frat man. Plays football, right?"

She laughed at his omniscient description of Rudy. A typical alpha male, she thought, the type that gets the pick of the food and the females. The natural order of things, according to Darwin and most of the civilized world, in spite of the Scopes case in that Tennessee backwater last year. "Yes, but he loves music, too. We met at a dance at his fraternity house."

"How's he feel about his girlfriend being a—what is it again? A medical researcher?"

"He says he'd love to see a Hoosier come up with a cure for cancer, especially if it was a Hoosier girl."

"Well, that's jake. Sounds like your life is all set." He smiled up at her again, but something unsaid seemed to lurk behind his eyes.

But it never really is, she thought, like she always did when Rudy would start talking about their future. Things could happen, cataclysmic things that no one ever planned, and everything could change overnight. She thought of tornadoes ripping houses off their foundations and flinging them into the greenish sky, floods carrying off cows and cars and people, people who if they were lucky enough to survive were left with nothing and had to start all over again.

"You, too. You're on your way to becoming a great musician."

"Musician?" He laughed. "I'm just a musical degenerate. Hey!" He pointed to the line, which had suddenly stiffened, straining in the water. "Looks like we got something."

ଚୀଔ

Between them they hauled up five fish that day, good-sized lake perch that Harriet would bring to Mrs. Traub to make for dinner. Bix strung them on a line and dangled them in the water alongside the canoe to keep them cool while they finished the blueberry pie and Bix finished the beer.

By the time the mosquitoes started getting fierce and fireflies began spangling the bushes and trees along the shoreline, Harriet realized she'd done more talking than Bix. He'd made her feel comfortable enough that she'd told him everything—about school, Rudy, her family, her dreams, even a little about her fears and misgivings and the shyness that she'd managed to bury under the easygoing words and the friendly smile. He watched and listened, eyes on her face, smiling and interjecting a word here and there. He thought the idea of a woman doctor was just jake, and she had him half-convinced that going back to school was a good idea, as long as he could take lots of music classes. Although she couldn't really say she knew Bix, she'd learned enough about him to know she liked him a lot—which she found unsettling and confusing in light of Rudy.

The sun was starting to set as they rowed back to the pier, the windows of the dance hall already throwing golden squares of light out onto the surface of the lake.

"Gotta hustle," Bix said as they walked down the pier, the string of fish dangling at his side. "We go on at eight." He looked at Harriet, the white of his shirt glowing ghostly in the shadow of the boathouse. "Why don't you stay and hear the band? We can talk between sets."

"I'd love to, but the Traubs will be worried. And I have to get these fish back."

His eyes were earnest. "Some other time?"

"All right. And when Rudy comes up...."

His smile turned wry. "Yeah, yeah, I know."

"And you've got Joy."

"So? We can still be friends, right?"

She laughed. "Fishing buddies."

His hand went up as if to touch her face, then dropped to his side. He looked confused, as confused as she felt about him. Then he laughed, too. "Fishing buddies. Come on, I'll take you home."

Chapter 7

Joy

I knew I shouldn't have gone into town that day. That's what made me so blue again, and took me away into South Bend and that's the day it started to happen between Bickie and Little Sister.

I was just gonna go to the movies over at the Castle in South Bend, only ten cents and it was Lon Chaney in "The Phantom of the Opera," supposed to be real spooky. And I figured I'd go shopping and look at the stores and just fool around town for the day. It's nice being here, but sometimes when the boys are busy it gets kind of lonesome, and then I miss being in Chicago. Especially on weekdays, when it was so damn quiet you could hear old lady Smith's cow mooing out back by the cottage, and that reminds me way too much of the ranch.

I hitched a ride into town with Ryker, who had to do it on the sly so his old lady wouldn't get the wrong idea, and then he dumps me off downtown on the corner of Michigan and Washington like I'm a goddamn hooker or something. They say it's pretty busy here during the school year when all the kids from Notre Dame are around, but weekdays in the summer in South Bend are pretty slow and quiet, at least to a city girl like me. Still, there were some office workers going to lunch from the Singer Sewing Machine Factory and the place they make Studebaker cars, so it wasn't totally dead.

They had a sale at Ellsworths' Ladies Clothing so I picked up a couple of cute tub silk dresses, and stopped for lunch at the Christiana Tavern for their famous spring chicken dinner, only the spring chicken I got tasted more like last Thanksgiving's leftover turkey.

The Castle was right on Washington, and it was nice and cool inside so I bought some gumdrops at the drugstore on the corner and went in.

Well, the Phantom was spooky, all right, especially when he whipped off that mask and Mary Philbin fainted and a couple of ladies in the show screamed when they saw Lon Chaney with his face all warped up like that. I didn't scream because I read in *Photoplay* that he did it all with putty and makeup, nobody's really that ugly, though if Bickie had been there I probably would have screamed and grabbed his arm just to hear him laugh and call me a fraidy cat and hold my head against his shoulder until the spooky part was over.

But after the Phantom, instead of the Felix the Cat cartoons they usually had, they ran some color slides of Harry Langdon in "Tramp, Tramp, Tramp" and then started another movie. That horrible, awful goddamn movie.

It was called "The Black Stork," and from the cards outside it looked liked something good, a society melodrama, with a rich boy and a poor girl, something you'd see Norman Kerry or Adolph Menjou in. But no.

This was an old picture, you could tell from the clothes and the hammy way the actors played their parts. It was about some guy who gets married to a girl because they love each other and they have a baby, but there was something wrong with the guy and their baby turns out to be deformed. Just horrible. And the doctor wants to put the baby out of his misery but the mother stops him and the baby grows up and becomes a bum, a degenerate, no good, a drunk, a dope fiend, and in the end he goes and shoots the doctor for not killing him in the first place.

Well, after that horrible movie was over I just sat there and put my head down on the seat in front of me and cried and the usher had to tell me to leave and I was crying so hard the sun outside hurt my eyes.

Ryker was due to pick me up around five, but I couldn't let him see me like that so I ducked into a church, of all places, just to sit and calm down. But the place was full of old Polish *stata babas* rattling their rosaries, and that reminded me of being a little girl back in Billings so that didn't help, either.

On the way back Ryker kept asking me what the hell happened but I couldn't tell him. I couldn't because it wouldn't make sense to him, it really didn't even make sense to me. So when we got back to the hotel I went over to the cottage looking for Bickie and he wasn't there and then I really felt blue. And then I saw him come walking up all dressed in white and humming to himself and I started crying all over again because I knew right then what was happening, even if he didn't.

It wasn't over right away. Harriet was busy working. It wasn't like her and Bickie were hanging around together all the time. And Bickie told me right off he'd taken her fishing, she was just a nice kid like his sister back home, he wasn't interested in her, anyway, he said, she wasn't his type at all.

So at first things stayed pretty much the same, with the boys rehearsing and playing and me hanging around the cottage and singing while Bickie practiced outside. But sometimes all the things in my mind would start pressing down on me, that horrible movie and the thought of Bickie with Harriet, and the goddamn mooing of that cow, and I'd start crying and couldn't stop.

Because everything was going to change, and I just wanted things to stay the way they were right now—with me and Bickie and the music and Hudson Lake, and nothing or nobody else coming between us.

The first time it happened, Bickie came hurrying in to see what was wrong and I tried to tell him, but it got all mixed up and didn't make sense and he ended up tickling me and laughing and we ended up doing it and then I felt better.

But after awhile, when the thoughts just got blacker and blacker, he stopped trying to cheer me up and instead would just go off with Pee Wee or Itzy to get the hell away from me, although he never said so. And then I was really alone.

And the more the thoughts turned black, the more I started to think about that goddamn horrible movie. The beginning of it, where the grandfather way back when gets a servant girl in a jam, and that's where everything starts to go bad, because of that bad blood.

And isn't that what they'd said about me?

That's what she told me, Millie, my sister-in-law, over and over again. That it was like a bad strain of cattle, you gotta keep books and be careful of which bull and cow you put together. Otherwise you get two-headed calves, or even worse, ones with diseases you can't see, even though they look pretty and normal on the outside with their big brown eyes, but carrying that bad blood inside where you can't see.

Millie thought it was bad breeding, just like animals. Some stock is better than others. Genetics, she called it, something we studied about with pea plants in high school. But people, too; some are just meant to be dumb.

The lady from the American Eugenics Society said the same thing, only fancier, when she pulled out all those pictures of the sides of people's heads, the shapes of their foreheads, she took a tape measure and measured everything on my head and wrote it all down and made a chart and that's what she called it, Slavic stock, like I was a cow, and other stuff I didn't understand, but it all added up to what Millie said, anyway.

And after remembering all this stuff I started thinking about the day it was just me and the rope. The day I left Montana. The day I tried to kill myself.

It had been a beautiful sunny day, clear, the sky so blue and clean, like it just came out of the washtub and hung up to dry. I'd been crying for days in the bedroom with the blinds drawn, just crying and crying about everything—Vern's drinking and never speaking to me, Millie and her talk about what I must have done to make it come out that way, and Michael, always him. His beautiful brown eyes—I'd never known where they came from, not mine, not Vern's, not like anyone in our families. And his headful of beautiful blond curls, such a blessed baby, my angel baby, even named after an angel, until they'd found out and made me give him away.

The barn had smelled so sweet, from all the fresh hay Vern and the farmhands had gotten in. I remembered times when me and Vern had gone up to the hayloft, with the sun coming through, and made love. Only Vern hadn't touched me in over a year by then.

I'd gone to the hayrack and looked around at everything hanging on the walls, everything in its place—buckets and shearers and brands and coils of heavyweight rope that Vern used to hog-tie the sheep when he was shearing them. I found the milking stool and stood up on it to reach the rope, feeling the cording under my fingers like a snake's skin, pebbly and smelling of hemp.

Outside I'd heard the sheep and the cows in their usual way, moaning on and on. Michael used to make a noise like that when he was hungry. Always that noise, slumped in his high chair, head to the side like it was too heavy for his little neck to support it, a baa or a moo, like a baby pen animal would make, no matter how many times I'd say, "Food, Mommy, I'm hungry, Mommy, please feed me, Mommy," trying to get him to say it back. He never said nothing.

It had been easy to throw the rope over the crossbeam until it caught tight, looped around twice, three times, so when I'd yanked one end it held, good and strong. Vern showed me how to tie the knot just so, back that year we were shearing for the first time, and he'd laughed in his quiet way about how I was scared of the sheep. *You tie it like this and they aren't going anywhere*, he'd said, his big red hands moving to loop the rope around and around and through, then tugging the loop open big enough to fit the sheep's legs through.

Then I'd sat on the milking stool and looked at the rope dangling in that square of sunlight. It had seemed right to me, even though the Holy Roman Catholic Church said it was the worst sin you could commit; they'd have to bury you in a potter's field away from all the good dead Catholics. But by then I didn't care; all I could think of was the nurse in her hard white uniform taking Michael away, down that long hall with the black-and-white tiled floor, her rubber-soled shoes squeaking and Michael just mooing and baaing, his head with its bright blond curls limp on her shoulder. To me he was still Michael, but to them he was a Mongolian idiot. That's what they'd called him. That's what was on the papers.

They'd told me to sign so I signed. Vern had already signed. I had watched his hands, red from work, thick fingernails scrubbed pink and clean, spread out on the paper as he slowly wrote his name on the line and added the 20 after the 19 on the year. I'd looked down at Vern's solid, sure black signature and leaned down to write my name next to his, just like on our wedding certificate.

And then it had been time to go get back into the Ford and make the long drive home to the ranch. I remembered the drive because it was so quiet, because even though Michael never talked, he'd make his noises and most times he sounded happy. Now there would still be no talking because me and Vern didn't have anything to say to each other.

It had been like that for a year and a half. Vern started drinking heavier than ever and sleeping on the sofa in the parlor and I stopped trying to stop him. Millie blamed Vern's drinking on me because I was a lazy wife, what man wouldn't drink with a dumb Polack like me, a millstone around his neck? In the morning he'd get up to take care of the animals and work with the farm hands, and I'd lay in bed, counting the crows on the telephone line like beads on a rosary and listening to the sheep noises outside.

After years of getting up at four in the morning and working alongside Vern, and taking care of Michael, I just couldn't get out of bed anymore. I'd just lay there all day under the covers like a pile of dead sticks and count the crows, listening to songs going through my head and wondering if Michael ever learned to say "I'm hungry, Mommy" to someone.

I wasn't even thinking. My hands were working on their own. I stood on the milking stool and tugged at the rope once more, making sure it would hold. Then I took the loop and put it around my neck. It felt warm and scratchy, like the high lace collar on my wedding dress. I pulled down the loop so the knot was right next to my ear, and the oily hemp smell was on my hands and in my hair.

I listened to the sheep and the birds outside, already feeling so far away that when I kicked down the milking stool it would feel more like flying than anything else, like flying free right out that hayloft window, out into that square of bright blue and away.

And then something happened, I still don't know what. Maybe it happened when I smelled the hemp, or heard the birds, but all of a sudden it was like waking up hard and fast after being asleep for years and years, like an alarm clock went off and I jerked back into my body from a deep sleep saying, "Yeah, yeah, I'm up, I'm awake, what happened, where am I?" I looked down at my hands and saw them trembling. I wiped them on my red calico dress and looked at the stain they left. I looked down at my black shoes, which were dusty from crossing the yard. And then I felt the rope, although I didn't remember putting it there. I couldn't get it off my neck fast enough.

Then I jumped off that milking stool and just stood there a second, watching the rope sway, its shadow moving on the barn floor. And then I heard a funny sound, one I hadn't heard in years. It was a laugh. At first I didn't recognize it, it sounded so strange. But it kept coming, getting louder and funnier, and then I knew. It was me, laughing.

I looked up at that rope again and pointed and laughed and laughed, so hard I doubled over and tears shot out of my eyes. The rope had been empty, but something had happened. Mrs. Dolores Schoenhof had died, and that was just dandy. Because I came back to life, me, Dolly Walensa, the loud, coarse Polish girl who loved to dance and have fun, not like that old Schoenhof pill who had tried so hard to be the perfect wife and who never, ever could be.

So I went back to the house and straight to the flour bin in the kitchen where Vern kept his wad of cash he thought I didn't know about. There was over a thousand bucks there. I shook the flour off each bill, rolled the money into my stocking and went to get my coat. It was a long, cold walk down the access road to the train station in town, but I didn't care. I was still laughing, and that kept me warm.

And it worked, too, the laughing and the running away, at least for a while. But it worked better when I knew I had Bickie, back in Chicago, or here at Hudson Lake. Having him close, hearing his music, made it easy for me to hold back the darkness that would come over me as fast and as black as a thundercloud over the flat Indiana horizon.

I tried not to think about any of that stuff anymore, after I came to Chicago and started laughing again, but that goddamn horrible movie made me. And after that, there was no going back.

Chapter 8

"Jesus Christ, Tram, just let me play." Bix reached out to the music stand in front of him and rearranged the chart for "Singin' the Blues," settling the pages into place with a soothing *pat-pat*, as if trying to calm them down. Tram walked over to him, sweating in his shirtsleeves like the rest of them. He prodded the charts with a forefinger. "You're not even on the right page," he boomed, hovering over him, making Bix feel like cringing into himself. He hated it when people hovered. It reminded him of the fifth grade at Tyler Elementary, and Miss Rozella Brown standing over his desk, tapping the page of his geography book with her ruler. *What's the capital of Spain?*

"Valencia, I don't know," Bix said. "Come on, let's start again."

"Valencia? We're not doing that song. What're you talking about?"

Next to him, Fuzzy sighed and fingered the valves on his trumpet. "He's all right, Tram. Really."

"He ain't readin' the charts!" Tram yelled, and Bix saw a vein standing out on his forehead. His voice echoed in the empty dance hall. "He's already been fired once for not being able to read. This is a band, fellas. If one guy stumbles, everyone falls. Doesn't that bother you?"

He heard Pee Wee chuckle from his spot out front. "It don't bother you, boss. You and him sound great together."

"I stand here and watch him, and his fingering drives me up the wall. All wrong. What other cornet player uses his third finger like that? That's not right," Tram said.

"So don't watch him," Itzy muttered, softly playing the opening chords of Chopin's funeral march on the baby grand piano, a move that made Bix laugh under his breath.

Tram turned to Fuzzy, index finger extended like a fire-and-brimstone preacher. "You're the one working with him. Is he or is he not reading the charts?" A bead of sweat flicked off Tram's forehead and landed on the charts on Bix's music stand. Hit a B-flat, to be accurate. Who said he couldn't sight-read?

He again thought of Miss Brown, the way she'd talk to the rest of the class about him like he wasn't there, making him feel like he didn't exist—the way Tram was making him feel now. *What's the capital of Italy?*

"Rome," Bix mumbled. "Jeez, we're burning daylight. Let's play, huh?"

Fuzzy slid a glance at Bix, then looked away. "Sometimes his reading isn't the greatest, I admit. But it really doesn't matter. He just..." he paused, waved a hand in a halfhearted gesture, "...knows what to do."

"Yeah, come on, Tram," Pee Wee whined. "Just let us play. It's hotter'n hell in here. I wanna go swimming."

"Fine." Tram turned his back to the band, like they were getting ready to play hide and seek and he was "it." Then he picked up his C-melody sax. Everybody turned to their sheet music, and Bix followed suit, just to keep Tram happy. Tram stomped them off and they began to play.

Sometimes Bix watched the other guys as they played, sometimes he tried to follow the music, and sometimes he just watched the floor, or people in the crowd. At rehearsals like this, the floor was fine, or he'd gaze out toward the bank of windows at the back of the dance hall and dream of being up to his neck in the cool lake. It didn't matter, because after awhile he didn't see them, anyway; they became a blur as he sank into the music. It happened even quicker if he had a bottle.

As they launched into the leisurely 4/4 time of "Singin' the Blues," he watched as Pee Wee took his turn with Tram, watched them turn the pages of their charts in unison, like a vaudeville dance team.

Bix had a solo, but first he had to play in tandem with Pee Wee's clarinet and Tram's sax. And he knew that's what made Tram nuts, where Tram always worried he'd screw up. Bix had tried to hide it all summer, faking it with Fuzzy, faking it with the band at rehearsals. The truth was, he'd never read the music, ever. He just listened for the thread of melody that ran through all the arrangements, tracked it like keeping a finger on somebody's wrist to feel a pulse, and as long as he did, nothing else mattered. He just followed the melody and never got lost.

Like now. He put the cornet to his lips, took a breath and came in right when he was supposed to, up against the clarinet and sax, like cutting into line with everyone's permission. And then he wound himself around those other sounds, just as easy as can be, still hearing the melody somewhere in the back of his mind like a record playing, and then teasing it, embellishing it, but never forgetting it was there.

He knew what the other guys were going to do—jeez, that's why they had rehearsals. He never stepped on them while they played, never took more than his share of the music. They were all good, they were fun to play with. Sometimes they'd watch each other while they played, and sometimes stuff sounded so goddamn sweet they'd catch each other grinning, which is a pretty good way to screw up a song when you're a horn player, but having so much fun together it was hard not to smile.

And then it was time for his sixteen-bar solo, and the other guys cut him the space, pumping a soft background beat while he let fly out front. It was different this time from the last time, just like next time would be different than now. It wasn't like being chained to the forgotten notes splattered on the pages in front of him, lifeless black dots that had nothing to do with the synergy between what was inside his brain, and what he did with his lips and fingers, and what came out his horn. He didn't understand the process; it just happened, and after listening and playing all these years, he didn't care how. He never thought about what would happen if it went away; it was simply a part of himself, like his breathing and his heartbeat, something that would always be there.

They finished. Bix shook the spit out of his horn; everybody else looked at Tram.

"Go on," he said, lifting an arm and pointing toward the door. "Leave. Go swimming."

Pee Wee whooped and was gone.

೮೦ఇ

"Come on, guys, we're all cooled off now. Let's go back and try 'Five Foot Two' again, what do ya say?" Bix called to them from shore where he was sitting on a PROP'TY HOTEL HUDSON towel. "I got an idea for a passage in the middle."

Pee Wee dove under the water, surfaced, and flipped his wet hair off his face. "Kiss my ass, Beiderbecke," he jeered. "I ain't gonna work all goddamn summer when there's a lake and janes swimming in it. Christ, you're a worse slave-driver than Tram."

"Come on, then, Fuzzy, how about you? I was thinking we could pair up right after the first chorus, and...."

"Maybe later, Bix, all right? It's too hot to go back in there." Fuzzy elbowed himself up into an inner tube and turned his face to the sun, drifting.

"Aw...." Bix groaned. He picked up a stick and began stabbing it into the sand in rhythm to the thumping tempo of "Five Foot Two." Goddamn it, he could practically hear the cornet and the trumpet playing in tandem right after that first chorus, in a jagged spill of notes that followed the scale up, still adhering to the melody, then scattering apart like an exploded firecracker. He'd been noodling around with the idea on the front porch for the last couple days, but every time he tried to get the guys to listen, or to work it out with him, they just ignored him.

Maybe he'd go into the dance hall and work on the piano piece. Over the past couple of weeks in the echoing, deserted space, a melody had taken form; at first amorphous, but gradually sprouting extremities, features, fingers and toes. By now it had enough substance for him to tentatively play it for Itzy, who found it interesting, although he admitted Bix's untutored fingering gave him cramps in his hand just watching him. Bix was hoping that by the end of the summer the fledgling little melody would be able to fly on its own. Maybe then he could get Fuzzy or Tram to transcribe it for him, to nail it down with ink and paper so it couldn't get away from him like everything else he played. It would only be the second song he ever wrote, next to "Davenport Blues," back in the Wolverines days. He didn't have a name for it yet; Bix wasn't good with names.

"Well, well, if it ain't Little Mary Sunshine. Woo-hoo! Oh, Jo-oy!" Pee Wee yodeled.

Bix turned to see Joy come tottering out of the bath house, clutching her robe closed with one hand and carrying a stack of movie magazines with the other. She clumped down next to Bix, pushing him over on the PROPT'Y HOTEL HUDSON towel, and flapped open a *Photoplay* with Bebe Daniels on the cover. She didn't look at him.

"Oh, Jo-oy," Pee Wee called from the water, "howza baby today, huh? Ain't you gonna give your ickle little Bickums a big, wet smooch? Mmmmm-wah!"

"What a goof," Bix laughed, shaking Joy's arm. "Hey, want something to eat? Tram had some sandwiches sent up for rehearsal, and...."

"I'm not hungry." She stared out at the water where Pee Wee, all gawky arms and legs, was launching himself against Fuzzy's inner tube, trying to pull him under. Bix heard female laughter and glanced down the beach. Mitzi Trumbauer and Norma Ryker sat under a big Japanese umbrella, heads together, deep in conversation, blatantly staring at them.

"Hey, I got an idea," Bix said, putting an arm around Joy's neck. "Why don't we go into South Bend after the show and make a night of it? We'll go to the movies, go get some Chinese, and...."

"I don't wanna." Joy pulled up the magazine so it hid her face. "Gimme a cigarette."

Bix pulled a crumpled pack of Camels from his pile of clothes and shook one out for her. *So much for trying to cheer her up.* She drew it from the pack, not looking at him, and accepted a light. A sudden burst of splashing and swearing made him look up to see Pee Wee shove Fuzzy out of the inner tube, stealing it for himself. Bix began massaging the back of Joy's neck, running his fingers along the knobs of her vertebrae. *Why was she acting like this, anyway? He didn't do anything wrong.* "Hey, listen, you want to take the train to Chicago this week? Maybe catch Jimmy at the Nest? Whaddaya say, it'll break the monotony. Come on."

She buried her face deeper in the pages of the magazine, not answering.

Bix sighed and took his hands off her. "What's eating you? Jeez, kid, I wish you'd...."

She turned on him, green eyes narrowed and fierce. "You wish I'd what? Cheer up? Stop being such a crepe-hanger? Something like that?"

He chewed his lip and watched the water, elbows on knees, chin in hands, thinking about how Joy was different now, had been for days. Crying all the time, eyes puffy and red. Stopped taking care of herself. Fingernail polish all chipped, her red hair fading and dingy. She'd put on weight. Her clothes hung all lumpy on her now. She wasn't fun to be around anymore, didn't want to sing with him and the boys, didn't even want to sit and talk music when Harriet would come down to the dance hall after her work at the hotel.

The way Joy was acting, you'd think it was something serious, like he was cheating on her, or like he'd gotten her in a jam. He thought of how Ruth had cried and moped around before she'd told him, and then the hard chill of shock he'd felt, staring out the window of the taxi, her soft, apologetic voice chasing around in his head. *I'm pregnant, Bix. I'm sorry, honey. What are we going to do? Bix?* But Joy couldn't be in a jam. She'd had an operation, she'd told him that first day here at Hudson Lake.

"You've been like this for awhile," he said. "I just wish I could help, that's all."

She laughed. "No, you don't. You just wish I'd stop being such a flat tire. You and all the rest of the guys. I'm takin' all the fun out of your summer, ain't I?"

"Don't put words into my mouth," he said, breaking the stick and throwing the pieces toward the water. "I never said...."

"No, you never said. You never said nothing. Not to me. I'm too stupid to understand. I'm no college girl."

"Jeez, Joy, what the hell are you...."

"But I'm good enough for some things, ain't I?" Her smile was bright and artificial, something with rhinestones bought in a dimestore. "Like sticking it into anytime you want, right?"

He looked at her and grinned back. "I never heard any complaints."

She shot to her feet and started walking away. *Christ, now I've gone and done it, but good.* Bix flopped down on the towel and stared at the sun, hoping it would sear away the image of her face wearing that idiotic smile. There was something unsettling about it, something strange and just on the edge of being crazy. "Hell with you," he muttered.

What the hell was wrong with her, anyway? Was she jealous of Harriet—a college girl who already had a steady boyfriend? He'd never laid a hand on Harriet, never would. Sure, Harriet was pretty, he couldn't kid himself about that, and he liked talking to her. But beside the fact that he and Joy slept together, they were friends, real friends. She'd been good to him, back in Chicago and here, too. Joy liked him just the way he was, and he felt the same way about her.

He turned his head just enough so he could see her. She paused at the bath house, turned around to see if he was following her. Then she stood there a moment, shifting from foot to foot, her face puckered into a look of sadness that made her look like a scolded child. Seeing that made him want to get up and go over to her, jab her in the ribs and tickle that sad look off her face. It would have been so easy to do, and then put his arm around her and tell her he was sorry and walk back with her to the cottage. He almost did just that.

But then he heard Pee Wee in the water. "You just don't love me anymore, ickle little Bickums," he whined in his annoying fake falsetto, using just the right reproachful tone, sounding just like Joy. "I'm gonna go cry now."

And I didn't do a damn thing to deserve this, Bix thought. He sat up and looked at Pee Wee and laughed. Then he went plunging into the lake headfirst, diving to the muddy bottom, holding his breath as long as he could and listening to his heartbeat thudding in his ears. When he surfaced again and looked toward the boathouse, Joy was gone.

Chapter 9

Harriet was the first to notice Buddy Smith as he limped up the road toward the hotel. She'd opened the back door to dump water when she caught sight of him. His left arm was slack and bleeding and he cradled it like it was a dog that had been hit by a car and left in the road to die. One side of his face was a bloody smear, the eye swollen black and shut. The knees of his pants were shredded and beneath the frayed fabric, his own knees were torn and bloody.

"Buddy! Oh my God, Buddy!" She ran out and helped him into the kitchen, an arm around his waist. Mrs. Smith, who had been washing dishes, screamed and dropped her best serving platter to the floor, where it exploded like a bomb into shrapnel.

"Buddy! Oh my darling little boy, who did this to you, son?" she cried, swabbing at the blood on his face with the edge of her apron.

Harriet rolled back his shirtsleeve, wincing at the sight of the swollen purple flesh. "Does this hurt?" she asked softly, testing the arm for mobility by gently moving it up and down. He gasped and went pale. She lifted his lids and peered into his eyes, checking to see if his pupils were dilated. Then she turned to Mrs. Smith.

"I think you'd better call a doctor. His arm's broken, and you want to make sure he doesn't have a concussion. If you have some Mercurochrome and hydrogen peroxide, I can get these cuts cleaned up."

As soon as Mrs. Smith waddled off, sobbing under her breath, Buddy grabbed Harriet's arm.

"One of 'em was that goddamn Trent Walker, I could have sworn it was. Cyrus Walker's kid." He looked at his arm again and groaned. "So much for swimming and the Scout campout."

"Look on the bright side," she said, filling a basin with water from the tap. "You're off wood chopping for at least five weeks."

"It's nothing to laugh about. Cyrus Walker's head of the whole South Bend Klan klavern. The grand high exalted cyclops, or whatever they call themselves."

Harriet sat down and began to gently swab Buddy's bloody face with a cool washcloth. "But why would they pick on you?"

"They probably seen me with Bix and Pee Wee and the guys. 'This is what you get for hangin' with nigger-lovers, Jews and rapists.' That's what he said." He wiped his nose on his shirtsleeve. "Then three of 'em knocked me into the gravel on the road and started kicking me. I got one of 'em in the balls, though—oh, sorry, Harriet."

"We have to report this to the police, you know. This is serious."

Buddy barked out a laugh. "The police? Cyrus Walker is the police. He's a big man on the highway patrol. Think he's gonna bring in his own son?"

"Dr. Mason is on his way," Mrs. Smith said, carrying in a clutch of brown medicine bottles. Harriet felt Buddy nudge her and she nodded at him. "And I called the police, too. I'm not going to let any thugs do this to my little boy and get away with it."

"Aw, Ma—why'd ya call the cops? I'll be all right."

"Now, Buddy, you have to tell mother the truth. Did you recognize any of those hoodlums who did this?"

"I told you, Ma, they got me from behind. I went down before I could get a good look at any of their faces."

There was a soft knock at the screen door. Harriet turned and saw Bix and Pee Wee standing on the step. Her stomach dropped at the sight of Bix. She hadn't seen him in days and she didn't especially want to see him now. Not after all the escalating talk in town about what the band had done to Crystal Hawkins on the Fourth. Instead of fading away, the incident had festered into an open sore. And now, this with Buddy.

Buddy looked up and grinned. "Hey, fellas. How they hangin'?"

"Buddy, what kind of talk is that? Yes, what can I do for you two?" Mrs. Smith asked.

"Is Buddy all right?" Bix asked in his laconic voice. "We seen him come up the road from the beach, and...."

Pee Wee came barging in, eyes wide. "Jesus H., kid, what the hell happened to you? Were you in a car accident or something?"

"He was attacked," Mrs. Smith said, nostrils flaring. "Now please leave my kitchen."

"We're friends of his, ma'am," Bix said, pushing the screen door open. "We just wanted to see if there was anything we could do."

Mrs. Smith swelled up to her full height and glared from Bix to Pee Wee. "You can stay away from my son! You boys have been nothing but trouble since you came here." Her eyes went red and began leaking tears. "Why didn't you leave that horrible Crystal Hawkins alone? Don't you understand that you're not in Chicago, or St. Louis, or New York City?" She ran from the room, crying into her apron.

Bix and Harriet exchanged glances over Buddy's head as Pee Wee crouched next to him, and Harriet looked quickly away, unnerved by his eyes. And she'd trusted him, told him everything about herself, things she'd never told anyone else, she thought. It was as if she was standing there naked, but only he could see.

"Come on, kid, give," Pee Wee said to Buddy. "Who did this to you?"

"Why? What can you do about it?"

"We'll see. Just tell us. Who did it?"

Buddy scuffed his shoes against the green speckled linoleum. "Couple of guys from town. One of 'em I go to school with. His father's on the goddamn highway patrol. The other three I didn't recognize."

Pee Wee stood, his face grim. "You know where this son of a bitch lives?"

"Why? What can you...."

Mrs. Smith came into the kitchen with the doctor, a portly man in shirt-sleeves, who was carrying a black bag and sweating profusely.

"You can go now," she said to Bix and Pee Wee, pointing to the door. They filed out, and Harriet followed them. The boys sat down on the wooden steps of the back porch and stared at the little yellow cottage.

"Did he say why he thought it happened?" Bix asked.

"Yes, he did," Harriet said, forcing herself to meet his eyes. "It has to do with that girl you fellows think so highly of. Crystal Hawkins."

"That skunk!" Pee Wee muttered. "Somebody oughta paste that jane, and it might just be me. You know what she gave me? That lowdown...."

Bix punched Pee Wee hard in the arm. "Jesus, shut up, you idiot." He looked at Harriet. "So Buddy said they were getting even for what happened with Crystal?"

Harriet sat down on the steps next to him, keeping her distance. "No. They just said something about nigger lovers, Jews and rapists. Do any of you fit the bill?"

"Nice talk! Those goddamn yokels. I say we go get 'em, Bix. I'm not gonna take any of this layin' down. Let's you and me and Itzy go get a car, and...."

"Are you nuts? Wasn't what happened over the Fourth enough trouble? Hell, Tram's screaming about business falling off. You want to kill it completely?"

Pee Wee leaped up and started walking toward the cottage. "I don't give a damn. Nobody's gonna beat up my pal Buddy and get away with it."

Harriet stood and peered through the screen door, watching as the doctor wrapped Buddy's broken arm with lengths of plastered gauze. The boy was biting his lower lip, his face pale and set. "Poor kid," she murmured. "Looks like he should have been more selective about his friends." Me too, she thought.

"Hey, nobody wanted this to happen," Bix said.

She glanced at him, in his usual rumpled attire, smelling of gin, and wondered why she'd ever found him so interesting. Maybe Mrs. Smith was right about the musicians, she thought. They didn't understand they weren't in St. Louis anymore. And now innocent people were hurt because of their disregard for local convention.

"What's the matter with you?" Bix asked. "I didn't beat the kid up."

"He wouldn't have gotten beaten up if it wasn't for what the bunch of you did to that girl."

"Hell, I didn't do anything to her. I wasn't even...."

"Bix, this is a small town. People remember things like that, and they're still talking about it. Everybody in town is saying it was a gang rape."

He fell back a step.

"And even if you didn't do anything to her, you didn't do anything to stop it, either." She stood and opened the screen door, glancing at him once more before she went in. "Please stay away from Buddy. He's a good kid. I don't want to see him get hurt anymore." And then she went in to help the doctor finish taking care of Buddy, the dismayed look on Bix's face burned into her mind.

I was wrong about him, she thought, heart sinking. He isn't what I thought he was at all—a gifted, good-hearted young man with a lot of potential who just needs a second chance. If he was, he would have never let anything like that happen to a girl, no matter how bad her reputation was. Poor Joy, she thought. *If I feel this bad, her heart must be breaking.*

Chapter 10

"Vaffanculo, you bitch." Jack McGurn slammed the door of the Lincoln and glared through the window at Louise, who fluffed up the pelt of her summer fur and turned away from him.

He walked a few steps away from the car, fuming, and adjusted his jacket, then pulled the brim of his fedora down further over his face. He felt Tony's eyes on him from where he sat behind the wheel of the Lincoln.

It wasn't good to lose face in front of one of the guys, especially over a *co-mara*. Not that he didn't trust Tony—the runty little driver knew how to keep quiet, that was for sure. But to have her mouth off like that in front of him—it was disrespectful, that's all. And things like that could get around.

I should pull her out of there by the fucking hair and kick her ass down to the beach, he thought, crunching over the gravel in the parking lot. But the hell with it. He looked at the dance hall across the road, with its brave new coat of paint and the sagging banner draped across the front shouting TO-NITE! FRANK TRUMBAUER & "BIX" BIEDERBECK!

Maybe she had a point. The joint sure as hell didn't look like much in the harsh light of day, McGurn thought. Just a dumpy little dance hall that looked like it had seen better days. There was nobody around. True, it was a Friday afternoon, and the band didn't go on until eight, but it still looked like a morgue. Hot day like this, there ought to be lots of people on the beach, which would mean good concession money and a ready-made crowd for the show later. But now it was dead. Shit, the only sound he could hear was the distant mooing of a cow. He laughed. A cow, for Chrissakes!

He turned around and looked at the hotel behind him, a three-story frame building with peeling paint and old-fashioned gingerbread trim, shrouded by bushes and trees that needed a good cutting back. "Looks like a goddamn haunted house," he muttered. Still, if somebody with some moxie was running the whole shooting match, this place could hum. Could *mint* money.

A car door slammed behind him. Tony stood against the driver's side door, cap crooked, chewing gum and smoking a cigarette. "She wants to go back," he said, the corner of his mouth twitching into a grin.

McGurn felt the fury burst in his chest and almost ran over to the car to yank her out. But the sight of Tony's smile—was he laughing at him?—forced him to tamp it down. No goddamn broad was going to make a fatmouth out of him. He grinned back. "Let her walk," he said.

The back door of the touring car opened, followed by a curvaceous length of silk-stockinged leg. "I mean it, Jack," Louise said, standing there with the afternoon sun shining through her sheer summer dress, silhouetting that body, madonn', like cut glass, McGurn thought. The bitch.

He forced his smile to go bigger, showing teeth. "You wanna go back, sweetheart? Fine, you go back. But he ain't driving you. You can take the train."

She huffed and looked around. "Look at this dump," she said, waving a braceleted arm at the haunted-house hotel. "It's strictly from hunger. I coulda been shopping on Michigan Boulevard, havin' lunch at the Drake with my girlfriends, anything but this." She readjusted the white fur boa which had cost him a C-note at Marshall Field's last Christmas. "I thought there was gonna be a band. So where's the band?"

"They don't start til nighttime, you stupid cooze." She stiffened at the word and McGurn was pleased to see Tony laugh. "All's I know is this place was a gold mine on the Fourth. They were turning 'em away at the door."

"It's still a dump," she said, leaning over to check her makeup in the touring car's side mirror. "And I ain't staying."

McGurn reached for his billfold and peeled off a sawbuck. "Take the train. Here. I'll see you back in town." He held the money toward her, arm outstretched, rubbing the bill between thumb and forefinger.

She huffed again and paused an instant, then slowly, inevitably, came walking over to him, taking her time, as if it was her idea. For a second they stood nose-to-nose, close enough so he could smell that expensive French perfume she always doused herself in. Her blue eyes were chinked in anger; she stared at him without blinking. He had to hand it to the broad, she had guts.

He gave first, exhaling a laugh. She snapped the bill from his fingers and turned to walk away. He grabbed her arm, pulled her back against him and ran a hand over her tight curves, settling on her ass. And then she gave, eyes going soft, letting him pull her against him. "I'll be back Monday," he said, squeezing her until she gave a little yelp of pain. "No funny stuff while I'm gone. *Capice?*" He slapped her ass as she walked away, and Tony got busy getting her suitcases and hatboxes out of the trunk.

McGurn turned back to the dance hall, his mind automatically clicking off the anger over Louise and onto business. He remembered the ads he'd seen for the Blue Lantern, what they called "park plan dancing." Which meant that any *cetriolo* with a tin lizzy could park it in the lot over here, ante up the buck and a half admission, and dance his galoshes off all night long without having to lay out another dime.

Back at the Green Mill they packed them in on Friday nights, their "Professional Night" when he ran seven vaude acts plus a band. It cost the mopes a buck fifty admission plus a two-drink minimum, plus another two bucks if they wanted to eat. The rest of the time the club got by with a band and their "big novelty nights"—crap like the old-fashioned waltz contests on Wednesdays, and the fifty-dollar ladies' hat competitions, crap that didn't cost McGurn anything. And they still packed them in.

But this place had a hot band, and hot bands pulled in crowds, and crowds drank and spent money. That's why McGurn was here. He liked hot music himself, liked to listen and dance, and had plenty of opportunity to do both at the clubs he ran for Al—the Sunset Café, the Dreamland, the Panama, the Plantation, the Fiume, the Elite, the DeLuxe. He knew what a good band sounded like compared with a sappy one, appreciated a hot horn solo and a good backbeat, fueled by drums or tuba or upright bass. But most of all he liked the music as a means to an end—because it made people want to dance, drink, fuck. And those were all things McGurn could make money on.

He peered into the window and saw a jasper behind the soda fountain, digging in his ear with a matchstick and reading a racing form. The guy looked like a horse himself, with his long face, drooping lips and dumb expression. McGurn knew they sold local mule out of here—the soda jerk was Ray Reynolds, who fronted for an Indy bootleg ring that supplied him with the stuff, all strictly local brew. The cops had cracked a couple of heads last month for show, but the outfit was still operating, thanks to dirty public officials. It shouldn't take much to squeeze in here, bringing the stuff up from Chicago, or even buying up the local talent. All depended on how much business this place could generate.

McGurn pushed open the front door; a bell jingled and the soda jerk looked up. "Help you?" he asked, pushing the racing form down the counter.

"Sure. Gimme a Green River," McGurn said, looking around at the marble-topped tables and wire-back chairs. Nice little place, well kept.

The jerk fizzed seltzer into a soda glass, followed by the viscous green syrup. He looked up at Jack and paused as if he recognized him. "Hot out there, huh? That'll be a nickel."

McGurn held up the glass at eye level and studied the green concoction. "Hot. Makes people thirsty, you know?" He glanced down the hallway. The dance hall must be back there. "Mind if I look around?"

The jerk shrugged and began wiping down the counter with a bar rag, still watching McGurn. He flashed a mouthful of fake-looking teeth in a smile. "Be my guest."

McGurn walked down the hallway, through the doors and into the dance hall. It was a decent-sized place, with lots of room for dancing, although he personally would have crammed a couple dozen more tables in it to fit more people who would eat and drink and spend more money. He looked at the bandstand, with its backdrop painted to look like a night sky, complete with a crooked yellow moon.

"Not bad," he murmured, looking around. "Not bad at all."

On his way out he stopped at the soda fountain again and tossed a fin on the counter next to his untouched Green River. The bell on the door jingled again as he left.

A kid about eight years old wearing a red wool bathing suit came running up to McGurn. "Mister, that your car?" he gasped, out of breath.

"Yeah. Who wants to know?"

The kid shrugged. "Just wondered. What kind is it?"

"Lincoln touring car, '26 model. Cost me eight grand. Tell your old man to get one. Here's a down payment." He tossed the kid two bits and laughed as he scrabbled in the dust to pick it up. "Where's the beach, kid?"

"Right over there. Hey, thanks, mister."

That's the beach? he thought, thinking of Oak Street Beach laid out at the foot of Michigan Boulevard like a long, expensive carpet. This sure as hell wasn't much of a beach, and neither were the people on it. Just an old couple looking like a pair of walruses with identical chin whiskers, a couple of kids digging in the sand with buckets and shovels, and—okay, *she* wasn't bad.

He didn't plan on walking out on the sand and scuffing his brown-and-white spectator shoes. But the redhead down there by the shoreline, the one in the red bathing suit with the big tits, she wasn't bad. Not bad at all.

McGurn walked over the sand, threaded around the kids, and stood a couple of feet away from her. She looked familiar somehow, even her profile was familiar. She sure as hell didn't look like she belonged here in the sticks, with the goddamn cow mooing back behind the dumpy hotel. She had style, you could tell. It stood out like a sore thumb in a place like this.

She was staring at the water as if in a trance and he wondered if she was drunk or just a dizzy broad. He watched broads like that all the time, come into his club and start acting goofy, hitting the gin and...

And then he remembered. "Hey, you used to work at the Green Mill. One of the waitresses." She finally looked up, and he saw she had green eyes. Or maybe blue, or gray. Eyes like a cat, narrowed up like a cat's eyes, too.

He walked over to her and reached down to shake her hand, leaning over just enough so that he got a good look down the front of her bathing suit at that big pair of melons. Nice.

"Jack McGurn," he said, smiling his best Valentino grin. "I own the Green Mill."

She looked up at him, face expressionless. "Oh. Yeah, I guess I remember you now."

"You used to sing at the club. You had a nice voice, too. What are you doing out here in the sticks?"

She shrugged her round white shoulders and stared back at the water. "Wanted to get out of the city for awhile."

"Well, this is a nice little place. Nice and peaceful. Maybe a little too peaceful, you know what I mean? Hell, I even heard a cow. You ever heard a cow before?"

She laughed mirthlessly, not looking at him. "I seen all the cows I ever want to see." Finally she looked up again, and the green-blue-gray eyes were more curious than angry.

"What brings you here? Slumming?"

"Business. It's hard to tell when it's this dead, but I heard this joint jumps on the weekends. That right?"

Her face went sad again and she looked away. "There's a band. People come out to hear them, I guess."

McGurn hunkered down on the sand next to her. He could always brush off his shoes and his trousers when he got back to the car. This broad might be able to give him the real story about what went on here. And besides, she was a hot little piece, easy on the eyes, and it wouldn't be any hardship to spend some time and money on her.

"Well, listen. I'm thinking of investing in this place, if it's everything it's cracked up to be. If this band draws hot and cold running crowds out of Chicago every weekend, that's a good sign." He stood and brushed off his pinstriped trousers. "So what do you do for fun around here during the week, besides listen to the grass grow?"

She shrugged again, gave him a crooked smile. "Go into South Bend. Go to the movies. Sleep. What else?"

"Well, it's a long drive from Chicago and there's nowhere around here to get any lunch. Hey, what do you say, uh—what'd you say your name was again?"

"I didn't. But it's Joy."

"Okay, Joy. I got my car over there, and the whole afternoon to kill. What do you say we go into South Bend, tie on the feedbag, and you tell me everything you know about this place—what do you call it? The Blue Lantern?" He thought of her sitting next to him in the back of the Lincoln, her red hair blowing in the breeze of the open window as they tooled along these hick back roads. A fast car would impress a broad like this, a city broad. And he thought of Tony, and what he'd think when he saw that Jack McGurn didn't waste any time on any one *comara*, that he wasn't any fatmouth for any one woman, and never would be.

She looked like she was thinking it over, lower lip between her teeth. She glanced back over her shoulder toward the hotel, eyes narrowed. And then she looked up into his face and smiled, a big, healthy smile that lit up her face like a movie star, just like that Clara Bow, McGurn thought.

"Just give me a minute to go back to the hotel and change," she said, standing up and giving him a good view of the big melons, nice, round ass, shapely legs. "I'll be right back."

Chapter 11

Joy

Sure, I went with him. Why not?

After all, I been sitting out on that beach by myself every day for two weeks now, like a real sap, a lovesick sap who had it bad and couldn't get it out of her system. And drinking too much up in my room, and moping around so much that nobody could stand me anymore. Not that I cared what they thought of me, those goddamn musicians. The hell with all of them.

I remembered this guy right away when I seen him. McGurn. Everybody knows he's a bodyguard for Big Al Capone. Al even came into the Green Mill a couple times when I was working, had all the doors locked and made the band play requests, handing out twenty-dollar bills like they was candy.

Let's face it, those boys have the mazuma and they know how to spend it. I remember one of the gals who worked with me went out with this McGurn a couple times and got a diamond bracelet out of the deal. I never asked her if she slept with him, but so what if she did? Maybe it's about time us girls got something for sleeping with fellas, besides knocked up, or a case of the clap, or a broken heart.

So I went back to the hotel, put on one of my new tub silk dresses so he doesn't think I'm that impressed with him, and went with him to South Bend.

He had a hell of a car, and even a driver—a little sawed-off runt who kept staring at me as bad as old lady Smith's punk kid but never said nothing, just sat behind the wheel and drove like a goddamn maniac all the way to South Bend, and those roads just whipped by underneath us, wow! Jack said he could get that big old Lincoln up to eighty-five miles an hour, which came in handy in his line of work, so I asked him why a big businessman investor like him needed to make any fast getaways and he just laughed.

He had a nice laugh. He was a good-looking guy, though you could tell he knew it. Big, white teeth, black hair, a guinea, sure, but nice-looking. And a snappy dresser, oh, his clothes were nice. Tailored suit he had on, and a silk shirt, and shoes that must have cost a fortune. A big gold wristwatch and a pearl stickpin and rings that could choke a horse.

We got into town and went to the Chink joint where the waiters all know me from being there with the goddamn musicians. So he kidded me about it, and right away started ordering everything off the menu. We were the only people in the place, and those Chinks were stepping and fetching to beat the band once they saw him peeling some big bills off a diamond-studded money clip he pulled out of his breast pocket.

Well, we ate everything, chop suey and egg foo yung and pickled ducks' feet and eggrolls and green tea. And over the fortune cookies and lychee nuts he asks me, hey, where can a fellow go in this burg to wet his whistle? So we went over to that speak on Indiana Avenue where the goddamn musicians go, where they know me, too, and he asked me all kinds of questions about the Blue Lantern.

Why shouldn't I tell him? It's no secret. I told him about all the crowds that came on the weekends, and how Charlie Horvath is running the place this year for Jean Goldkette, but how the local yokels preferred Joe Dockstader's corny band and so it was dead during the week. I told him about that old bitch Mrs. Smith and how she didn't want anyone to have any fun out there, wanted to run the joint like it was a YMCA. And I told him about Ray Reynolds, and how he wasn't just no soda jerk, but in tight with the local moonshiners and a pretty important guy at Hudson Lake.

And then he asked me about the hot band, and I told him the truth, about how most everybody came up to see that goddamn Bix. He looked hard at me when we got to talking about that goddamn Bix, and he asked me, hey, what's wrong, aren't those guys any good? And I told him yeah, they're damn good musicians, but pretty sorry excuses for human beings, you ask me. And he smiled in this sweet way and put his hand over mine on the table and held my hand real nice, didn't try any funny stuff or anything.

And anyhow, having somebody like McGurn paying attention to me was nice and took my mind off how Bickie had been spending more and more time with Harriet, talking about music and a lot of other stuff that was over everybody else's head. I almost started crying right there in the Chink joint just thinking about it, but then I looked at Jack and thought, I'll be goddamned if I cry one more tear over any man.

On the way back to the lake Jack sat with his arm around me, just nice and light, rubbing my shoulder while the breeze blew through my hair. And when he dropped me off, he told me he'd be back out here next Saturday to check out the crowds, and that I should be waiting for him, dressed nice, and he'd take me back into Chicago for a late dinner after the show.

When we pulled into the parking lot in front of the hotel, that goddamn Bix and the rest of the guys were sitting out on the porch of the cottage and everybody came out to stare as I got out of that big old Lincoln. So I leaned in and gave Jack a peck on the cheek and said real loud, "See you next week," and then just walked back into the hotel like I didn't even see them, even though I could feel them all staring a hole into my back.

And then I went upstairs, put some hot jazz records on the phonograph, and hennaed my hair. I needed it.

Chapter 12

"Shame something like this had to happen to the boy." Cyrus Walker hitched up his khaki uniform pants, making a point of showing off the .45 revolver on his hip.

"Yes, I know." Mrs. Smith sighed and moved to the cupboard, putting things away. "My poor little boy. Who would think something like this would happen in New Carlisle?"

Cyrus put the notepad back in his pocket and looked at Loretta Smith. He'd known her back when she was Loretta Wilkens, the prettiest girl in their class. He'd had kind of a crush on Loretta back in school. She was the kind of girl who loved to dance, moving easily to the rhythms of the fiddles and the banjos. She could make even the biggest clodhopper feel like he had wings on his heels, just by putting her little hand in his and stepping onto the dance floor.

Now as she shuffled around the cramped kitchen of the hotel, the floorboards squeaking under her ponderous weight, her gray hair frizzed around her face, there was no trace of that girl of almost thirty years ago. And Cyrus Walker was here on business.

He hitched up his pants again. "Loretta, beggin' your pardon, but having that band living out back don't help things. Bad element coming out from Chicago, a lot of boys doing a lot of drinking and hellraising—well, there's bound to be trouble, that's all."

Her creased face drooped and she looked like she was about to cry. "I told him. I told that Charlie Horvath there was going to be trouble. And now this—my poor little boy...."

"Now, now, Loretta," Cyrus said, clumsily patting her arm. "We'll get to the bottom of this. And summer can't last forever. September'll roll around, those boys'll pack up and leave, and all of this will be a bad memory. Mind if I have a look around before I leave? Might come up with some evidence."

"Not at all, Cyrus. And thank you for coming out."

He heard her blowing her nose as he walked out the screen door and headed back toward that ramshackle cottage behind the hotel. *Her poor little boy.* Cyrus knew for a fact the Smith kid was forever dogging the heels of those out-of-town musicians, running their errands, driving them into town, getting up to God knew what with them. "The little whelp probably had it coming," he muttered.

Too many changes, he mused, thinking how Loretta Smith's face and figure weren't the only things different these days from the LaPorte County of their youth. Everything had changed. Everything. And none of it for the better.

The .45 slapped reassuringly against his hip as he walked through the weeds and mounted the wooden porch steps. He hammered on the screen door. "Police officer," he called. No answer. But then they were probably all out at the beach or in town this time of day. He tried to peer around the window-shades. *Good God, what a mess. How could anyone live in that sort of filth?*

As he walked back through the weeds toward the dance hall across the road, Cyrus remembered coming here years ago, back when the kids were still little and Betsy still alive. They'd bring the family out on summer afternoons to swim off little Bluebird Beach and picnic in the grove. There'd been a band then, too, local fellows playing a mixture of waltzes and nice, danceable tunes, out in the gazebo before Bill Smith built the dance hall. Even a couple of years ago, after the Casino opened, a white man could still come to Hudson Lake and feel at home.

But not now. Cyrus had come out here the day after the big Fourth of July event just to have a look around, and was disgusted by what he saw. Half-naked girls and boys from God knew where, as young as his son Trent, all laying out on the beach, smoking cigarettes and necking in broad daylight.

And that music! He crossed the road and walked through the deserted soda fountain to the dance hall. Cyrus liked a good tune as much as the next man, but he'd heard that St. Louis band play. If you closed your eyes, you'd think it was a bunch of jigaboos. And on the weekends, all sorts of riff-raff came out from Chicago to hear that band, couples dancing with moves that were one step removed from actual fornication.

The dance hall was empty now except for a whelp playing some strange sort of piano music on the bandstand, his head bent low over the keyboard, greasy hair flopping in his face. Cyrus grunted, shook his head and walked back through the soda fountain.

And that was another situation. Ray Reynolds was the fountain man, nights he was here.

Everybody on the force knew Ray as the man to go to for bootleg liquor here in New Carlisle, but he'd never been caught red-handed with the stuff so they couldn't make the pinch. Bootlegging was a big problem here in LaPorte County, as much as the department denied it. The police in the cities had staged a few raids, mostly in South Bend, but some of those farmers out in the backwoods who'd been moonshining for generations kept a steady supply flowing to the cafes and blind pigs. And places like the dance hall right here.

Hudson Lake used to be a nice place, a family place, where you could take your kids on a Sunday and not have to worry about seeing women all tricked out like whores, or stepping on used condoms on the beach, or having somebody try to sell you bootleg liquor, or having to listen to jigaboo music. These days, Hudson Lake was starting to look more and more like Chicago—a city Cyrus had visited once and couldn't leave fast enough.

It was bad enough America was becoming a country of dark-skinned foreigners who worshipped the Pope in Rome and anarchists who thought they were too good for an honest day's work. But now, this nigger jazz was putting crazy ideas into the heads of otherwise sensible kids. Even Trent listened to that garbage and wanted to dress like a dime-store sheik, all tricked out in baggy pants and patent-leather hair, like these boys hanging around Hudson Lake. Like that whelp back there playing piano in the empty dance hall.

And that was exactly why the Hundred Percenters existed, Cyrus thought, to clean up things like this, to step in when the police couldn't or wouldn't. Well, the police force might not be able to do much about the situation at Hudson Lake, but the Hundred Percenters could. And it was something Cyrus, as Exalted Cyclops of the Valley Klan Klavern #53, planned on bringing up at the very next meeting.

Chapter 13

Joy

Oh, they were a piece of work, those Klan guys. Prancing around in their
bedsheets, hating everybody who wasn't just exactly like them. I seen enough
of their type back in Billings, although it wasn't the Klan back then, just
ignorant ranchers and farmers who hated us because we were Polish. There
was Polish in South Bend, too, and these Klan guys hated them, and Catholics
in general, although you usually think of 'em hating darkies and Jews, but
when there ain't any darkies and Jews to speak of, ya gotta blame somebody
for everything that goes wrong, don't ya?

I picked up one of their newspapers once when I was in South Bend, some
rag called *The Fiery Cross*, and it was full of bitching and moaning about how
His Holiness the Pope wanted to take over the country (God should strike
them down dead for that), and how they needed to stick together to fight
against foreigners and anarchists. Well, I wasn't any star pupil in grammar
school, but I remember the story of the Pilgrims; seems to me like everybody
here in America is a foreigner one way or another, except maybe the Indians.
So what the hell are a bunch of backwoods Hoosiers getting so high and
mighty about?

Seems like most of those Klan people were men, or I should say, a certain
kind of man—overblown windbags who liked to talk about Americanism and
business and the best way to keep this country great, meaning great for them.
If Vern lived in South Bend, sure as shooting he'd be a member, because to
those guys it was like a social club, like the Fraternal Order of Moose, or the
International Organization of Odd Fellows, a place to go sell each other stuff
and tell each other what swell guys they were.

I know what they're like because I seen them come breezing into the Blue
Lantern one afternoon on the way back from their big picnic at Island Park.
Carsful of 'em, with their wives and kids wanting ice cream from Ray's soda
fountain, wearing ribbons with their klavern number on it, and some of 'em
in their bedsheets and all. And Ray was playing right up to them, all grinning

and polite, you'd never think he was making his big money on bootleg hooch. Butter wouldn't melt in his mouth. It was yes sir and yes ma'am, and what a sweet little tyke you got there, enough to make you puke. And I wondered just how many of those good upstanding law-abiding citizens had some of Ray's hooch stashed away at home for entertaining purposes, and how many of 'em had seen the inside of a South Bend speakeasy. Probably most of them, truth to tell.

The older women all looked like WCTU dames, sour-faced killjoys like the old Smith bitch. But even the younger ones all looked alike somehow, neat and smiling and clean, like they'd never gotten a good stiff one in their lives.

And I heard 'em all whispering and looking around while they were waiting for their ice cream. It was right after the gang-shag with that little whore from Evansville and they were buzzing about it, you could tell it was a big dirty thrill for them, being in a place where they played hot jazz, the same place where that girl had gotten it. You could practically see them drooling.

And they gave me that look, the one I know so well, like I wasn't good enough to be on the same planet with them, let alone standing at the same soda fountain. They all reminded me of my sister-in-law Millie and her husband Roger. Dressed like them, talked like them, even had the same bland faces, like dolls lined up on a shelf at Woolworth's. Oh, they were always polite, but they made it clear by the way they looked at me that I was different from them, not as good somehow, and nothing I could do would ever change things. With people like that you could have a million bucks, be wearing the finest clothes, driving the best car and talking French, but it wouldn't matter. You're different from them, and somehow they can smell it on you.

I remembered when I was married to Vern, trying to fit in with his friends and relatives. We'd have them over and I'd sit there all quiet and smiling, dressed in something modest with a lace collar and cuffs, my hair still long and put up in the back, serving them my homemade poppyseed cake, the kind Ma taught me to make. They never did complain about my cooking. "So is this a Polish dish, Mrs. Schoenhof?" they'd ask, all polite, like I was a servant they'd let sit at the dining room table on special occasions like Christmas and Easter. And then they'd shake hands and leave, and I'd never hear from them again. They'd never invited us back to their houses, they'd never let us into their little social circle. Especially after Michael got a little older and it was clear to them he wasn't a nice, normal kid like theirs were.

Because to hear them talk, it was all for the sake of their kids. Their kids had to be protected, and kept clean and pure, away from corrupting influences like foreigners and anarchists and liquor and jazz. According to them, their kids were all smarter and prettier and better-dressed than anyone else's kids. Even though most of their kids ended up pie-eyed in speakeasies and in the back seats of sedans with their pants off, just like the rest of us.

So these Klan guys were nothing new to me, you see. Seems like I'd lived with 'em all my life.

Well, after the Klan people finally got their fill of ice cream, they went and stood on Bluebird Beach and looked around and pointed to the cottages and the hotel, whispering among themselves, and then they took their ribbons and their bedsheets and their perfect kids and got back into their cars and drove away.

But you know, I had a feeling right then that they'd be back. And as it turned out, I wasn't wrong.

Chapter 14

By the time Bix got back to the little yellow cottage, Pee Wee was around the back, grimly hammering nails into the ends of two-by-fours.

"What the hell is this, the armory? You're frigging nuts, Russell."

"We'll see who's nuts," Pee Wee muttered, standing up to wipe his hands on a rag. "I'm gonna get those stump-jumpers who beat up Buddy."

"What do you think you're gonna do with this stuff?"

Pee Wee picked up a board, laid it on his shoulder, and swung the business end like Rogers Hornsby taking aim at a strike. "Bust some Hoosier heads, what do you think?"

After the show that night, Pee Wee insisted on piling into Ryker's Dodge, not telling Ryker why he needed it, and recruited Dan, who was big enough to take care of himself. Bix, who'd been drinking the last of his gallons bought from the sisters, was fueled by self-pity and the flask of Chicago scotch they were passing, and starting to feel mean.

They'd finagled out of Buddy where Trent Walker lived and they took to the back roads, baseball bats and two-by-fours piled in the backseat.

"Think they're dealing with a bunch of pussies," Pee Wee said, flooring the Dodge and bouncing down the graveled road. "We'll show 'em."

"Slow down, Russell, you're rattling my teeth," Dan said, downing another swallow and handing Bix a half-full bag of chocolate macaroons he'd picked up from Ellwood's, the general store down the road from the Hotel Hudson.

Bix ate a cookie, then shot back a mouthful of scotch, wiping his mouth on his sleeve. The Blue Lantern had been almost empty tonight, the third night in a row. The only real business they were seeing now was on weekends. Tram was having kittens, moaning about how Jean was going to can them all, how he'd pull out of the Blue Lantern deal even before the summer gig was up if he couldn't turn a profit. If that happened, God only knew what he'd do.

And the people in town actually believed they'd raped that girl. Even though he hadn't done a goddamn thing to hurt anyone that night. He'd been on stage just when he was supposed to be, playing pretty goddamn good, for that matter.

Then, after almost ten hours on the bandstand, he got Benny, Dave, Mezz, Tommy and a couple others to jam with him in the cottage. They played everything, from old original Dixieland Jazz Band numbers to the stuff the Goldkette band was playing now, even some of the stuff Bix was working out on the piano. People had come and gone while they played, to dip into the dwindling gallons of moon and to visit the bedrooms, in pairs, in groups. Bix had just watched the traffic over the valves of his horn, laughing to himself, and kept playing. And why not? There wasn't anything he could do to control them.

Control. The word rang in his mind, making him feel uncomfortable, helpless, angry. For a second he couldn't figure out why. Then he remembered his old man standing in front of the mantelpiece in the parlor, arms folded across his chest, smelling like cut lumber from the coal yard, stone-faced and silent while Bix tried to explain. And the feeling low in his bladder like a prodding, frigid finger, like he was five again and about to piss himself because, although the old man never yelled, his silences were deafening, and his cold contempt a more brutal weapon than any stick or belt could ever be. And how Bix had to go through the ritual self-flagellation of explanation and apology before the vast yawning silence was replaced by words again, by civility and normalcy and a semblance of affection. *I'm sorry, Dad, I know it was wrong, I'll never do it again. Yeah, I know I did lousy on that test, Dad, but I promise I'll try harder next time. I didn't study enough, that was stupid, Dad, and then we had to play a dance the night before the test, and I was so darn tired I fell asleep in class, isn't that nuts? I'm sorry—yeah, I'm sorry. It won't ever happen again.*

But it *had* happened again, again and again, over the years—at Tyler Elementary, when he couldn't keep any figures straight in his head and flunked all his math classes, and at Davenport High, when he'd been caught smoking and drinking. Or when he finally got kicked out of Lake Forest Academy and instead of coming home in disgrace, ran off to join a band. The icy shock as he sat on the bandstand in some café and looked up across the smoky room to see his father, dressed in his dark topcoat and homburg, arms folded across his chest just like he was back in the parlor at home, as incongruous amidst the gaudily dressed revelers as a raven among peacocks. His father, waiting until the song was over, and then threading through the dancers, up to the bandstand, and laying a heavy hand on Bix's shoulder. "Put the horn away, son," he'd said, his voice dead. "It's time to go home."

And the time the really bad thing happened, the thing that happened before Lake Forest Academy, right before the summer on the riverboat. The time his father wouldn't even let Bix try and explain, just watched, silent and expressionless, while Bix trembled and cried like a little kid, snot bubbling out of his nose, and his mother's voice pleading, "Herman, please—Herman—he's your son." And the old man speaking softly, almost gently. "Is he, Agatha? Is he? I always wondered." And then turning to Bix. "I can't control you or understand you anymore. I'm not even going to try. I don't even want to look at you. You sicken me. You're not a kid anymore, you're a man. Leave. I don't care where you go or what you do, just leave."

Bix took another deep swallow from the bottle to try and wash the words out of his mind. But his father's face remained, then melded into Mrs. Smith's dewlapped scowl, Norma Ryker and Mitzi Trumbauer whispering and staring at him, Tram turning red as he yelled about Bix's sight-reading, Joy's lip quivering with suppressed tears, Harriet saying, "Everybody thinks it was a gang rape."

More goddamn explaining, that's what they wanted. Just like the old man. *Gee, Mrs. Smith, I'm sorry I had to use your sacred shithouse because you have us out living in a goddamn shack with no toilet, and gosh, Mrs. Ryker, I know you and the other ladies think I'm nothing but a drunken slob, I'm sorry my existence offends you, and hey, Tram, I can sight-read, oh shit, no, I really can't, I've been faking it all along, but I'm sorry, and Joy, jeez, yeah, I said something stupid, but why should that keep us from fucking...and Harriet. I'm sorry you don't think I'm a nice college boy anymore, go talk to Mrs. Ryker and she'll tell you what a degenerate I am, but I'm sorry, I'm sorry, it'll never happen again...*

Then he thought of Buddy's black-and-blue face and worst of all, the vacant looks worn by the handful of locals in the audience tonight. Pee Wee was right. These goddamn rubes didn't deserve them.

"Fuck Joe Dockstader."

"What'd you say?"

"Joe Dockstader. Fuck him. And Lola Trowbridge, too."

"He's all right," Dan said, chuckling. "Got hayseed growin' out of his nose, but..."

"They're all a bunch of ignorant hillbillies." Bix jammed another cookie into his mouth, mumbling around it. "They got the best goddamn band west of New York City right in their backyard and what do they want? Joe

Dockstader, jacking himself off to 'Japanese Sandman.' Fuck 'em. Fuck 'em all."
He gestured at Dan for the bottle and took another pull. "I think I wanna bust
some Hoosier heads, too. Klan bastards. Know what they call us? Jews, nigger
lovers, and rapists." He laughed and dug into the bag for another cookie. "You
know what I call them? Rednecks, peckerwoods, and sister-fuckers."

"Hey, my girl's from Indianapolis," Dan said, sounding pained. "Not everybody's like that."

"The hell they're not. Christ, did you see 'em tonight? Faces like a bunch of
sheep. That's what comes from fucking the livestock."

"Go get 'em, Bix!" Pee Wee hollered.

"Come on, that's too much. Irene's a nice girl, and...."

"Yeah, and I bet her brother thinks so, too."

"All right, Beiderbecke, that's going too far!"

"You tell 'em, Bix! They're all ignorant yokels! Hey, look at the mailbox.
Ain't this the place?"

Bix shone a flashlight on a mailbox painted with "Walker." Down the path
in the darkness he could make out a white frame house and hear the distant,
guttural barking of what sounded like a large dog. Pee Wee pulled along the
side of the road and killed the engine. The country silence, which was anything
but silent, pressed down on him with the combined noise of crickets, cicadas,
tree frogs, and the wind in the trees. They passed the bottle again, the sloshing
adding to the night sounds.

They looked at each other. "So what are we gonna do?" Pee Wee asked.

"You stupid jackass. Wasn't this your idea? Here." Bix handed him a baseball
bat. He lurched out of the car, jamming the almost-empty cookie bag into his
back pocket. "Here, doggy-doggy-doggy..." He started walking into the darkness around the back of the house, not giving a damn if Pee Wee and Dan
were with him or not, his hands wanting a horn in them, or some other blunt
instrument that he could use to do some damage. He gestured at Pee Wee who
handed him a two-by-four, which he swished against some flowers along the
house, beheading them, scattering ripped leaves and petals in his wake.

"So what're we supposed to do if they're home?" Dan whispered.

"Christ, grow some balls, will ya?" Bix hissed over his shoulder. "They ain't
home. We know they ain't home. So we're gonna leave 'em a little message."

"Jeez, Bix, I'm glad to see you getting into the spirit of things," Pee Wee
whispered, going into a crazy laugh. "I thought I was in this by myself."

They reached the back of the house, and a neatly fenced-in yard flanked by a concrete birdbath and a blue glass globe on a stone pedestal. Bix raised the two-by-four to his shoulder and swung. The globe shattered, spraying them with blue shards.

"Shit, Bix, he's on the goddamn police. You really think this is a good idea?"

"It's a little late now," Pee Wee laughed, attacking the white picket fence with a baseball bat, bursting several pickets into raw wood.

They heard the barking again, and suddenly the dog was there, a fair-sized German shepherd. The dog flung itself against the fence, barking so frantically that it gasped between barks. They fell back at the sound, until Bix pointed to the collar around its neck; the dog was tethered to a stake in the yard, and could only get as far as the fence.

Bix gestured to Pee Wee. "Here, gimme that bat," he said, tossing aside the splintered two-by-four.

"What are you, nuts?" Pee Wee said, backing away. "It can't get at us, for Chrissake."

Bix took the bat and slapped it against the palm of his hand.

The dog was hysterical now, bouncing up and down behind the fence, straining against its collar, drops of spittle spraying from its mouth, its barks growing in ferocity.

"Jesus, Bix, don't," Dan said, grabbing Bix's elbow. He shoved him away, catching him off-balance, and Dan landed in a flowerbed.

"Hey, it can't get at us," Pee Wee repeated, backing away from the fence. "Come on, let's get the hell out of here."

Bix ran at the fence, slamming at the pickets with the baseball bat, until several of the slats were gone. He stood there catching his breath, the blood pounding in his temples. The dog backed away, yelping. Then it cowered at the stake, hackles raised, growling, its eyes gleaming like heated marbles in the glow of Pee Wee's flashlight.

He kicked in the slats on the fence and advanced on the dog, lifted the bat to his shoulder, hands tensed on the grip. The dog whimpered, cringing. Man and dog stood there sizing each other up. Then Bix took a deep breath and swung.

The bat spun off into the darkness, landing with a thump somewhere in the distance, and Bix felt the hard glass bubble of anger shatter inside him. He looked down at his hands, which were trembling, and reached into his back pocket. He raised his hand and shook the bag of cookies at the dog, which was now staring at him, ears perked up in anticipation.

"Here, you stupid son of a bitch," he mumbled, panting, hand extended, a macaroon balanced on his fingers. "Have a cookie." The dog advanced, sniffed, and took the cookie daintily between its teeth, crunching, then swallowing. Then it looked up at Bix with a dog grin, tail wagging, eyeing the bag. Bix flopped down in the grass next to the dog and scratched it behind the ears while it thrust its muzzle into the bag and crunched down the rest of the cookies.

Chapter 15

McGurn leaned back in the wooden-slatted chair and puffed expansively at the Havana cigar in his mouth. Now this is more like it, he thought, scanning the crowd in the Blue Lantern—jammed shoulder to shoulder on the polished dance floor, drinking at the tables ranged along the promenade on either side of the room. It was a Saturday night, and the South Shore cars were still unloading gaiety-seeking passengers, and this is what he had heard about, why he'd come up to this jerkwater town to begin with.

He nudged Tony, who was swiveling his head back and forth, eyeing every broad who danced by. Some were real pigs, looked like local meat, big old farm girls who were probably accustomed to heavy labor. Others you could tell were from Chicago. Dressed snappy, all made up, hot jazz babies. Tony didn't care. Eight to eighty was his range.

"The joint's jumping," McGurn said, and Tony nodded, made a show of scanning the tables.

"You talked to the yokel at the sody fountain about the hooch?" he asked, talking out of the corner of his mouth in his ongoing attempt to sound tough.

"It's all set. We can start shipping in our own stuff now that the South Bend rubes are out of the picture. And I got to Horvath about paying for some more publicity. He ain't beefing."

Tony jerked his chin at the French doors opening onto the pavilion.

It was the jane he'd met here last time, that Joy. He didn't even know the broad's last name, just that she'd worked at the Green Mill a while back and that she sang. She'd sure pulled out all the stops tonight.

She came across the floor at him with a movement like a well-oiled, expensive Swiss watch, all hips and melons, in a dress that could knock your eye out, green satin, cut low, with lots of sparkle. "*Madonn'*," McGurn murmured, standing up. He slapped Tony on the back of the head. "Hey, you *cetriolo*, get off your ass. Stand up when a lady is present."

"Well, hello, Mr. McGurn. It's a pleasure to see you again. You too, Mr....."

"Accardo."

"Yeah. Tony, isn't it?"

"Here, honey, have a seat. You gonna sing up there tonight, sweetheart?"

She laughed, showing bright white teeth, throwing back her head and making her dangly rhinestone earrings dance. "Well, only if the boys'll let me. And who knows about them!"

"Well, maybe if a paying customer puts in a special request. Anyhow, I heard you sing before and I know you're a helluva lot better than that anemic broad they got with the other band."

She sat, and McGurn nudged Tony to go get them setups. She glittered, this jane, she was full of personality, not at all mopey like the first time he met her. She even looked better—younger, full of pep, and McGurn would bet she was a good stepper.

"Well, was I right?" she laughed, winking at him. "This a big enough crowd for ya?"

"I'll say. You couldn't squeeze in another jamoke with a shoehorn. But see, you could put more tables in through here, and if you give 'em some food to buy, and up the cover charge, you just watch. This joint'll mint money."

Tony returned and deposited several pop bottles on the table. McGurn took a gold-plated hip flask from his breast pocket and passed it to Joy, making no pretenses about hiding it. "Have a taste, baby. Bet you find it's a big improvement over the local poison you're used to." She took the flask and tilted back her head to drink. The mama can put it away, he thought, watching her soft white throat work around the slug of booze.

"You're not kidding, Mr. McGurn. That's smooth."

"Like it? Get used to it. That's the kinda stuff this area's gonna be seeing from now on." He leaned back in the chair again, grinning. "Yep, there's gonna be some changes made to little old Hudson Lake."

"Here comes the band," Tony muttered.

McGurn glanced up and saw the tuxedoed musicians filing up to the bandstand. The crowd took up a chant of *Bix, Bix, Bix,* and people started stomping their feet in time to the chant.

Who the hell is Bix?, he thought. Then he saw the guy get up on the stage with his horn, a moon-faced, jug-eared jasper in a tux that didn't fit him right, and he waved at the crowd and everybody started clapping for him. "Hey, I think I know that guy," he murmured to nobody in particular as the band swung into a heated-up version of "Coquette." The guy stepped up and took a solo, plenty of pep to it, all right, and there were people just standing around the stage clapping and hanging onto every note he played.

He was good, no doubt about it, almost as hot as the niggers that played in the South Side joints McGurn frequented as part of his work for Al. It wasn't often you heard a white guy play like that, with a sock-time beat that made you want to grab a broad and dance, laying everything you had right up against her, like this Joy. What a soft, slow ride that would be....

And then he sat forward and stared at the horn player and it clicked. The Greyhound in Cicero, must have been about a year ago. He'd gone over to collect from the owner and check out the band while he was there. The place wasn't much to look at, couldn't hold a candle to the Mill, more like a shot-and-a-beer place with a lot of working stiffs probably on their big Saturday night out after a week's work at the Western Electric plant on 22nd and Cicero.

But the band was hot, a six-piece group with a horn player who could blow up a storm. The same guy who was up on the bandstand now. "Why, that little son of a bitch," McGurn laughed, remembering.

That little son of a bitch could drink like a fish, that much he remembered. McGurn had bought the boys a couple of rounds, then sent up a big gallon jug of wine, and asked them to play a couple of his favorite songs, stuff like "Melancholy Baby" and "You Made Me Love You." The moon-faced fella sucked up plenty. But it didn't affect his playing; if anything, the hooch made him play hotter. As the night wore on, a couple of Al's fellas came in to wet their whistles. Everybody was having a good time, laughing it up, yelling at the band, making a hell of a racket.

And then the little son of a bitch got mad. He jumped off the bandstand and ran up to the table in front where Al's guys were drinking, feeling up their broads and cutting a deck of cards for change. The guy called them ignorant bastards and told them to shut up while the band was playing.

Al's guys clammed up because they couldn't believe it. McGurn had been sitting at the bar and heard enough to know that the little son of a bitch had just told off Bottles—Ralphie. Al's brother.

Ralph was all for carrying the horn player outside and kicking the shit out of him or worse, but McGurn smoothed it over, telling him it would be bad for business. The little bastard had been stripping off his jacket, rolling up his sleeves, getting ready to take on the whole table, but the other musicians settled him down. Lucky for him he'd had his friends around to talk him out of it.

And now, here he was again. What a laugh.

"Hey," McGurn leaned over to Joy and stroked her arm, "who's that fellow playing the horn so hot? Boy, he's good."

She turned to him, cat eyes slanted in a grin. "Bix Beiderbecke. Ain't he something, though?"

He leaned back in the chair and reignited his cigar. "Yeah, he sure is."

When the band took a break, McGurn shouldered his way through the crowd, zeroing in on the guy. He was in his own world, checking out the valves on his horn, head tilted like he was listening to imaginary music.

"Hey," McGurn said, loud enough so that people sitting at the tables turned around, "you Beiderbecke?"

The guy looked up, a flummoxed look on his face. "Who wants to know?" he said, reaching under his chair for a bottle of pop.

This little shit has brass ones, McGurn thought. "Jack McGurn," he said, extending a hand. "I run the Green Mill on the north side of Chicago."

He shook his hand, staring at McGurn as if trying to place him. "Pleasure," he muttered and took a swig from the bottle.

"You sure play some hot horn. Almost as hot as that time at the Greyhound in Cicero."

Now he had the guy's attention. He looked up at McGurn and laughed. "Hey, yeah, I remember you," he said. "You saved my ass there that night. Here, lemme buy you a drink."

"Just what I was gonna suggest," McGurn said, extending his flask. "Here, have a snort. Fact is, we're probably gonna be doing business in the very near future."

He took a swallow of hooch and slid his glance over to McGurn's table, where Joy was jabbering away at an expressionless Tony. McGurn caught the barely perceptible tightening of his lips, his eyebrows pulling down. So that's how it is, McGurn thought, laughing inside.

"How do you mean?" Beiderbecke mumbled, still staring at Joy.

"I'm sinking some money into this place. Investing, expanding the entertainment. Hot horn player like you could work out great, here and at the Mill, too."

"I work for Goldkette," he said, and stood to walk away.

"Wait a minute. I know that. But I know Goldkette only leased this joint for the summer. What are your plans after that?"

"I work for Goldkette. I'm not looking for any other job right now."

"Don't get ahead of yourself," McGurn said, putting a hand against the guy's chest to keep him from walking away. "What I'm getting at is...."

"I know what you're getting at," he said, and the moon-shaped face turned hard. "And I'd appreciate it if you took your hand off me."

"Hey, kid, back off. I don't want to get into an *imbroglio* here. I just figured you might like the opportunity to make some real dough after this gig is up. I don't give a damn that you're working for Goldkette. You got a price. Everybody does."

"Break's almost over," he said. "And I gotta use the can. Excuse me, okay?" The guy brushed past him. McGurn watched as he stopped briefly at his table and leaned over to say something to Joy. Heated words were exchanged; McGurn could tell by the way the jane was waving her hands around, getting red in the face.

So the little son of a bitch was pumping her. He should have guessed it, thinking back on how she'd badmouthed the musicians that day they'd met. He was pumping her, and they had a fight. Well, that made it even sweeter, in McGurn's book. Stolen goods were the choicest.

Anyhow, he didn't give a shit one way or the other about either of them. The broad was his for the price of dinner and maybe a bauble—they were all that way. And he'd find Beiderbecke's price, too, maybe not now, but soon. He couldn't let him get away at the end of the summer, not after how he packed them in here on the weekends. It was easy enough to make inquiries from the owners of the places he'd played to find out his price, and his weakness. Booze, that was for sure, and probably broads, too, from the looks of him with Joy. Easy enough. Those were just the kind of people guys in McGurn's line of work catered to.

McGurn left halfway through the second set, carrying Joy away on his arm like a beautiful hothouse corsage. He felt Beiderbecke staring daggers into his back and laughed to himself just thinking about it. Yeah, everybody had their price; it was just a matter of figuring out what it was. McGurn knew that very well, since he had had his own price once, not so long ago.

If the Six Terrible Gennas hadn't drilled his old man in 1923, Jack McGurn would have never been born. He probably would have stayed Vincenzo Gebardi and followed his old man into business in the grocery store on Vernon

Park Place. Or if he'd been lucky, maybe he would have made something of his welterweight boxing career.

But the Gennas drilled his old man, right in front of the grocery store, over an *imbroglio* about the price of bulk sugar he sold to the Gennas for their alky-cooking business. And McGurn had wanted revenge.

It took a lot of balls for him to make that first visit to the Metropole Hotel, past the armed thugs at the front door and up into the double rooms on the fourth floor, fragrant with marinara sauce.

The fireplug-shaped man, dressed in a hundred-dollar suit, was sitting behind a carved mahogany desk the size of a battleship, the office decked out in Oriental rugs and Italian marble.

McGurn knew he was nothing but a neighborhood kid, another *stoonad* from the Circus Café gang on North Avenue, good with his dukes, with a rap sheet for minor-league stuff like breaking and entering and assault. But Capone was at war with the Gennas, and Jack had come to enlist.

"What's your price, kid?" the big man asked.

"My price? Hell, I'll pay you for the chance to kill some Gennas."

The big man just laughed, showing an octave of white teeth. But McGurn persisted and convinced Capone he was serious, pledging his loyalty if he could only help eradicate all the Gennas from Chicago.

He rose quickly. Starting as a driver and foot soldier, then a lieutenant, McGurn proved himself. By 1925, three of the six terrible Gennas were dead, and the remaining three had decided the weather was better back home in Sicily.

Al took a shine to McGurn and promoted him to bodyguard. Al and McGurn, dressed to kill, became a familiar sight at all the events around town—boxing matches, horseraces, opening night at the opera. McGurn took over muscling the South Side nightclub owners for protection, a job he liked so much he ended up investing in his own place.

Before long, McGurn was wearing hundred-dollar tailored suits from Sulka's, specially cut to accommodate whatever heat he was packing, setting himself up in a modern flat on North Sheridan Road, buying the Lincoln, buying Louise, a leggy showgirl. Vincenzo Gebardi had come a long way from the tenement on Halsted Street, where the weekly bath came in the kitchen sink and you were lucky to have a pair of shoes that fit to keep off the ash-blackened slush in the winter.

But it wasn't enough. Just as he'd worked his way up in the fights, McGurn aimed for the title—nothing less than Capone's second in command. He knew that wouldn't happen by getting greedy. Instead, he was content to keep proving his loyalty to Al, in whatever way he had to, to build the big man's faith in him.

Now that the Gennas and Deany O'Banion were out of the picture, the only world left to conquer was the North Side, where Weiss and Drucci and Moran still had a stranglehold. Al had everything south from State and Lake to the Indiana border at the Lake Michigan and 106th Street, down to Chicago Heights—but Al wanted more. Handing him this profitable little pocket of Indiana would be like laying a tribute at a king's feet, designed to get McGurn his own fiefdom. Ease Weiss and Moran out, and maybe that North Side territory could be his, all the way up to Evanston and maybe even beyond, into those tree-shaded enclaves like Wilmette and Lake Forest.

And he wasn't stopping at that. Prohibition couldn't last forever, and by the time the Volstead Act had breathed its last, McGurn would be a legit businessman, running a string of exclusive nightclubs where he'd shake hands and slap the shoulders of swells in tuxes and Brooks Brothers' suits, dance with broads who went to Northwestern, golfed, sailed, rode horses.

He'd live in one of those houses set far back along the North Shore lakefront, with servants in the carriage house, a Junior League wife, blond and slim and aristocratic, who devoted her days to charity and supervised the raising of their children through a live-in nursemaid. All his money safe in blue-chip stocks and lakefront real estate. And a hot broad like this Joy on the side for fun. Mr. Jack McGurn, Esquire.

But until then, he was enjoying himself. And when Al started seeing the profits come rolling in from this little corner of Indiana, it would get McGurn in even better. Meanwhile, he'd play around with Joy. It was a nice way to pass the time.

Chapter 16

"This meeting will now come to order."

Cyrus Walker banged the gavel and looked out over the robed audience of Hundred-Percenters who were gathered for the weekly meeting of the Valley Klan #53 Klavern. Place Hall, at the corner of Michigan and Washington Streets in downtown South Bend, was up on the third floor, and hot. The oscillating fans mounted on the walls stirred robes and ruffled graying hair but did little to alleviate the heat. Wilmer Banks was fanning himself with the latest issue of *The Fiery Cross*; Bob Richmond kept sticking his finger under his celluloid collar and pulling it away from his goitered neck.

Fewer members in the house this week, Cyrus thought, always one or two fewer. Not like in '24, when the chapter first got its charter and membership was well over a thousand. Despite the last recruitment drive, the official rolls of Klavern #53 stood at a little over eight hundred, and that included the Ladies of the Invisible Empire Auxiliary.

"Kligrapp Collins?" Cyrus called. "Please read back the minutes from last week."

The chapter secretary, known as a "kligrapp," was Claude Collins, a real estate agent under his robes. He cleared his throat and flipped back several pages in the big black ledger. "Monday, July 20. Weekly meeting of the South Bend chapter of the Invisible Empire will come to order. Point Number One. Kleagle Williams reports twenty-five new applications put in for naturalization. Twenty-five applications read and passed."

"And I see some new faces here tonight," Cyrus beamed. He spotted Clyde Burgett, an auto dealer from Mishawaka, Preston Raymond, a chiropractor, and Ronald Warner, who Cyrus might have pulled over for speeding somewhere outside New Carlisle. "Please continue, Kligrapp Collins."

"Uh, yes. Point Number Two. Uh, Klokan Smith reported that the new robes were ordered, and dues collected through the end of August."

And they're way down, in spite of a measly twenty-five new members, Cyrus mused. Even the Fourth of July picnic had failed to muster enough interest to stir the chapter's sluggish membership beyond the official eight hundred point. Cyrus was under pressure from both the regional kleagles, who recruited new members, and state headquarters in Indianapolis to get more names on the rolls. It didn't look good. Especially since Cyrus was hoping to use the Klan membership for a voter base in the upcoming election for sheriff. It was a spot Cyrus had been eyeing for years, and a big part of the reason he'd gotten involved in the Klan in the first place.

"Point Number Three. Exalted Cyclops Walker stated that members should in the future kindly put on their robes in the cloakroom before entering the Klavern. This not only avoids a lot of confusion and time, but is far more impressive." Collins blinked over the rims of his spectacles like a schoolboy successfully reciting a lesson. "That's it for old business."

"Very good," Cyrus said. "Well, I'd like to welcome all our new members to the Invisible Empire. As you know, our mission is to promote four-square Americanism, support law enforcement, and fight with every fiber in our being the encroaching menace of anarchists, Papists and all things anti-American. You new Hundred-Percenters will be awarded your official Klan pins sometime later this summer in a special ceremony. Pins will be worn just above the fiery cross insignia on your robes, right over the heart. Congratulations, gentlemen." He looked over the room and mopped his brow against the heat. "And now, is there any new business to discuss this week?"

A hand shot up. As usual, Mitch Johnston. The butcher had a never-ending list of useless comments that he stored up all week long, then spewed out at every Monday meeting, Cyrus thought.

"There's a situation in Mishawaka with those Jews," Mitch said, long face red with outrage. Cyrus thought it must get tiring being so outraged all the time. "It's bad enough we got all those polacks and bohunks out on the west side of town by that St. Stephen's Church, but now I hear tell those Jew shopkeepers in Mishawaka are looking to buy property in South Bend. And I don't like it." He looked around, expecting support. The newer members nodded in polite agreement, but everyone else pretty much ignored him.

"Thanks, Mitch. We'll take it under advisement. Anything else in the way of new business?"

Davis Woodburne raised his beefy hand. "I'm worried about the Pope," he said. "Most of those foreigners working at the Birdsell wagon works and Studebaker plants are Catholic. If they ever decided to gang together to put over their religion, there wouldn't be an American Protestant could stop them.

And you know what they stand for. Trade unionism and anarchy!" There was a mutter of agreement.

The constant paranoia about the Pope annoyed Cyrus. Granted, he wasn't any fonder of the local Bohunks than any of the rest, but some fellows like Mitch Johnston figured the Pope to be coming into South Bend on the next *Monon* train. That was just plain stupid, especially considering the very real problems facing the area right now. Something he was about to get into.

"Well, thanks, Davis," Cyrus said, smoothing down the folds of his robe. "I appreciate everyone's concerns about Jews, and the Pope, and all of the other threats to Americanism we face every day. But we got problems right here got nothing to do with any foreign influences. And I'm talking about bootlegging and licentiousness and that situation over to Hudson Lake."

Several heads bobbed at the mention of the resort. The town was still gabbling about what happened to Crystal Hawkins, even though Cyrus knew the stupid girl had brought it on herself. But he also knew folks were expecting him to do something about it.

"Ain't Loretta Smith runnin' it no more," called out Clem Clarke. "Some fella from St. Louis, slick-looking fella name of Horvath." He grunted. "Sounds like some kinda hunky name to me."

"You been out there since that new band come to town?" Mitch said. "Sound just like niggers."

"I'm friends with Joe Dockstader," said one of the new members. "He says what goes on out there isn't to be believed, especially when those other bands come over from Chicago. We're not just talking about some bootleg liquor. We're talking drugs and prostitution!"

Cyrus had to bang his gavel repeatedly to get them to simmer down. Looks like I hit a nerve, he thought. "For those of you who don't know, there's a real problem out there," he said. "It used to be a nice place to take your family on a Sunday afternoon. Now there's jazz, and a bunch of city boys living out there that are up to no good all hours of the day and night. Let's put it this way. I wouldn't want my daughter going there anymore, not even in broad daylight."

The members fell into a sea of murmurs and whispers, probably about Crystal, Cyrus thought. That's all right—whatever it took to get things done. He went on, just warming up.

"And then there's bootlegging, gentlemen. Let's not turn a blind eye to this modern plague. Used to be a man could have a drink if he chose, even put up some home brew if he was so inclined. But the government in its wisdom made liquor illegal, and as law-abiding Americans, it's our obligation to follow the letter of the law." Cyrus noted support of this notion wasn't quite as unanimous as cracking down on the behavior at Hudson Lake. But the law was the law, and as Exalted Cyclops Cyrus was charged with upholding it.

"I say we put a torch to the place!" hollered Mitch, always itching for a fight. "Burn it to the ground, with those punks in it." The meeting erupted into chaos, and Cyrus was forced to use the gavel again.

"Gentlemen, order please," he called. "Yes, it's true there's a disruptive element at Hudson Lake. But Loretta Smith and her son have done nothing wrong. Yet the boy was beaten up, badly, too." He looked around to make sure he had everyone's attention. "And my own home was vandalized."

A gasp went up from the collection of fluttering white robes.

"Your place? No!"

"Think it was niggers or Jews?"

"Anybody hurt, Cyrus?"

He made a soothing gesture with his hands. "Now, friends, settle down. Nobody was hurt, that's what's important. But it's just a sign of how much things are changing in the Valley—and a call to action to put a stop to it."

"Burn 'em out!" Mitch hollered again. "And let's hit the west side of town and take care of those bohunks, too."

Cyrus slammed the gavel again. "Now wait just a minute, Mitch. Those people are our neighbors, most of 'em law-abiding citizens. They're not the problem. Nossir, it's the bad element that comes and goes and treats our town and our people like something to wipe themselves off with and throw away. That's what's causing the trouble. And we need to stop it right now."

"Boycott the place!" Clem shouted.

Cyrus nodded. "We need to hit these people where they live. Unless that dance hall has local support, business will suffer. And that's the only way we'll get our point across."

He had to bang the gavel yet again in the resultant hubbub, but he was pleased at the response. Membership may be down, true, but this group was red-blooded and ready to go, all right, he thought.

"So where do we start?" Jim Dawson called.

"Right here, with you men. It's simple. Just tell everyone you know about what's going on at the Blue Lantern. Raping, loose women, bootleg liquor and flaming youth. We'll get the word out to all our members to raise the name of any Hundred-Percenter seen patronizing the Blue Lantern, and read his name out at the next meeting, and every meeting, until he stops going there. I'll speak to Reverend Tufts and some of the other clergy in town about addressing the issue from the pulpit. And for God's sake, keep your children away from this den of iniquity." He slammed the gavel one last time. "Meeting is adjourned."

⠿⠦⠿

Cyrus tried to avoid William Bates in the cloakroom, but the chicken-necked little teacher cornered him. Out of his Klan robes, in his threadbare store-bought suit, Bill Bates was someone he wanted to avoid, but couldn't.

"Cyrus, I've been meaning to call you," he said, tone apologetic, eyes bright behind his silver spectacles. "It's about Trent, you know."

He laid a hand on Bates' stringy shoulder. "Bill, I'd love to talk right now, but I need to get back to headquarters. I'm on the late shift tonight, and...."

"I'd prefer you came out to the school to discuss this, but I understand your hectic schedule. We need to get some sort of plan in place to help your boy when school starts again in the fall. He needs to take English and algebra again. And then there's the truancy problem...."

Cyrus felt his mouth tighten, and the gathering storm in his stomach go from rumbling threat to directly overhead. "I've already disciplined him," he said, staring directly into the teacher's watery blue eyes. "Repeatedly, and hard. There isn't much else I can do besides send him to reform school. Which isn't out of the question, either."

"I think Trent just needs some of your attention. Perhaps if you did something with him, some sport or activity...."

"Sport?" Cyrus snorted a laugh. "Sport! What was your sport when you were a boy, Bill? Pitching hay? Slopping the hogs? Those were my sports, that and a lot more. And just enough time after supper to finish my schoolwork and fall into bed. I didn't have any trouble sleeping. Neither did you. Because we were bone-tired from all that work."

Bill reached out and patted Cyrus's arm, like the old woman he was. "I understand, Cyrus. But times have changed. Things are different for boys today. There's more...."

"That's right, more trouble for them to get into when they don't have enough to do. Idle hands are the devil's workshop, Bill. That's why my son has a job after school and all summer long, instead of giving him the leisure time to idle around the movie show or the football field, or that Blue Lantern dance hall."

"Yes, Cyrus. Except according to Malcolm down at the hardware store, Trent hasn't shown up at his job in a week or more." The teacher smiled with what Cyrus perceived as a touch of smugness.

He carefully folded his robe and hung it on the wall peg, deliberately avoiding Bill's eyes. Then he smiled into the teacher's face. "Thanks for the information, Bill," he said. "I'll be sure to straighten things out with Trent."

"Uh, Cyrus, I'm sorry to be the one to tell you this, but there's more." Bill was positively beaming now.

Cyrus felt his innards grow cold. More? What more could there possibly be? The truancy, the shoplifting, the running around with that wild crowd of bohunks last fall—he was sure he'd beaten it out of the boy. Trent had been toeing the line ever since, or so Cyrus had thought. He sighed. "All right, Bill. What else do you think you know?"

The teacher licked his pale, dry lips. "Well, several days ago when he was supposed to be at work at the hardware store, Malcolm and some others saw Trent in downtown South Bend in the company of some men. In the vicinity of that cafe on Indiana Avenue that's been raided as a speakeasy. And it wasn't the first time, either."

Cyrus said nothing. What could he say? He wouldn't put it past the whelp. He couldn't understand what motivated the boy. Emma was such a good girl—graduated from high school with honors, engaged to Bradford Wood, a decent boy who would make a decent husband. And Trent? Just plain bad, ever since he was old enough to toddle. Not that Cyrus would give Bill Bates the satisfaction of admitting as much to him.

"Well, thank you for the information. I'll be sure to get to the bottom of this." One way or another, he thought.

Chapter 17

Jean Goldkette stood on the landing of the stairwell and turned his face toward the music drifting from the top floor. He noted the regularity of the double-time rhythm, the synchronization of the reed section, the steady throb of the upright bass, and the fact that the cornet solo came in promptly when it was supposed to. Grunting with satisfaction, he laid a hand on the banister and scuffed up the remaining marble steps to the third-floor broadcast studio of WSBT, the radio station of the South Bend Tribune, housed in a four-square chocolate brick building in the heart of downtown South Bend.

The frosted glass door to the auditorium was propped open against the heat and he gently pushed it open to peer in on the rehearsal.

"Ah," Goldkette said, and smiled. There on the stage, facing a hall of empty seats, was his band.

Off to the side was the engineer's booth, manned by a bald little fellow working the knobs and controls that would broadcast the music as far north as Niles, as far south as Michigan City.

Goldkette nodded at the man and stood watching a moment before the band knew he was there. They looked so serious up there on stage, working hard in shirtsleeves and stockinged feet, which prevented uncontrollable foot tapping from disrupting the sound of the broadcast. A grand piano stood on the stage for the Eastwood Lane solo Beiderbecke was scheduled to play.

He tapped the engineer on the shoulder. "The broadcast begins when?" he asked.

"Another fifteen minutes."

"Ah." Just enough time for a word with Trumbauer. That individual spotted him first, looked up from his charts and came hurrying over.

"Jean," Tram said, thrusting out a big square hand for him to shake. "Great to see you. Charlie should be here any minute. He's working out some last-minute business with the station manager."

Goldkette dipped into a breast pocket for a gold case and affixed a cigarette to an amber holder. "And business at the Blue Lantern?"

Tram flushed, flicked him a glance, then turned back to the band. "Not so hot. Charlie figured this broadcast might drum up some interest. It's getting a lot of play in the newspaper."

"Horvath advises me business has declined sharply since July Fourth," Goldkette said. "Any idea of why?"

"Well, it sure isn't due to the playing. These boys are working hard every day. You can hear the results."

"Ah, yes." Goldkette nodded at the band. "I'm pleased with their progress. So poor attendance at the Blue Lantern may be due to elements out of our control." He blinked at Tram from behind his round tortoise-shell spectacles. "I hear there was some sort of local disruption that could be affecting things."

Trumbauer fiddled with his suspenders. "I don't pay attention to gossip," he said. "All I know is my men are working hard every day, doing just what they're supposed to do."

"And our two Peck's bad boys? Mr. Russell and Mr. Beiderbecke?"

"Same deal."

Goldkette stood there a moment, watching and listening, as the band ran through another take of "Hoosier Sweetheart." They certainly sounded very well rehearsed, he mused, as good or even better than they had at the Arcadia. No faulting them on that count. "So perhaps some promotional efforts are in order," Goldkette said. "Giveaways. Contests. Other such devices."

"I suppose we could work up something."

"Well, you had better. The organization is beginning to lose money on this venture. We need to increase attendance significantly between now and Labor Day, before our lease on the place is up for the season."

"Or what?" Tram said. "With all due respect, I mean."

"I may be forced to discharge some of the men. Or perhaps dissolve the band completely."

Tram jammed his hands into his pockets and glared at his boys.

"Not you, of course," Goldkette said. "But Beiderbecke may have to go again. I'm assuming his sight-reading has improved?"

"He's doing a lot better," Tram said, talking faster. "You can't get rid of him, Jean. He's our biggest draw."

"But Farrar is the lead brass man. Beiderbecke is becoming a luxury I can't afford." He rubbed his chin, thinking. Trumbauer was probably right about Beiderbecke. The man was a machine on the cornet, in spite of his weakness as a section man. Russell, though—he was still unseasoned, needed to be brought along. An endeavor that perhaps someone other than Jean Goldkette should undertake. "Russell, then. He's less experienced. Expendable. Ryker can do double duty."

"What about the section?" Tram exploded, face going red. "How do you expect me to play these arrangements with only one other reed man?"

"Better the loss of a reed man than the band folds. And tell Beiderbecke he's on probation, unless he can get his reading up." The little man turned to the engineer. "Are we just about ready?"

ဆာလ

Pee Wee crumpled to the bench in the hallway, hands dangling limp between his knees. His face was slack, eyes dull. Bix sat next to him and nudged him with his flask. Pee Wee ignored it.

"He must have found out about that skunky Crystal or something," Pee Wee mumbled. "Why else would he have fired me? Hell, I'm playing better than ever!"

"Jean's not like that," Tram said, standing over them. "It's got nothing to do with your playing or anything else. Things are tough now, that's all. He's losing his shirt, and we still got til Labor Day to go here." He looked away. "I'm really sorry, Pee Wee. I'll ask Charlie about trying to get you in at one of the other ballrooms back in St. Louis, or something."

Bix poked at Pee Wee again, sloshing the flask under his nose, but Pee Wee didn't move. *Jeez, he really is down. And I can't say that I blame him. He's gonna be losing his salary for the next month, and*—Bix sat up straight, an idea hitting him. "Hey, listen to this. Tram, you still need a full reed section, right?"

"Sure, I don't want to lose Pee Wee. But...."

"Well, I'll chip in part of my salary to keep Pee Wee on for the rest of the gig."

Bix slapped Pee Wee on the back. "Whaddaya say, pal? Will that help?"

Ryker walked up, unclipping his sax from the holder he wore around his neck. "Maybe Jean don't care about wearing out my chops, but I do. I need you around, Russell. You can have a slice of my pay, too."

"Hell, who else is gonna do the hooch runs for us?" Dee said, passing Pee Wee a fin. "Here, this should help tide you over til payday. I'll ante up part of my paycheck, too."

Pee Wee looked around at the guys, then ducked his head. "Jesus H., you guys," he muttered, as if afraid they'd hear him. "Thanks." Then he went back to the studio to pack up his instruments.

Tram sank down next to Bix and folded his arms over his chest. "Your butt's on the line again, too," Tram said. "Guess Jean figures we can tough it out with just Doc and Fuzzy."

"I'll prove him wrong," Bix said, pulling out of his slouch and straightening on the bench. "I'll work up my reading so damn good, he'll...."

"I think it's more than that now. Now it's a matter of economics." He looked at Bix. "Can you line up something quick if it comes to that?"

Bix thought a moment, drawing a blank. Where could he go? Not back to the Rendez-Vous in Chicago—Charlie Straight had fired him for the same reason Jean had that first time. Not back to the Wolverines—Jimmy McPartland had taken his place, and the Wolverines were on the verge of breaking up, anyway. So where? He knew the guys in the pit orchestras at all the big movie houses in St. Louis, if he wanted to go back there, but he didn't want to, because of Ruth. Or maybe the Chicago Theater, they might have him. Maybe he could tide himself through the winter that way and when spring and summer came again, what the hell—go back to the riverboats, as a last resort. Back where he started. And face the old man and his wall of silence.

He looked up. Tram was staring at him, frowning.

"I guess I could go back to Davenport," Bix said.

"Davenport? What's back there?"

Bix shrugged and looked at the floor. *Home. The place they have to take you in.* He laughed. "Oh, I could always gig around. Or there's the old man's coal business. I'm sure he'd be thrilled to have me there."

Like that one year his mother had persuaded the old man to take him back. He'd spent the summer with Burnie, writing out bills of lading and arranging coal deliveries, trying like hell to do everything right so the old man would approve of him. But every night he'd sit in with whatever band was playing at Danceland, or the Col, even the black-and-tan joints in Milan. And while everyone else in town came out to hear him, excited that a local boy was making a name for himself, the old man never did. He'd just give him that cold-eyed stare next day, then find endless fault with everything he did at work, and carp at him about *that damn music. And what are you going to do when your good-time friends have had enough of you and you can't play horn anymore? How are you going to make a living? How will you support a family?*

Tram punched him in the arm. "Don't talk crazy. You're a horn man, the best in the business. You wouldn't last a week away from music, and you know it." He clapped Bix on the shoulder. "Come on. We got a big Saturday night show to do."

The two of them walked down the stairway, Tram with his arm around Bix's shoulders. They met Charlie Horvath coming up, in a hurry.

"Just the man I gotta see," Tram said, grabbing his arm. "Jean's getting panicky about the take. We gotta figure out some gimmick...."

"I got it handled," Charlie said, frowning, eyes shifting. He looked at Tram, then at Bix, then away, preoccupied. "I got it handled," he repeated, and ran up the stairs.

"Handled how?" Tram hollered after him.

Charlie turned on the top step and looked down at them. "Every which way. Newspaper ads, billboards, you name it, here and in Chicago and all over the place. And I worked out a contest with the radio station manager. There's a big prize for the listener who writes the best letter on why they like the Jean Goldkette band."

Tram grunted. "Looks like Jean ain't doing as bad as he claims if he can throw those kind of shekels around on publicity."

"It's not Jean's money," Charlie said, raising his eyebrows meaningfully. Then he walked down the hall, heading for the engineer's panel.

"What's eating him?" Tram muttered. "Jeez, things around here sure are getting screwy."

They sure are, Bix thought, thinking about how much he was contributing to the screwiness. And how he should try and put things right.

Chapter 18

Harriet woke at three in the morning to cramps and the approaching, menacing mutter of a thunderstorm. She got up to close the window and use the bathroom to check and see if her period had started yet—it hadn't—then slunk back into bed, wondering why the natural order of things had to be so damned painful and messy at times. And not just the cramps, but the way she'd left things with Rudy.

By the time the storm came crashing overhead, pelting the attic roof with a mixture of rain and hail, she decided it was all her fault somehow, and cursed her stupidity.

"Maybe we should slow things down a little," she'd said to him the last time he'd telephoned her at the Traub's.

He was momentarily silent, and Harriet could practically hear the telephone wires buzzing in the void. "What the hell? Why?"

Now she slammed her fists into the pillows and asked herself the same question, over and over.

Why? Just because they hadn't seen eye to eye about everything since the last time she'd seen him on the Fourth of July weekend? True, there was the argument about her hennaed hair, first thing, and the snotty way he'd talked to Joy, and the way he'd laughed at Bix's wrinkled tuxedo.

"Jeez, Harriet, you've been out in the sticks too damn long if these people are looking good to you," he'd said. "Don't you remember high-school biology? The Jukes and the Kallikacks. White trash." That had made her so mad she'd stormed off and left him sitting in the dance hall. And even after he'd caught up with her and apologized, things weren't the same. They hadn't been the same since, in their telephone calls or letters.

Rudy was different now. They'd only been apart for two months, but he'd changed. He'd grown thinner, and looked older, didn't smile as often, and seemed more impatient with her and everything else, everybody else. He didn't talk or write about music anymore, but about work—business associates, and the new friends he'd made in Indianapolis, friends he said would be able to help him get ahead once he was working full-time. But when she'd tried to point this out to him, he'd just laughed. "Welcome to the real world, kid," he'd said. And then she remembered her reliable analogy of Rudy as an alpha male, and knew that alpha males sometimes did whatever they had to in order to survive.

As Harriet snuggled deeper into the bedding, she thought about how the summer that had started out so innocent and fun was turning out to be a disaster for just about everyone. The Crystal Hawkins mess. Buddy getting beat up. Joy locking herself in her bedroom, playing an old record of Fanny Brice singing "My Man," over and over. And then going off to Chicago with a stranger in a big, expensive auto, spending most of her time in the city.

And Harriet hadn't spoken to Bix since the incident with Buddy. She didn't want to. It had been a mistake trying to befriend him, to assume he was just like her, to think she could ever understand him. But although Harriet rationally knew this, the memory of that evening on the lake, and all the other times they'd talked and she'd watched him play, made her viscerally feel she was right, that under the drinking and the wildness he *was* a good person.

And then there was the way her body felt when she was with him, a longing for physical closeness she barely acknowledged to herself, let alone to him or anyone else. For a long time now, she'd wanted him to touch her the way she'd never let Rudy touch her, in part because she felt he instinctively knew the shadow-Harriet, the one she never showed to anyone anymore. But now it seemed that both Rudy and Bix were out of her life.

The noise of the storm faded and the rain grew long and steady, suggestive of a full day of nonstop gloom. She must have dozed awhile because the next thing she knew Mrs. Traub was tapping at her door, and Harriet was saying she was sick and couldn't go to church today, she was sorry, she just wanted to sleep. She listened half-dozing to the sounds of them walking back and forth as they got dressed, inhaled the aroma of brewing coffee, bacon and biscuits from the kitchen, and finally heard the clunk of the front door and the roar and rattle of the Ford telling her they'd left. And then nothing but the somnambulant swish of the rain against the windows and the roof and the trees outside.

∞∞∞

When she woke it was still raining, the windows showing a slate gray unmarked by sun or blue sky. She heard a car grinding down the gravel driveway and glanced at the alarm clock. Nine thirty-eight? The Traubs always went straight from church to their son and daughter-in-law's for dinner and didn't get back until evening. Harriet listened as a car door slammed and feet clumped up the wooden front steps. She slid out of bed and peered around the curtains.

Bix was on the front porch, pushing an envelope under the door. He looked around as if afraid someone would see him, then turned to go back to the car.

She opened the window. "What do you want?" she called, still behind the curtain. A rush of apprehension washed over her, and she felt her stomach knot up the way it had that evening on the lake, before they'd talked and she'd gotten to know him.

His pale, upturned face was an ill-looking blotch in the dimness. "You're home. Thought you'd be at church."

"What do you have there?"

He shrugged and started back-pedaling off the porch. "Letter. Hey, I'll see you later, okay?"

"No. Wait there, I want to talk to you." Before she could think, she snatched up her faded pink bathrobe, scuffed into slippers and ran down the stairs and into the hallway. For a moment she hesitated, watching him through the front-door window. Then she threw open the door and huddled behind it as the wind and the rain blew in.

He wiped the rain from his face and handed Harriet the envelope. Then he turned to leave.

She laughed, not wanting to, but it burst out of her like a belch. "Come in and have some coffee," she said, walking ahead of him through the dim hallway toward the kitchen. He just stood there, not moving, dripping rain, staring at her.

"Bix? Come on. Please have some coffee."

"Where's the folks?"

"At church."

He pushed a hank of rain-blackened hair off his forehead and looked at his feet. "Gotta get Ryker's jalopy back, anyhow. I'll see you later."

How stupid this is. Harriet took his arm, feeling him flinch beneath her touch. "You're soaked. Please come and sit by the stove, just for a minute, to dry off." She led him into the kitchen and pulled up a chair next to the cast-iron stove, still warm from the Traubs' breakfast. She lifted the grate, stirred up the embers and put the coffee pot on to heat.

Mrs. Traub had left some biscuits and bacon on the table so Harriet added butter and raspberry jam, pushing it toward Bix. He hesitated a moment, then picked up a knife, split a biscuit and slathered it with jam, stuffing the whole piece into his mouth. *He's such a kid,* she thought, *even though he's older than me. Like a little boy who will never grow up.*

He looked up, a blotch of jam in the corner of his mouth. "Suppose you're mad at me," he muttered, spraying crumbs. "Seems like everybody always is."

"No," she said. "Just confused, I guess. About me and Rudy. About you and Joy."

He scowled under the wet forelock of hair, fiercely buttering another biscuit. "Hell, she's off in Chicago with that goddamn gorilla. I never see her anymore."

"Bix," she said, reaching across the table to touch his arm. "She cares about you."

He pulled away from Harriet's hand and rubbed the bridge of his nose. "Yeah. Joy's a sweet kid. A good friend. And...."

"You sleep with her." The words almost stuck in Harriet's throat. "She's your lover."

"Yeah. But we're friends, too, me and Joy. It's not like she's a—I mean, I *like* her. But my lover? Well—look, I gotta go. Just read the letter, and...."

"Bix." She took his arm, his hand, and the feeling washed over her again, the feeling she always got whenever they touched. Her hands trembled as she reached out to stroke his hair. "Bix—look at me."

"No, goddamn it. No." He pushed out of the chair, knocking it over, and strode out toward the front door. "No, I won't. Read the letter, and...."

I must be insane, Harriet thought, as she grabbed his hand and pulled him toward her. She felt the tension in his arms dissolve and then he put his arms around her waist and her hands went to his face, caressing. *I'm insane, but I can't fight anymore, can't fight my body, don't want to anymore. It's too hard, and I'm too sick and tired of pretending.*

Bix pulled her against his chest and she finally allowed the feeling to flood over her. It radiated from her groin and warmed her whole body, turning her limbs languorous. She molded herself against him, feeling the perfect fit of his compact body against hers. He put down his head and kissed her. The moment crystallized, with only the ticking of the big schoolhouse clock on the kitchen wall and the sibilant sound of the rain at the window giving evidence that time still moved at all.

Whenever Harriet thought about losing her virginity, she always pictured her wedding night, to Rudy or some other faceless-but-handsome man. She'd be wearing a flowing white silk peignoir and he'd carry her into a bedroom that looked like something out of a Gloria Swanson movie, lay her on the bed, tell her in the most eloquent language how beautiful she was, how much he loved and wanted her, and then the moment would fade to black.

But reality was now, with her running up the stairs of a farmhouse wearing her oldest nightgown, wet between her legs, and the man about to take her was an itinerant horn player who had never even finished high school, who would never woo her with words. Harriet was tired of words, tired of hearing them, tired of speaking and thinking them, and the silence and this moment and Bix all suited her perfectly.

They spoke with touch instead. He was as gentle as she'd imagined that evening in the rowboat on Hudson Lake, when he'd held his hand in front of her face and talked about music, his eyes glowing. And now as they lay across the bed, his hands were everywhere on her, lifting up her nightgown and tugging it off and away. Naked, she sprawled open to him, mindlessly, as uninhibited as a child, her body learning its needs under the touch of his lips and his fingers.

She wasn't sure what her untested body was capable of—she hadn't even experimented that much with it herself, and she'd quickly terminated the few furtive gropings between her and Rudy. Not because she didn't respond, and not just because she didn't want to get pregnant, although a sensible girl like Harriet always thought of things like that. She stopped because she was afraid of losing control, of being betrayed by her treasonous body and the natural force that drove it, an omnipotent force that would dwarf her intellect and render her helpless before it.

But now, instead of worrying about catastrophes, she thought of his hands on her, her hands on him, as a fascinating new empirical observation, curious as to what would happen if she touched this, or kissed that, or stroked something else. Action and reaction, like a science experiment. She unbuttoned his shirt, his trousers, his underwear, wanting to see him naked, and he shrugged out of his clothes and eased down next to her.

She guided his hand and his fingers effortlessly found the spot, moving so gently against her that she felt as if she was melting into the bed. She found him, too, and she knew she was doing it right because of the feel of him hardening in her hand, and from his sudden sharp inhalation, the faintest trace of gin carried on the warmth of his breath.

Even in her inexperience, she knew what would happen if he kept on. She didn't care; she wanted it, and wanted to bring him there, too, first this way, to watch and see it happen, and then deep inside her, the real way. But first she wanted to savor the delicious power she wielded over his flesh, a power just as potent and real as the control he had over the cornet when he played.

Now that she knew how things worked, she was intensely aware of the possibilities, the variations, how they could improvise this act the same way he improvised on a melody; always following the beauty of the basic musical line, but turning it, twisting it, making it better. The possibilities stretched out in her mind like a blank musical chart, like reams of graph paper awaiting a formula.

It happened to him first and he pressed himself against her side, panting. And then it was her turn and she reveled in it, shuddering, clenching him hard against her flesh. And then without hesitation he was inside her. She felt a stretching at first and a momentary pain as he tentatively inched forward and in. And then they were as close as they could ever be, rocking together in an easy rhythm, yearning into each other's bodies. She felt a steady reaching, a climbing, a peaking, and then an exquisite, quivering fall, and she cried against his bare shoulder and he kept calling to God against her neck as he caught up with her, and then he was there with her. Then they lay together, limbs enmeshed, bodies cooling, finally at rest.

The rain kept falling and they dozed, arms around each other, belly to wet belly, face to face, warm breath against each other's mouths and eyelashes. As if coming awake from ether, she blinked her eyes open in slow motion and gazed at his sleeping face, blurry in its closeness.

"Bix?"

His eyelids twitched. "Mmm?"

"What are we going to do now?"

Eyes still closed, he smiled and pulled her in closely, decisively. "Sleep, I guess. I'm bushed. Aren't you?"

ॐ

You stupid goddamn idiot. Bix punched the steering wheel of Ryker's Dodge, then shook his fingers at the pain. *Why did you do it?*

He started the engine and splashed through the puddles in the Traubs' front yard, now a quagmire of sodden grass and mud, and pointed the car back to John Emery Road. It was still raining, and he'd have to go back to the cottage to change before the show, and if Joy was there she'd be able to smell it on him. If she knew about this...

Bix tried to steer the Dodge clear of the potholes that lay in wait across the graveled road. He didn't know why he did it; especially not the way he did it, with no protection. Crazy, after what had happened with Ruth. And, like Ruth, Harriet had been a virgin. A nice girl, a girl he liked, in love with another man so she was safe, all he'd wanted to do was talk to her, look at her, not go to bed with her, my God, he'd just wanted to explain, smooth things over, make things right –

And suppose she did get in a jam from what they did today? Would he have any say about what happened this time? Ruth was just a farm girl turned secretary, sweet and naïve. Harriet was a smart girl with an education and a big career ahead of her. If Ruth didn't want to be tied down to a traveling jazz musician, why in God's name would Harriet? If she got in a jam, she'd probably get rid of it right away, whether he wanted her to or not. She probably wouldn't even tell him. Just like last time.

He shook his head, went to punch the steering wheel again, and then thought better of it. He didn't want to hurt his fingering hand. The *double-entendre* belatedly sank in and he muttered, "Shit."

It was different with Joy. She'd been around. And she'd told him right from the beginning not to worry, she'd had an operation. She'd laughed when she said it, but he'd never thought it was funny. And now, thinking of Joy, he felt even worse about betraying her.

Even if she wasn't the old Joy anymore. Gone half the time, God knew where, with that snaky McGurn. He missed her, missed her singing and her laugh, missed what they did in his bed on those hot afternoons, passing a bottle and shutting out the world.

"Shit," Bix hissed, this time really punching the steering wheel, hard enough to bruise, welcoming the pain in his right hand, hoping he'd feel it as he played tonight.

It had been enough for Joy just to be there with him. She didn't care if they did nothing at all. She just wanted to sing, listen to him play, and screw. He didn't feel like he had to say all those goofy things to her, things that always got him into trouble with women. Or those things he wrote in the letters home to Burnie and Sis and Mother. And, of course, the old man.

Dear Dad

I'm doing great here at Hudson Lake, swimming and fishing every day, getting a good suntan and putting on some weight. We're way out in the country, so there's not many ways to get into trouble.

Well you might not believe this, but I'm thinking of going back to school, right here at Indiana U. in South Bend, to get my requirements out of the way. School starts up in September, so don't be surprised if I ditch the Goldkette band for awhile and take a shot at the sheepskin.

Thanks for the dough you sent in yours of June 28th. I'm saving all the money I make this summer and putting it toward tuition in the fall, in South Bend or somewhere else. I can always go back to playing after I get my diploma, and I figure I can gig while I'm going to school, too, for the college proms and dances, like I did at Lake Forest. But it won't be like that again Dad, I promise. I was just a goofy kid then and didn't realize how important it was to have a decent education. Well I was wrong and you were right and I'll never make that mistake again, believe you me.

Give Mother and Sis my love and tell Burnie he has to come out here to hear us play some weekend soon.

Your loving son,

Leon

Lies, all goddamn lies. He'd actually sat down in the cottage and written out a whole sheet of lies, telling them just what they wanted to hear, and then convincing himself it was true. How could they be lies when he could see it all so clearly? He could picture himself in classes at the U. as the summer crisped into autumn; saw himself in the classroom with cute little co-eds like Harriet, impressing his teachers, getting great marks.

But the fantasy stopped right before the stacks of textbooks started weighing him down, before the faces of fellows four or five years younger started making him feel old, conveniently blanking out the classroom hangovers from gigging the night before, or the dry-mouthed feeling of waking up at two in the afternoon and realizing he'd slept through all his classes. And of course, the report cards with Ds and Fs and incompletes.

And now Harriet was another person on his lies list, he thought. The whole idea of going back to school had come from her. And before he'd left her, sleepy and naked in bed at the old German couple's house, he'd sworn he'd enroll, and he'd filled up her head with a bunch of bullshit—about how they'd break the news to her boyfriend, about how he could support her while she finished school, yeah, he made pretty good coin with Goldkette, enough to take care of them both, they could both have their dreams, hell, all the dreams they wanted, if they loved each other enough.

And the sick goddamn thing was, he really meant it when he said it. When he was with her, he *did* love her; he loved her that first afternoon they went fishing out on the lake, with her cute dress and her basketful of sandwiches. Who wouldn't love her? She was a terrific kid—kind, beautiful, smart. Everyone would love her. He'd be proud to have her at his side anywhere he went, whether it was at a ballroom to hear him play, or up the steep hill on Seventh Avenue in Davenport. He got a brief vision of Harriet in Oma's big house on Christmas, helping Mother and Sis in the kitchen, playing with Burnie's kids, sitting next to him on the piano bench in the parlor, her hand gentle on his arm.

But then it was time to go to work, and it was like everything outside of that was some crazy pipe dream. Like sitting in the movies. It seemed so real while you were watching it, like you were actually there. But then the movie ended and you walked out of the darkened theater and stood blinking and confused on the sidewalk in the real world.

He turned the car down Chicago Road and saw through the beaded curtain of rain the hulking dance hall, sleeping along the shore of the lake. It would feel good to go to work tonight, to sit under the hot lights back between Itzy on piano and Dan on drums and just slide into the music.

Because the real world was under the lights on the bandstand, and every-thing else that happened in his life was like the suspension of disbelief you practiced at the movies, where safes fell on comics who got up and walked away laughing; where Doug Fairbanks flew on carpets over magical Arabian cities; where Tom Mix and Tony rode the range and never got old or killed by Indians. Nice enough, and you believed it while you were watching it, but make-believe anyway.

He pulled Ryker's Dodge in front of the Blue Lantern, got out, and walked through the doors, into the empty dimness, past the soda fountain, through the French doors and into the dance hall, his footsteps echoing behind him.

And here, this was real. The smell of the dance hall, any dance hall, when it was dark and empty. The stink of stale sweat and dead cigarette smoke, piss from the toilets fighting it out with the chemical pine of the floor wash. And the people who came to hear them, here and other places. The drunken frat boys and their giddy dates from St. Mary's; the locals in their dime-store finery, always waiting for Joe Dockstader; the hard-faced working girls from the Studebaker and Singer Sewing Machine factories, licking their lips at the musicians and going down on the farmers out in the parking lot while the band sang about the moonlight, a June night and you; the local bootlegger selling his stuff at a fifty percent markup; the slick-dressed guys sitting up front with hard bulges in their breast pockets, sliding you twenty-dollar bills to play the sentimental crap that made them cry; the other musicians with their endless talk of racehorses and pussy, both of which always came across; the songs you played over and over and over until you knew exactly which note went where on every instrument's part.

And then that moment, the one you lived for, one moment a song, eight songs a set, four sets a night, when you got to hit a solo and let yourself be shaken and sucked dry by something you couldn't control, even though you pretended to, even though you'd domesticated it enough so it came when you called, but it was still something wild and unpredictable, something you didn't fuck with because it could turn on you. But when it grabbed you, by God, it made you feel like no woman ever could, it made the sound come out like jism, trembled you to your toes, and at the end of the night either left you limp and spent, or wanting to do it again and again.

He slid onto the bench in front of the piano and felt blindly for the keys. His melody was waiting there for him among the blacks and whites. All he had to do was find it again, sink into it, feel its rhythm, touch it just right, and hope he was good enough for it to stay with him this time.

Chapter 19

Cyrus Walker strode up the sidewalk to his little house and barely waited to pass through the front door before bellowing "Trent!"

Because Trent wasn't at the hardware store where he was supposed to be working, and he wasn't at the highway patrol office when Cyrus was supposed to take him home, and a neighbor woman said she'd seen someone who looked exactly like Trent downtown by that speakeasy on Indiana Avenue, just like Bill Bates had told him.

Cyrus walked through the tiny parlor, still cluttered with Betsy's collection of china cups and family photos, kept just like when she was alive. Only now everything was covered with a fine layer of dust because Cyrus wasn't much of a housekeeper and admitted as much himself. But what else could he do? He was a working man raising two children alone, and he was doing the best he could.

"Trent? Boy, if you're in this house, you'd better answer up right quick." Cyrus walked through the dark, narrow hallway that separated the parlor from the kitchen and bedrooms at the back of the house. He peered into the dimness of Trent's bedroom and walked in without a moment's hesitation. The kids used to whine and squeal about having their privacy, but as Cyrus always reminded them, there was no such thing as privacy as long as they were living under his roof. He'd grown up in a drafty farmhouse with four brothers and three sisters, and privacy was just a word you found in a dictionary, if you were lucky enough to have one and had enough school learning to be able to read it.

Last time he'd disciplined Trent, the boy had come in here and slammed the door, and Cyrus had heard a lot of muttering and shifting around of things in the closet. Later Cyrus went into the room and searched, thinking maybe Trent had hidden something there, something he didn't want him to see. But he didn't find anything.

Now, as he rummaged through Trent's bureau drawers, he remembered how Betsy used to chide him about hitting Trent. *Give the boy the benefit of the doubt, Cyrus,* she'd say, her big blue eyes wide and sad. *He's your son. He looks up to you. A kind word will go further than a blow.* Betsy had never believed in striking the children, and while she'd never interfered with Cyrus's form of discipline, she'd never condoned it, either. But the Good Book always said spare the rod and spoil the child, didn't it? Cyrus wouldn't think of going against the Bible. And besides, all Betsy's kindness had done nothing to make Trent into a decent son. The boy was just plain bad.

Cyrus walked to the closet, reached up to the top shelf and pushed aside boxes of winter clothes and Trent's old baseball equipment, reaching far into the back. Nothing. And then he caught a glimpse of something toward the back of the closet that crackled when he moved the boxes. He touched it with his fingertips and pulled it forward into the light. A big manila envelope.

He pulled it out, shaking loose dust. The envelope felt thick and heavy in his hands. He thrust a thick finger under the flap and pulled out the contents. Inside were eight stacks of banded greenbacks in large denominations—tens, twenties, even a thin stack of fifties.

Cyrus leafed through the bills, estimating in his mind how much was here. A couple hundred, at the least, maybe close to five. More money than Trent could ever make at the hardware store. More money than Cyrus made in a year when he first started at the highway patrol.

Stunned, he riffled through the money one more time, then stuffed the bills back into the manila envelope and put it back where he'd found it, thoughts slowly turning in his mind. Whose money was this? Trent's? Or was he holding it for somebody else? He suddenly thought of Ray Reynolds, dishing up ice cream, grinning like a spiteful monkey and all the while sneaking bootleg alcohol into people's drinks at a dollar a pop.

So it was true, after all.

⟨⟩⟨⟩

The teenaged boy looked up from the counter at the Blue Lantern soda fountain where he was loading vats of ice cream into the cooler. He gave Cyrus Walker a buck-toothed smile.

"Hello, Mr. Walker. What can I do for you? Ice cream, sir?"

"No thanks, Randall, I'm just looking to talk to Ray Reynolds. Is he around, son?"

The boy flushed red. "Uh, well, sir, he's off to South Bend on some business, I guess. Should be back in an hour or so. Sure there isn't something I can do for you?"

"He's off to South Bend on business quite a bit, isn't he? Even more than he's here tending to his job, if I'm not mistaken."

"Well, I don't know about that, sir, he-he's here most of the time, b-but...."

"Never mind, son. You just tell him I was out to see him, and that...."

The bell jingled over the soda fountain door and Ray came in. There was a brown paper sack tucked under his arm, a sack that clinked against the buttons of his shirt as he moved. His face stretched into a grin like an ugly rubber doll.

"Well, well, if it ain't the long arm of the law hisself. To what do we owe the honor?" He clinked down his package on the marble countertop.

Cyrus glanced over at Randall, and Ray jerked his head at the boy.

"Go on, Randall, take a break while I talk to the officer. Shouldn't take more than a few minutes or so, right, Cyrus?"

The boy blushed again and hurried out the door. As soon as he was gone, Cyrus reached into the pocket of his shirt, pulled out the envelope of money and flung it on the counter. "I have reason to believe this might be yours," he said.

Ray didn't move, just kept grinning and staring at Cyrus. "Well, I don't recollect losing anything, Officer. Why do you think it's mine?"

Cyrus opened the envelope and pulled out the stacks of greenbacks. "I found this on the back of the shelf in my son's closet," he said. "When I asked him about it, he admitted he got it from you."

"Why, that may be true, Cyrus, but it's not my money. It's the boy's. He earned it fair and square, runnin' some errands for me. All strictly honest, believe me."

"Nobody makes this kind of money honestly, and you know it. Trent wouldn't admit to anything more, so I figured I'd get it out of you. This is bootlegging money, isn't it?"

Ray laughed, showing a mouthful of teeth too white and symmetrical to be anything but false. "I don't know why you should suspect that. Why, you can go talk to Loretta Smith right now, she pays me my wages for tending the soda fountain here at the Blue Lantern, six days a week. I didn't give the boy that much money. Maybe you should be talking to him about where he got the rest."

"What's in the bag, Ray?"

He grinned again. "What bag? This bag?" He picked up the brown paper bag from the counter. "Damn, Cyrus, you got me dead to rights. I confess. Here." He passed the package to Cyrus, who hefted it in his hand before pulling away the bag. Inside were two pint bottles of cream.

Ray's laughter was shrill and loud. "Hell, Cyrus, why didn't you believe me in the first place? You think I'd try and implicate the son of the South Bend Klan chapter's Grand High Exalted Poobah, or whatever you brothers of the bedsheets call yourselves? Hell, don't you know how bad that would look? Especially when the Grand Poobah is also the law—and angling for the office of sheriff?"

Cyrus felt his face stiffen and he reflexively hitched up his gunbelt. "Stay away from my son, Reynolds. Because if you don't, I'll nail your bootlegging operation to the wall."

But Ray just kept laughing. "Yeah? Then you're gonna be runnin' in your own son right along with plenty of others. Because he's in deep, deeper than you think. Here." He flipped the envelope of money back across the counter at Cyrus. "Give this back to the boy. He's earned it. He's a damned good worker."

Cyrus stared at Ray, ignoring the envelope of money on the counter between them. As he walked out into the hot afternoon, the music from the band in the dance hall followed him out like Ray's braying-jackass laughter.

Chapter 20

McGurn watched as Joy's jiggly round ass twitched through the gilded lobby of the Palmer House Hotel. He didn't like the way she kidded with the doorman, or the way the bellboy looked at her—shit, the way everybody looked at her as she flounced along, her tits bouncing unfettered under a white silk dress.

On the way up to the room the elevator boy leaned toward her as if whiffing her scent, then glanced at McGurn with an evil grin.

"Wait in the car," he told Tony, who was carrying the boxes of clothes he'd just bought her. He deposited them in the room and McGurn barely got the bellboy tipped and the door closed and locked before he had her on the bed, pulling up her dress, undoing his fly, and her laughing the whole time in that loud way of hers, the way that made you want to crack her one –

It was over in less than five minutes. He got up and went to the toilet to wash up. She sat on the edge of the bed, looking sore, her skirt still ruched up around her waist. What the hell did she expect, a performance like a goddamn gigolo? He was no gigolo, and wasn't about to spend the whole goddamn afternoon in bed with this broad. There was work to do.

"You goin out?" she asked in that whiny voice.

"Got business to attend to," he said, leaning over to slap her ass. "I'll be back."

"What'll I do?"

He laughed. "That's a song, ain't it? You're a singer. Sing it for me."

She pouted, looking like a dyspeptic Kewpie doll. "You brought me all this way just to do that and leave me alone?"

"I said I'd be back, what the hell else do you want?" Fucking broads. She'd just cleaned him out of a couple of C-notes with clothes and shoes and jewelry, and the jasper behind the counter at C.D. Peacock gave him a big smile of recognition since Louise practically had her own table there. So McGurn introduced Joy as his sister, not that he gave a shit what the jeweler thought, but he sure as hell didn't want Joy and Louise crossing paths, no matter how remote the possibility. But then he'd think, goddamn it, what the hell do I care what one cooze finds out about the other?

She went into the bathroom and closed the door, running water into the tub, and he picked up the phone to call the Hotel Metropole.

He didn't plan on telling Al anything about the Hudson Lake deal until it was up and running, but he didn't want him to find out through second-hand information, either. He'd tell him today when he went over with the protection collections from the South Side joints. He was a little nervous, but he'd lay it all out for Al, show him how much they stood to make out there. He knew he'd get Al's blessings.

A knock on the door. "Hey, can't you read? Do not disturb," McGurn said, the phone's mouthpiece against his chest.

"Me."

He opened the door to Tony, who stood out in the hallway, obediently making sure the boss was done banging his girl before he went in.

"Didn't I tell you to stay down with the car?"

"I gotta talk to you," Tony said, eyes shifting both ways down the hallway, then over McGurn's shoulder, looking for Joy.

"She's takin a bath, she can't hear you. What do ya want?"

Tony walked into the room and looked McGurn in the eye. "That rube is gonna double-cross you."

He had to think a minute to understand what Tony was talking about. "Oh. Ray? You mean Ray from Hudson Lake?"

"He's in tight with that Indianapolis ring and he ain't gonna give it up that easy."

McGurn waved his hand in disgust. "Bullshit. What can he get outta those hicks? I'm givin him twenty percent. He's got no beef."

"I'm tellin you. You let me handle it, you won't have nothing to worry about."

"Handle it how? Don't do nothing goofy, Tony. I need this guy out there to oversee, unless you wanna spend your days out in the sticks at fucking Hudson Lake."

He watched as Tony's face went as hard as granite; his perpetually moving mouth, always with a load of gum, even stopped. *What, is this punk getting goofy on me?* Tony had a temper, that much he knew. Sometimes the littlest thing would set him off. Back in their Circus Café days, McGurn had seen

Tony drag a guy out into the alley and pound his face into a pulp one night, just because he'd looked at him funny.

"You hear me, Tony? Nothing goofy. We'll talk to the guy tonight at the Green Mill and get everything straight."

Tony turned and went back down the hall to the elevator. And McGurn resumed dialing up the Hotel Metropole, practicing in his mind how he'd lay it out for Al to put it all in the best possible light.

Before he left he tucked a wad of money into Joy's hand. "I might be awhile," he said, grabbing a tit, ignoring her hands pushing him away. "Keep it warm for me, huh?"

On his way downstairs, the elevator operator slid him a look and gave him that evil grin again.

Chapter 21

Joy

So I laid there on the bed in my new black silk kimono, staring at the face on the fifty-dollar bill and thinking how quiet it was up here in this top floor suite. You could barely make out the sound of traffic from State Street down there; it sounded like waves on Lake Michigan, with some honking car horns thrown in for variety.

I held out my arm and looked at the new gold bangle bracelet there, then slipped off the platinum necklace Jack just bought me and brought it up to my face. The links were made to look like a rope, and there was a square-cut diamond right in the middle, where the knot would be on a lasso. Jack had picked out a string of pearls for me, but I didn't want them. Just this necklace, because it reminded me of that day back in Montana.

Jack didn't think I was listening when Tony came in, but I heard what he said. And even if he hadn't, I knew what was going on, anyway. I didn't spend all that time at the Blue Lantern and not listen to anything that was happening around me.

Ray Reynolds was a snaky bastard. I'd been watching and listening to him since I first got to Hudson Lake, and I knew from the start how snaky he was, even though he tried to act like the stupid hick to try and fool people. And I knew for a fact he was planning to pull a fast one on Jack since I heard him talking to some fellas one day at the soda fountain. Even though I was sitting right there, they acted like I was deaf or something and just kept talking.

I would have told Jack about it, but he was just like Ray, anyhow. He wouldn't have believed me. Like everybody else, he thought I was just some dumb broad who didn't have the sense God gave a sheep.

And that was okay with me, because that's just what I wanted him to think about me, that I was safe, too stupid to figure out anything, a dumb bunny he could keep around to play with. And meanwhile he'd take care of me, give me money and clothes and just the fact that I was with a guy like him would keep anyone from trying to find me and bring me back to Montana.

Because I'd be goddamned if I'd ever go back to Vern and Montana. There was no reason for me to go back now. Michael was in an institution and they wouldn't let me see him, and if Vern had his way, that's where I'd be, too. They might even throw me in jail, or worse. After all, I took his damn money, didn't I?

And Jack wasn't so bad. Maybe he wasn't as nice and sweet as when I first met him that day out on Bluebird Beach, and maybe he got a little rough sometimes, especially after he'd been drinking. But he treated me good, bought me anything I wanted, was proud of having me on his arm when we went to all those places where he was collecting the ice. Besides, he wasn't even around that much, between his work and his real girlfriend. See, I'm no dumb bunny. I knew there was someone else, I knew it right from the start.

And anyhow, what I really wanted was to be back with Bickie again. But Bickie was gone now, gone to Harriet, and I had to change direction again, spinning like a weathervane, feeling the wind against my back lift me up and off to somewhere else, someone else. And now there was Jack. I looked at the necklace again, pressed the cold stone against my lips, and wondered how it would feel to press the hard mouthpiece of a horn there. Or the muzzle of a gun.

Chapter 22

Harriet shifted against the hard seat of the pew as the Right Reverend Hammond Tufts of the Methodist Church expounded on the importance of maintaining both a clean body and a clean mind in order to best serve Christ—to stay away from all temptations of the flesh, whether they be the sin of gluttony, or the soul-consuming sin of lust! Sins that traced their roots back to ancient Babel, and the temples of the pagan sinners of Rome, but sins that were being played out right here, today, in this little corner of Indiana—through drinking, licentiousness, and jazz. Yes, jazz, the Devil's music, which spurred its listeners to acts of debauchery and unbridled lasciviousness.

His verbosity hung heavy in the humid confines of the church, while the tightly packed parishioners plied cardboard fans from the local funeral home and the ladies of the choir, arranged behind the good Reverend like obedient seraphim, surreptitiously shook air into the folds of their black robes.

Finally came the benediction, and the congregation went from sitting to kneeling. Mrs. Traub grunted with the effort of changing positions.

As she knelt next to the wheezing Mrs. Traub, Harriet tried to focus on the service, or at least the angels on the stained glass windows. It was sunny and hot and the rainy Sunday afternoon she'd spent with Bix seemed far away, like a fantasy she'd dreamed up.

Given the minister's tirade, he could have been preaching directly to Harriet. Because weren't jazz and sex her two biggest sins? Part of her believed if she died right this minute, according to Reverend Tufts' God and the God of her own childhood, she would go straight to hell because of what she'd done with Bix. But another part of her looked dispassionately at what they had done as a straightforward and natural physical act, as the whole reason of how the male and female bodies were designed to work, whether you believed those bodies were formed by the hand of God or eons of evolutionary progress.

And then there were the most unlikely times when she'd be at the sink doing dishes, or shaking a dust mop out the back door, and a fragment of memory would dislodge itself and fall into her consciousness—the feel of a hand on flesh, the thought of the noises they'd made together, the glimpse of his naked body under the sheets of her prim little bed in the Traubs' attic bedroom—and she'd find herself weak, leaning against the sink, wishing he was pressed up against her, all reason and sensibility gone, just as she'd always feared.

She hadn't spoken to him since it happened. Mrs. Smith had cracked down hard on both Buddy and Harriet, as if she was her own daughter. Harriet didn't mind. She stayed close to the hotel and did her work, thinking of Rudy and the letter she'd gotten from him, the one she'd read over and over until she'd memorized it, the one that crackled in the pocket of her Sunday dress. *Why don't we cut out all this bull and just get married? We've waited long enough.* She wondered if he'd still be in such a hurry to marry her if he knew she'd thrown away her virginity on a traveling jazz musician.

After Bix had left her bed that morning, Harriet had been ready to pack her clothes and follow wherever the music took him, to give up school and Rudy and everything else, just to be with him. But common sense returned quickly enough, especially when Bix seemed to be avoiding her. They'd had no chance to talk since that Sunday morning.

But it didn't stop her from thinking about him—not just about what they'd done in bed that day, but about his thoughtful face as he played the piano in the empty dance hall, about the way his smile lit up his eyes, and the patience of his hands as he'd helped her cast her fishing line out on the lake that very first day. She felt there was a power in Bix that was bigger than just the music, a power he didn't even realize he had, a steady calm at the core of his being that translated into a strength that could take him anywhere.

And to make things even more confusing, here was Rudy coming to her with a proposal that seemed more like an ultimatum. He wanted an answer from her by the end of the summer. Only a month ago she would have seriously considered marrying him right away, even though they'd both agreed how important it was for both of them to finish school first. If she married Rudy now, would she ever finish school? Or would she simply sink into the inevitable morass of babies and housekeeping and bills, just another respectable middle-class Indianapolis matron, a girl with some college education who married an architect? If that happened, she would fade away completely, she knew—the shadow-Harriet would win and the Harriet she'd worked so hard to become would be put away forever like a spangly dance dress that was impractical for a wife and mother. And no matter what she did now, with or without Rudy, how could she ever forget that Bix was out there in the hugeness of the world, living and making music without her?

Her mind was a tangle of guilt, and regret, and defiance, and lust. And something else, a vague longing for something more, for something she was afraid could never be: a life with Bix. Nothing like the life she'd so carefully planned for herself, or the life that she and Rudy had talked about; but a messy life, unplanned, tumultuous, its rages and floods carrying them along like flotsam on the tide of a storm on trains and cars from town to town, Bix's music the only raft they could cling to. It would be exasperating, exhausting, wonderful.

And she wondered if Bix thought of her at all.

ဆဝ03

On their way to their son's house for Sunday dinner, the Traubs offered to drop Harriet back at the farmhouse, but she wanted to walk, and think. She took the long way down Holling Road toward the little Hudson Lake cemetery that dated back to the 1840s. As she approached the weedy graveyard she thought she heard the sound of a horn playing. It wasn't her imagination.

He sat under a twisted apple tree, his back against a headstone, cornet gleaming in the light filtering down through the leaves. He was playing one of his solos from a dance number, turned around so the melody was inside out, upside down. He put down a phrase. Stopped. Played the same phrase again, slightly different this time. Stopped again, looking for a moment at the horn, fluttering the valves soundlessly, then put it to his lips again and blew the phrase, added to it, lengthened it. He stopped once more, nodded to himself in affirmation. Then he looked up and saw her and she suddenly felt embarrassed, as if she'd caught him in a private act.

They didn't speak. She walked closer, touching the tops of the headstones along the way.

"Haven't seen you in awhile," he said with his usual guileless smile. "Guess the old lady really has you working your tail off, huh?"

She stood there, feeling the breeze lifting the ribbons on her dress, under her skirt, around her legs. She walked closer and stood over him.

"You're just going to pretend nothing happened," she said softly. "I can't believe it."

He looked straight ahead, and his face went flinty, the smile gone. "I'm not pretending."

"You're sorry it happened, aren't you?"

His lips twitched. "It wasn't right," he said. "For a lot of reasons."

"I'm not sorry. Even sitting in church today. I just know God didn't give us these feelings and not want us to feel them. Give us these bodies and not want us to use them."

He finally looked at her, eyes narrowed. "Yeah? Well, take a look around. This is where we all end up, no matter what we do with our bodies when we're alive."

She smiled. "Some of my family on my mother's side come from around here. I even have relatives buried in this graveyard. Over there, back by that tree? There's my great-aunt Thelma. Beloved wife and devoted mother, it says on her stone. She lived a good life. I don't think it's sad here. I think those stones tell the stories that God wanted them to tell."

"Sure. And what about all the little stones with the lambs and the angels on 'em?" He pointed, voice rising. "Look, there's the Borden kids. James, one month, five days. John, two months, nine days. And this one. Didn't even have a name. Infant Borden. Two days old." He abruptly stopped talking, face bunched in a frown, and began ripping up handfuls of grass, sifting the blades between his fingers. "I come here a lot. It's quiet, and I can hear myself play and think. And every time I see those little headstones—all those dead babies—I think about God's plan. And I think God doesn't know what the hell he wants any more than we do."

He sounded disgusted, she thought. Why? "You can't stop death. Or life. And if you really do believe in God, you have to believe he didn't put us on earth just to be sad."

"I thought you were modern and scientific," he scowled. "This sounds like old-time-religion talk to me."

"Just because I believe in science doesn't mean I don't believe in God. Oh, maybe not the kind of God we learned about in Sunday school, but a caring father who made us in his image. Don't you believe in God, Bix?"

He sighed and leaned his head against the tombstone, gazing at the drift of clouds overhead. "Yeah, I guess I do. But people screw up an awful lot on him. Keep disappointing him, even if they're not doing it on purpose, even when they're trying like hell to do what's right. Like what happened to all those dead babies. Somebody should have stopped it."

She reached out and put a hand on his arm. "If you believe in God, then you believe everything happens for a reason. Even those dead children." She swallowed, blinking hard to keep tears from spilling from her eyes. "Even us, Bix. You and me."

He finally looked at her and his face softened into a smile, and she sank down next to him in the hot, moist grass under the tree. He put an arm around her and pulled her close, and she laid her head against his neck, listening to the beating of his hard, strong pulse.

They sat, not talking, for a long time. She remembered everything he'd said before he left her bed that Sunday. He'd talked about a life together—about both of them finishing school, and his working to support her, about both of them reaching their dreams, each helping the other. But he probably didn't mean it. Right now she knew he felt more comfortable not saying anything at all. And right now, so did she. Just being with him, his arms around her, momentarily drove out all the conflicting thoughts in her head, forced her to focus on what was happening right now—on the clutch of orange monarch butterflies floating through the graveyard weeds, the smell of earth and green, the feel of his warm, living body against her side.

"Bix?"

"Mmm?"

"What do you want out of life, anyway? Just to play music?"

"Mostly, yeah. But other stuff, too."

"Like what?"

He gazed up into the branches of the tree over their heads. "Well, a wife and kids someday, I guess. A family. Like everybody else."

"Do you think you could still play music and have a family?"

"Well, it works for Tram and Mitzi. And for Doc and Norma, and for lots of other people. Why?"

"Because Rudy asked me to marry him. Not when I'm done with school, but now, right away."

He looked down at her. "Do you love him?"

"That's just it. I don't know." She covered her face with her hands, smelling the dusty odor of the limestone from the grave markers still clinging to her fingers.

He gently pried her hands away from her face, looking into her eyes. "Hey, listen, I want to know. What *are* we, you and me? Lovers? Friends? Fishing buddies?"

She didn't answer; what could she say? She could never tell him the truth—that the idea of losing Rudy didn't mean anything compared with the thought of losing Bix, of never seeing him again.

He picked up his cornet from the grass and stood to leave. "It's your call. If you want to see me later, I'll be here tonight right after the show."

ୟୁଓଷ

She came back under the haloed glow of a full moon. The wind was high and hard, rocking the trees, pressing down the grass, pushing her along the side of the road. She swung the flashlight back and forth in the darkness, pointing the beam of light downward and turning her feet, her legs, the graveled road she was walking on, into a jerky black-and-white movie clip.

She wasn't thinking anymore because she couldn't answer his simple question, even though she'd thought about it all day. She had finally concluded that there were no answers, and that although she wanted him forever, she'd settle for having him right here and now—that she wanted his naked body next to hers, wanted him inside her, again and again. Right now. She didn't care about anything else.

The car was parked next to the graveyard, headlights on. The weeds slashed against her bare legs as she started running, the wind pushing her, the moon drawing her, until she was there at the car where he leaned, waiting, white shirt glowing in the darkness.

"Didn't think you'd show," he said.

"I didn't think you would, either."

"Yeah. Let's not talk. We already talked enough." He pulled her against the car. She felt the hot metal of the hood under her dress. He stood between her legs, pressing against her, and kissed her, their mouths open, both of them breathing hard. He tried to steer her into the open car, but she eased out of his arms.

"Not here," she whispered. "There. In the grass. Under the tree."

Running ahead of him, she scanned the area with the flashlight and found the spot. She reached up, pulled her dress over her head, spread it on the ground and laid down on it, head thrown back, opening herself to him. On top of her great aunt Thelma, she thought, the beloved wife and devoted mother who had been dead almost forty years.

Her great-aunt Thelma's bones were their bed that night, and all the rest of the summer.

Chapter 23

Wish that ratty little bastard'd stop staring at me. Ray Reynolds lifted the shotglass to his lips and swallowed a gulp of oily bourbon, trying to ignore the eyes of McGurn's driver.

He looked down at his glass. Capone crap, probably cut with gasoline to give it the beaded texture in the glass that Lake Shore Drive swells took to mean it was the real McCoy. Ray didn't care; this trip to Chicago was on McGurn, a goodwill gesture designed to cement the deal on Hudson Lake and serve as a taste of things to come. Everything was on McGurn—the dinner and show at Colosimo's, the drinks here at the Green Mill, where indirect lighting and heavy velvet draperies gave the place the glow of an underwater grotto. Maybe even the big-assed blonde who was giving him the eye from a table across the room.

"Like it?" McGurn asked, stuffing a bulging envelope into the inside breast pocket of his chalk-striped suit.

Ray looked up, thinking McGurn was talking about the broad. But no, he meant the popskull Ray was nursing. He nodded and finished off the drink. "Straight off the boat, huh, Jack?"

McGurn laughed, showing big, square teeth and exuding garlic from the dinner they just ate. "By way of Taylor Street. We upped production, just for the Hudson Lake deal. We got everything. Bourbon like that, gin, beer, you name it."

"It's good, Jack. What's in it, anyway?"

McGurn reached down between his legs to readjust his package—a habitual gesture that made Ray want to laugh out loud. "Hell, I ain't giving away any trade secrets telling you what's in the stuff. How's it taste? That's what's important."

Ray took another swallow and considered the quarter-inch of amber glow remaining in the shotglass. It was a far cry from bonded pre-War stuff, but compared with the white mule and goat whiskey that was the typical product of the farmers of LaPorte County around New Carlisle, it was an improvement. "Damn good."

"Good. Then it don't matter what's in it." He leaned toward Ray and took his shoulder in a bone-grinding grip. "But I can tell you I seen 'em use burnt sugar for the taste, and even throw in a little iodine for color. But ain't nobody complaining, right?"

Ray grinned, feeling his dentures starting to slip off his gums. The goddamn shot of shellac he'd just drunk was probably melting the adhesive right off. "Yeah, yeah, it's damn good. And a deal at fifty bucks a case, Jack. Before you come along, it was all gallon goods, fifty cents a shot, all that white lightening and popskull, pure alcohol, most of it. And what the hell, those kids out at that dance hall will drink anything, right?" He laughed a staccato laugh, knowing he sounded nervous, unable to stop talking. "Oh, those South Bend rubes, Jack, you'd laugh at how they do business, I mean compared to a big-time operation like this. Stills out back behind their barns, for Chrissake, you get everything in there, dead possums floating around in the mash, my God, you wouldn't believe it! You know how much it costs them to make that popskull, Jack?" He laughed again, almost giggling. "Fifteen cents a gallon. And selling it for fifty cents a shot. Those hillbillies been putting up white lightning for years, way before Pro'bition, just for their own consumption, you know? So Pro'bition is like money from home for those old boys, money from home, hah!"

McGurn grunted. "Those musicians ain't no slouches, neither. They lap it up. They're stewed to the gills most of the time, the bastards." He squeezed Ray's shoulder again. "And twenty percent's a good number for you, ainnit? Twenty percent of every fifty-buck case of stuff you sell. We handle the trucking, you handle the distribution, and keep the locals out of the picture. And everything's copacetic."

"Sure, Jack, it's a terrific deal. And the stuff'll sell like wildfire, you wait and see. Why, those farmers'll get used to it before you know it, being they're accustomed to the hillbilly popskull. You'll spoil 'em, Jack, you'll just spoil 'em, that's all." He brayed a laugh, then looked around to see if anyone was paying any attention to him. Nobody but the ratty little driver sitting at the end of the bar, chewing gum and smoking a cigarette and staring, staring.

McGurn snuffed out a laugh. "We're thinking those local boys in South Bend that put up most of the stuff might need a little convincing. What do you think?"

"Oh, they'll see it our way. You don't gotta do anything rash, really, they got other markets, they don't need the Blue Lantern, it's just one dance hall, and...."

"Who said I'm stopping with the Blue Lantern?" McGurn's face was close enough now that his breath was a foul miasma in Ray's nostrils, a blend of cheap whiskey, wine and garlic. His friendly, toothy smile was gone, replaced by a tight-lipped grimace. "Fact is, I already greased the police captain in South Bend to stage another raid on some of the bigger stills. Let 'em put on a big show, bust up the equipment and the stills, just to send 'em a message. You oughta be reading about it in the South Bend newspapers any day now."

"Bust up the stills, huh? Just like Izzy and Moe, huh, Jack? Those big-time Pro'bition agents?" Shit, Ray thought. He'd told McGurn he'd handle the local leggers, and now this. But what kind of position was he into do anything? Chicago was calling the shots now.

"I ain't stopping with the Blue Lantern. You got that Playland Park there, and all those other joints around South Bend and LaPorte and Mishawaka. There's a lot of dance halls out that way. And guys like me just get greedy, you know?" He smiled again, teeth white and carnivorous. Then he shook Ray's shoulder one last time. "I gotta take care of some business. You have another drink, look around see what girl you like, take her upstairs and enjoy yourself. It's all on me." He stood and walked through the crowd.

Ray sat there, shaken, and looked blankly into his empty shotglass. The bartender came and poured him another finger, waving him away when Ray went to pull out his billfold and pay for it. Maybe he ought to warn the South Bend joints and the local leggers that trouble was coming, that they ought to lock down their operations so a raid wouldn't put them out of commission completely. But if they did, McGurn would know who tipped them off and Ray would be a stiff. Yeah, he knew from the start playing with Chicago was gonna be playing with fire. But still, he wasn't out of it yet. Not yet.

He downed another shot of bourbon and grinned, thinking of the squeeze play he was going to pull once McGurn got established at Hudson Lake. Hell, yeah, it was a gamble, but Ray was a gambler, always had been, wasn't afraid to take a chance, not like most of the rubes and the yahoos he dealt with back home. None of the other leggers would have had the balls to try and work out a deal with McGurn. Twenty percent? Shit. Once the Blue Lantern was established as the goldmine Ray always knew it could be, he'd work both ends against the middle, make the local bootlegging ring give him a fifty percent cut, just to stay in business.

The bourbon burning in his chest gave him the nerve to stare right back at

Tony. Ray gave him a big, friendly grin. "What's on your mind, Tony? You don't talk much." He lifted his glass to the little man.

The guy shifted on the barstool, his face as impassive as a piece of leather. "And you talk too much," he said, mouth barely moving.

"There's no reason why we can't be friendly, pal. We're gonna be working together now, right? You heard what your boss said. You're gonna be spending a lot of time at little old Hudson Lake. You might as well learn to like it. And me. Right, Tony?"

Tony squinted against the smoke from the cigarette plugged into the corner of his mouth. He leaned his arms on the bar and continued staring at Ray, saying nothing.

I hate these fucking guineas, Ray thought, all of them, with their greasy hair and their expensive suits, I hate the way they shoot the cuffs on their shirts so everybody can eyeball their gold wristwatches, I hate their big cars and the way they jabber at each other in Eye-tie and then laugh like they're putting a good one over on regular Americans, guys like Ray who put his life on the line fighting Over There while this greaseball was picking pockets in Little Italy. Ray laughed again, not nervously this time, confident in the knowledge that McGurn needed him for this deal, and that this punk was nothing but McGurn's lap dog.

"Hey, Tony?" he said, smiling like a traveling salesman. "How do you people say? *Vaffunculo?*"

The punk was coiled like a spring, ready to launch himself off the barstool at Ray, but just then McGurn came back, striding through the club, cutting across the dance floor.

"Tony, go on and bring the car around so's I can hit the South Side joints and collect the ice. Ray, make yourself at home. We'll be back in a couple of hours."

Good, thought Ray, as the slickly dressed little rat pushed away from the bar, car keys jingling in his hand, giving him one last scowl.

As he walked past Ray, Tony struck a match and flipped it towards Ray's pants legs, just quickly enough so McGurn didn't see. Then he gave Ray a feral grin and walked out onto Broadway.

Ray ordered up another free drink and crooked his finger at the big-assed blonde he'd had his eye on all night. "Hey, honey, come here," he said. "Come and teach me how to talk in Eye-talian."

Chapter 24

Bix watched as Joy walked into the Blue Lantern that night the way a movie star waves from the back of a train—dressed to kill, her smile with all the warmth gone, bright and glittering like a theater marquee, promising everything, giving up nothing.

She was alone this time, but he and everyone in the band knew she wouldn't be coming to the little yellow cottage anymore, to sing or drink or do anything else. Buddy Smith had told everyone how she'd come back from Chicago that morning with two new slick leather valises from Chicago Trunk and Leather Company, monograms and all, walked right up to Mrs. Smith and handed her a fat manila envelope. Then she had Buddy bring her new valises to Mrs. Smith's precious Room 4, the biggest room at the Hotel Hudson, where Mrs. Smith liked to jam extra boarders and charge them double. And she tipped Buddy five bucks just for hauling her luggage.

He watched her from the bandstand as she walked in late, alone but dressed for company. She laughed and talked to some of the patrons, just like the old Joy. But when he caught her eye, she returned his look with the same smile he remembered from that day at Bluebird Beach, the day he'd asked her why she was blue, the day he'd said something stupid and everything changed.

When the band took a break, he headed straight to her table before she could disappear. "Let's talk," he said, taking her arm and guiding her to the porch overlooking the lake. She didn't resist.

It was the sort of night they wrote bad Tin Pan Alley songs about—stars on the lake, a warm breeze, nightbirds calling to each other from the shadowy trees. There was enough light from the dance hall to see her, and to reflect off the new glitter on her wrists and at her throat. A diamond lavaliere, shaped like a lariat, with a square-cut stone in the center where the knot would be. He touched its coldness with a forefinger.

"Nice. What'd you have to do to get it?"

She just smiled again, elbows on the railing, head thrown back as if to give the full effect of the stone nestled in the hollow of her throat. "Nothing I didn't want to do."

Bix bunched his fists into his pockets. "He own you now?" he said, regretting the words the second they were out of his mouth.

She turned and glared at him over her shoulder. "Nobody owns me," she said, smile crooked. "Not even you."

He took a deep breath, trying to keep calm, wondering why he should care. He was sleeping with Harriet. What was the difference if Joy slept with someone else? She was right; he didn't own her, she didn't own him. It had never been like that between them. But McGurn was bad news. Dangerous. He didn't want her to get hurt. *Bullshit*, a deeper voice whispered. *You are jealous.*

"Don't you know who he is? Didn't you ever see him at that joint you used to work at? What do you think he is, some butter-and-egg man from Rogers Park? Christ, Joy, he's a goddamn killer. He works for Capone." For no reason at all he thought of the little yellow cottage where they'd spent so many hot afternoons, hiding away from the rest of the world, wrapped in a cocoon of music and sex and sleep. She hadn't been there in weeks. One of her red silk slippers was still there, though, half-hidden under the bed, along with crumpled newspapers, abandoned socks, movie magazines, empty bottles, dust.

"He treats me good. Yeah, he gave me this, and a trunkful of new clothes from Mandel Brothers, too. Even a fur for the winter. Chinchilla." She laughed, looking square at him now, a smear of red lipstick on her two front teeth. "What'd you ever give me—*Bickie?*" She spat out the name like an obscenity.

"You're playing with fire."

She laughed. "And you're not? Hell, you're pumping some college girl. For a guy like you, she's a hell of a lot more dangerous than Al Capone."

So she knew. "Don't speculate on something you don't understand," he said, wondering why he had to explain himself to Joy. It was something he'd never had to do with her before.

"Oh, I understand, all right. She's out for a cheap summer thrill before she goes back to school. And you're the cheap part. Don't you get it, Bix?" She laughed again. "You're her idea of slumming."

"She's not like that. She's just a nice girl from Indianapolis, like...."

"Yeah, I know, like your sister. And your high-school girlfriend. And that dumbbell in St. Louis." Joy bared her teeth, the smile pulling wider. "So you must have sold her on that crap about your respectable family back in Iowa, and all the good schools you went to. Did you mention you got kicked out of all of 'em? And *why* you can't go back to Iowa?"

He felt the blood rush to his face. The feeling of betrayal was like a frozen knife in the vitals.

She drew back, smile fading, voice sizzling down to a whisper. "Did you tell her about Ruth yet? About what Ruth did? About *why* Ruth did it?"

Before he could even think of what he was doing, he yanked her forward by the arm. "Shut your goddamn mouth. You're in no position to talk, and you know it." Then he dropped her arm, feeling like it had burned him. He sucked in a deep, shuddering breath and looked down at his trembling hands. "Leave her alone, Joy. Just leave her alone."

She pulled away and rubbed at her upper arm where the marks from his fingers faded from white to red. "Well, you don't have to tell her. I will."

୨୦ଓଃ

Harriet had just been with Bix in the cemetery early that morning, had snuck back into the Traubs to rinse the smell of him off in cold water, put on a work dress, and come back down to the hotel. She started mopping the kitchen floor, thinking about the conversation they'd had only a few hours ago, about what he'd asked her, about what she'd said. And how everything was different between them now.

They'd just finishing making love and were lying together under the tree in the cemetery, right before the sun came up, when she'd blurted out the question about him signing up for classes at Indiana U. He had promised her he would, and it was the one promise Harriet wanted to hold him to.

"It's for your own good, Bix," she'd said, watching his eyes. "You know it is. Even if you just take one class, just to help you read and write music better."

He'd immediately changed the subject. "Yeah? What about Rudy? You tell him about us yet? You tell him you're not marrying him? Or *are* you marrying him?"

And then he'd asked her.

"Do you want to get married?"

She didn't know what to say. "Eventually."

"To me?"

A brief second of hesitation, barely perceptible. "Yes."

"Not just because I took your cherry, right? Because that would be a really stupid reason."

"No."

"Well, why, then?"

Again, she hadn't known what to say, so she'd stroked his hair in the calming gesture of a mother soothing a needy child. "Well, if you insist on a list—because you're sweet, and you make me laugh. And you play so beautifully. And—well, because I love you, that's all. Do you love me?"

A brief second of hesitation. Barely perceptible. "Yeah. Hell, yeah."

"Well, then?"

He'd leaned over and kissed her. "Then consider us engaged."

Now, as she sloshed soapy water over the floor and pondered how she could be engaged to both Rudy and Bix, Joy sauntered in. She was smoking a cigarette, wearing a new black satin kimono and last night's makeup.

Harriet wondered just how much Joy knew about her and Bix. Probably everything. But she didn't seem to care. She grinned at Harriet as if nothing was wrong, while Harriet tried not to look at her. Although she didn't regret anything that had happened between her and Bix, Harriet did feel a shadow of guilt when she thought about how much Joy seemed to care about him. Joy had been her friend before Harriet had ever even spoken to Bix, and Harriet wasn't the kind of girl who stole men away from her friends. She wished she could just sit down with Joy the way they used to and explain that she'd never planned on falling in love with Bix, that it was something that had just happened, like an unexpected thunderstorm. She glanced up at Joy, and seeing the false smile on her face, decided that conversation could never happen.

"You're up early," Harriet said, concentrating on the mop and bucket.

"Couldn't sleep." Joy slouched against the kitchen sink, watching as Harriet swirled soapy circular patterns on the linoleum. "You got coffee? I could sure stand some." She clacked over to the stove in her high-heeled mules and poured a cup. They were silent a moment, the only sound the regular splat of the mop on the wet floor.

"How's Bix?" Joy asked, blowing on her coffee to cool it.

Harriet gritted her teeth and kept mopping.

"You two sure are seeing a lot of each other these days. Sweet guy, ain't he?"

Harriet moved the mop along the baseboard, poked it under the stove. She didn't answer or look at Joy. She didn't want to see that smile again.

"You know, little sister, I hope you're usin' Lysol or Zonite or Sterizol or something." Harriet looked at the bucket, then at Joy, puzzled. And Joy laughed, the old laugh she'd used back when they were friends. "Oh, no, not on the floor, honey! I meant to *douche* with. You don't wanna get in a jam, do you?"

Harriet felt her face flame, and concentrated on the floor.

"Well, didn't Bix tell you about what happened to Ruth? The girl in St. Louis?"

Harriet shook her head, not looking up. It didn't matter—she knew Joy was going to tell her, anyway. But what could she do? Run away? Tell Joy to be quiet? She knew it was going to hurt and she didn't want to hear it.

"She was a regular at the Arcadia dance hall, her and her two sisters. Cute kid. Nice figure, sweet face, innocent. Kinda like you."

Harriet flinched, but kept working. Joy kept talking.

"A friend of hers introduced her to Bix. Right away, she went gaga over him. One thing led to another and they were engaged just like that, and—does any of this sound familiar?"

Harriet stopped mopping for a second, but didn't look up. Joy kept talking.

"But she was dumb enough to go the limit with Bix, and wound up getting in a jam. Right before Christmas, just last year. Well, her and her sisters went home to visit the folks on the farm back in Illinois, and Bix went home to Davenport for the holidays, and when she came back, guess what?" Joy paused, blinked, smiled. "She wasn't pregnant anymore. She went ahead and got rid of it, just like that."

Harriet kept working, clutching the mop handle until her knuckles went white.

"Bix didn't want her to. Before she left, he begged her not to. He still wanted to marry her. She told him it was because she didn't want to tie him down because they were both too young. She was your age, little sister, just about twenty. But she finally came out with why. She thought there was something wrong with Bix. With his mind. And she didn't want to have a kid there was something wrong with." She took a sip of coffee and flicked cigarette ash into the soapy puddle on the floor at Harriet's feet.

Harriet leaned the mop against the wall and sank into a kitchen chair. She thought of Bix being a washout in school, his trouble with sight reading, his drinking, the way she'd seen him fall silent and immerse himself in working out songs on the piano, blocking out her and everything else but the sound. *Something wrong with his mind?*

She glanced up at Joy. Her red mouth just kept jabbering, the words a blurred stream of sound because Harriet's brain had stopped registering what she was saying. But some of it still filtered in.

"And did he tell you about what happened in Davenport when he was eighteen? Why the old man really sent him away?" Joy was saying. She took a deep breath and grinned, leaning closer to Harriet, as if relishing every word. "There was a little girl. Five years old. They arrested him, and there was a grand jury and everything. They said he took her off the playground and brought her back to the Beiderbecke's garage, and...."

"Stop it!" Harriet screamed, pushing her fingers into her ears so Joy's babble would finally stop, watching her red mouth keep writhing, soundless words spilling out in an obscene torrent, Joy now looking surprised, then smiling. Harriet took her fingers away. Joy continued.

"That's why he took the job on the riverboat. He had to get out of town. He never went back." She flicked her cigarette butt onto the wet floor where it soaked up the water and swelled into a sodden plug. "Mind if I have more coffee, hon?"

Harriet ran, out of the kitchen, out of the hotel, as far down Chicago Road as she could to get away from Joy's voice, still hearing the staccato delivery in her mind. The thought of what she'd done with Bix, what she'd craved doing with him, against those words made her stomach churn. Tears burned her cheeks as the horrible words seared into her brain, words Joy hadn't said because she didn't even known them, but words Harriet knew from school, from life. Alcoholic. Atavistic. Pedophile. She leaned over and threw up along the side of the road. Then she started running again, back to the farmhouse, wanting to hide, never wanting to see Joy or Bix or the Blue Lantern again.

Chapter 25

Joy

But that's exactly why I loved him. All those things about himself that he hated so much, that he wanted to hide from the world, were exactly the things I loved most about Bickie.

It didn't bother me that he'd gotten Ruth pregnant. It was before he loved me, so it didn't matter. Sometimes when we were in bed and everything felt so good, I'd wish it could be different, that I hadn't gone to Cook County Hospital and had that operation when I first came to Chicago. That I could get big and pregnant with Bickie's baby, the way she wouldn't do for him. But then I'd remember the stuff the doctors and the lady from the American Eugenics Society told me, and the things he said about himself, and knew it was better this way. Especially if what Bickie thought about himself was true.

He only mentioned it once, a night he was really drunk and feeling sorry for himself last spring in Chicago. He'd just gotten fired from Charlie Straight's band because his music reading was no good, and he was out of a job for awhile. He had nothing to do but drink. And he did—from the minute he got up in the afternoon to whenever he passed out again the next morning. It didn't matter what—gin, wine, scotch, it was all the same to him.

I was paying his rent at the Diversey Arms for awhile, and that just about killed him. I was working and I still had most of Vern's stash I came to town with. He could pay me back or not, I couldn't care less. But being out of work was really hard on him. It didn't matter it was only temporary and we both knew it. He hated it. And it changed him. He got sarcastic and mean, even to me. But mostly to himself.

One night I came over to his place and he was sitting at the kitchen table with a pair of scissors and a stack of those letters from Davenport. When I asked what he was doing, he looked up at me with these bloodshot eyes and gave me a crazy smile. "I'm getting rid of him," he said, and I looked down at the table and saw all these little squares of paper, and all these little holes in the letters and the envelopes where he'd gone and cut out every place his name was written, so all these little squares with "Bix" or "Leon" on them were scattered all over the table and floor.

Then he told me he was no good, he didn't belong in that good German family, maybe because his mother's father, his Grandpa Hilton, up and left when she was a kid. The Beiderbeckes, always worried about a scandal, claimed he was a riverboat captain who drowned on duty, but nobody ever found his body. More likely he was nothing but a drifter, a bum, and maybe that's where he got it, the bad blood on his mother's side, Bickie said.

Because he always knew he wasn't right, he said, knew it ever since he was big enough to know anything, when even as a little baby he'd rather go and sit on the trolley tracks in front of his house or pick out tunes on his mama's piano. Oh, he learned to fit in, he said, at first because it made things easier, and then later because he learned to like it. But he always knew he was different, and sometimes it scared him.

That just made me love him more, because that's always the way they treated me, too. Not at home too much, but later, after I married Vern.

Then Tram sent him the telegram about the job in St. Louis, and he came back to being his old self. But I never forgot the way he acted and what he said that night, about his not being right.

And the thing about the little girl—that was something he told me in the three a.m. hush of a winter morning walking under the L tracks on Van Buren, practically the first month I knew him. He blurted it out, like something he had to do or he wouldn't be able to breathe again. He told me all about it and said it had been a mistake, although he never said whose mistake it was.

And I didn't care. I still don't. All of us have some black secret on our souls, something we did that we can't even admit to ourselves, something that most of the time if we're lucky never sees the light of day. I know I did.

But right after I told Harriet, I felt bad. She'd been my little sister, the one I never had. If I'd been thinking straight, I wouldn't have told her anything. But I hurt so much about her and Bickie falling in love I couldn't help it.

It hurt most of all because no matter what happened between me and Bickie, no matter what we did together or what he told me or what black secrets we kept about each other, I knew he'd never feel that way about me, the way he felt about Harriet.

Because underneath it all he still wanted to be the clean-cut college kid—for Ruth, for Harriet, for his old man. It didn't matter he could never really be that person. With Harriet, like with Ruth, he could pretend to be that college boy, and make them and his old man love him for it.

He could never love me, though, because I made no bones about not wanting any part of that life. I learned long ago I could never fit in, no matter how much I wanted to. And even though it hurt for a long time, in the end it was a blessing in disguise because it forced me to figure out what really made me happy and go after it with all I got. Which I did for awhile, all the time I was with Bickie, in Chicago and at Hudson Lake. But once that was over, and I knew I'd lost him forever, it didn't matter where I ran or who I ran with. Only that I keep running.

Chapter 26

Kleagle Richard Livingston was a tight man—tight-lipped, tight clothed, tight with a dollar. He kept meticulous track of the dollars and cents coming into Valley Klan #53 Klavern. Kleagle Livingston didn't come to South Bend on a personal visit to socialize. He was here because of the dwindling rolls of Cyrus's klavern.

As he sat across the table from him over another dry spring chicken dinner at the Christiana Tavern, Cyrus tried to watch for an expression, any expression, to cross Livingston's face and give him a clue about how he really felt—and whether he was going to pull the Klavern #53's charter.

Something was wrong in South Bend. Cyrus had been struggling with it for a while now. It could have been the fracas that happened a couple of years ago, when ruffians from Notre Dame had started a riot with some Hundred Percenters. Or maybe it was the scandal involving Stephenson, the Klan's leader in Indianapolis, and that girl who ended up killing herself. Or maybe it was just because there were fewer and fewer true believers, even here in LaPorte County. Too many people were giving up the old ways for store-bought clothes and automobiles and jazz. Too many people were just giving up, period.

No matter—Livingston didn't care. He was charged with recruitment for the region, and he'd use any means at his disposal to increase Klan membership.

As Exalted Cyclops, Cyrus knew he should be stirring up the ranks and encouraging new membership. He'd tried, God knew he'd tried. A lot of things hung on the outcome. But no matter how hard he tried, interest in the Klan was dwindling.

As if reading his mind, Livingston looked up at him, and a smile twitched at his mouth. "It's not your fault, Cyrus," he said, wiping a napkin across his mouth. "But we need to get membership up, or headquarters might pull your charter."

"Dick, I'm trying," Cyrus said, his lunch a cold, forgotten mess in a pond of coagulated gravy on the plate in front of him. "But things just aren't the way they used to be around here. When the biggest thing to worry about is whether the Pope is going to come in and take over the town, that's not much to stir up interest."

Livingston smiled and sipped at his lemonade, which was on the sour side and made his already tight mouth look even tighter. "I like the way you got them enthused about that dance hall. Every preacher in town is sending the message out from the pulpit about the evils of jazz music and drinking."

Cyrus sighed. "Yes, and our members are keeping busy reporting anyone they see going into the place. Word of mouth is getting around that the Blue Lantern is a good place to stay away from."

"Good for votes, too," Livingston said, arching an eyebrow. "That is, if you're an office-seeking man. And it's Steve Brinton's last term as sheriff, isn't it?"

Cyrus felt his face go red. He wondered how Livingston had gotten wind of his interest in running for sheriff. "It costs a lot of money to run for office, Dick. I'm a widower with two children. I don't know if I can do it."

"With the support of a strong klavern, you're a shoo-in. And I don't have to remind you how important the Klan vote was in the election back in '24. But you have to get enrollment up, Cyrus. It's a fact."

"I don't know what else I can do. We had the Fourth of July picnic, and a membership drive in the spring, and...."

Livingston leaned across the table, smile practically tightening up to his ears. "That's not going to turn the trick, Cyrus. What you need is a little inspiration from some of the other klaverns. Not the ones here in the Midwest. I mean the ones down South."

"I don't know anything about those operations. Besides, things are different down there. You got niggers, and the natural trouble that comes from them. There's only a handful of Jews in Mishawaka, and the Polish and Bohemians out here are hard-working people." He snuffed. "Voters, too, most of 'em."

"But what about that Hudson Lake crowd?" Livingston asked, stabbing at a slice of peach pie. "There's a bad bunch of rabble. Especially after what happened to that poor little girl from Evansville."

"I'm here to tell you that poor little girl went there looking for trouble. Her aunts didn't dare file a police report because—well, between you and me, the girl had it coming. And everybody knew."

"That's not the point, Cyrus. You have to take advantage of an opportunity when it's handed to you. You're right, you can't wait for the Pope to come rolling into town on the next train, even though, let's face it, some of our members are unschooled enough to believe that it just might happen." Livingston pushed away the mangled slice of pie and signaled at the waitress for more coffee and the check. "I say crack down hard on Hudson Lake."

"We've been cracking down. I told you, we're reading off names...."

"For God's sake, Cyrus, I'm not talking reading off names!" Livingston finally lost his temper, a spring wound too tight that snapped. "I'm talking about bringing some of that good old Southern spirit right here to South Bend." He grinned again, leaning across the table toward Cyrus until he was close enough that he could smell his breath. "Now do you get me?"

Cyrus's jaw dropped. What was Livingston talking about? He thought of the stories he'd heard about the Southern chapters, of tar-and-featherings, of burning people out of their homes. And worse. Photographs he'd seen once at a regional meeting, of a crowd of white men grouped around a tree, everybody smiling for the camera, hats off, waving like they were at a baseball game or a picnic. And high up in the background, almost forgotten, the cause of the celebration—a naked, twisted form, bloodied and burnt almost beyond recognition as human, dangling from the stark black branches of the tree like a huge and hellish seed pod. *Lynching? He wants us to lynch someone?*

Cyrus swallowed, the taste of the chicken turning rancid in his mouth. "Dick, do I have to remind you that I'm an agent of the law? I'm paid to uphold the peace, not disrupt it."

"Who says it has to be you? Plenty of people are worried about the situation out at that dance hall. And you've got a firebrand right within your midst. Fella named Mitch Johnston."

"I wouldn't want to go too far," Cyrus murmured, rattling the ice in his lemonade, the image of that gnarled black body burned into his mind. But also thinking about how they wouldn't go that far, that maybe somebody like Mitch could be persuaded to front something dramatic but harmless. A cross burning. Right in front of the Blue Lantern on a Saturday night.

"I don't mean anything drastic," Livingston said, almost as if reading Cyrus's thoughts. "Just a little action to stir things up. I've been seeing ads for that Blue Lantern all over the Indianapolis newspapers. They're gearing up for some big show next week. So I say get a bunch of boys to swoop down that Saturday night and show those invaders what true-blue Americanism is all about. And then let all the registered voters know that the Valley Klan #53 under the leadership of Cyrus Walker was what helped clean up Hudson Lake."

Cyrus rattled his ice some more and reached for his billfold. "You might have a point there, Dick. I'll think about it, see what we can do."

Chapter 27

It was August, the time of year that always gave Bix the blues. Summer was coming to an end, even though it was hotter than hell, still high summer by the thermometer and the number and fierceness of the mosquitoes humming around the netting he had draped over his bed in the little yellow cottage.

There were already signs of impending fall. Leaves, dark green with heated blood, were starting to grow delicate edgings of brown, not from the heat but from age. Nights were starting to get an edge, too, a barely noticeable chill that blew off the lake and had girls begging their boyfriends for their jackets when they walked along the open promenade of the dance hall.

There was no reason for him to hang around Hudson Lake after the show on Friday night. He couldn't stand thinking of Joy and how he'd hurt her by being with Harriet; and he couldn't stand thinking about how he'd promised Harriet he'd marry her when all he really wanted to do was play the horn. And then there was the threat of Jean canning him, of letting down Tram because he couldn't sight read, of the possibility of having to go home to Davenport. He just wanted to be away from it all.

So he took the South Shore into Chicago, got off the train, walked up the steps to Michigan Avenue, and grabbed the first cab he could get to the South Side.

As he watched the streets slide by, he felt himself float free like bubbles shaken loose in a glass of beer, all the stuff that was starting to weigh him down at Hudson Lake dissipating into air. There was just him and the night and the South Side streets outside, where anything could happen. The promise of good music at the end of the cab ride—loose, unfettered music that didn't give a damn about charts and sight-reading—made him want to bounce in his seat like a kid.

He got out of the taxi on 35th and Sunset, right in front of the Sunset Café, his cornet under his arm, sidewalk glittering under the streetlights, the neighborhood throbbing with sound coming from beyond the awninged walkway up to the club's door. The doorman recognized him and grinned a welcome, holding the door open.

Inside, the patrons—black, white and every shade in between—belly rubbed on the dance floor to the sounds of a band where two big, black horn players took turns pumping a melody as hard and as high as they could, while sweating people stood on chairs, clapping and screaming for them to take it higher.

Bix was absorbed into a sea of light and smell and sound—colored spotlights, glittering women's dresses, mingled odor of sweat, tobacco and marijuana smoke and liquor—the noise level even between sets loud enough to make him squint. The crowd closed around him like an amoeba, making him a part of it, lifting him toward the familiar bandstand he remembered from his school days at Lake Forest Academy when he and the gang would come down here to worship at the shrine.

The floor show was just finishing up and a line of high-yellow girls, wearing swatches of bright silk and feathers over their bobbling breasts and buttocks, took a bow and headed backstage. He sidled up to the stage, where the boys were taking a break.

Louis spotted him first. "Say, look who's heah, fellas. *Mistah* Bix Beiderbecke." Bix accepted palm slaps, sweaty handshakes, claps on the back, Coty-flavored kisses from women who smelled like Evening in Paris and Madame C.J. Walker's hair pomade. He settled at a table in front of the bandstand.

"Man, you slept in those duds, or what?" Louis laughed, pointing at Bix's limp linen jacket and crumpled pants. He gestured to a round-eyed chorus girl who smiled into Bix's face and sat at the table with him, slipping her arm through his.

"How's bidness out there with the peckerwoods in Indiana?" Carroll asked, setting a bottle and a glass in front of Bix.

Bix looked from face to face, then down at his travel-stained clothing and laughed. He took his cornet out of its black velvet bag and set it on the table next to the bottle. "What are you playing tonight?"

"Shit, man, why don't you be a payin' customer for once?" Louis leered at the girl who had her head on Bix's shoulder, her hand in his lap. "Don't you ever get tired of blowin, boy?"

Bix poured a drink and downed it in a swallow, looking around the room at the crowd. "We've been working up some hot stuff out there," he said. "You oughta hear Tram and Pee Wee. Bet we could come down here and kick your asses."

Louis and Carroll looked at each other and screeched with laughter. "Lissen at the ofay boy!" Louis howled. "Well, you on. You welcome to come on up and kick our black asses anytime you want." He put his face up to Bix's and grinned. "Like how about now?"

He got up on the stage with the rest of the band and the lights hit him, so warm and comfortable and familiar, the crowd, the noise, and the other musicians. "Dippermouth Blues," Louis said, and stomped off the tune. Then he finished a solo and stepped back, sweeping an arm at Bix, introducing him to the simmering crowd. Bix stepped up, the horn weighty in his hands, ready.

And then it happened. He looked down at the cornet and didn't recognize it. It might as well have been a musical instrument from another world, alien, exotic—mute. He turned it around, studying it, totally at a loss as to how this thing was played. It was like holding a brick or a block of wood—it would be that impossible to evoke a sound from this instrument, playable neither by breath nor touch of fingers, this convoluted tangle of brass tubing and silent valves, lying dead in his hands.

His mouth had gone dry, tongue shriveled as if in the hollow cavity of a mummified corpse. His eyes locked on a couple sitting at a table in front, their faces almost touching, drinks in hands. They looked at him, eyes heavy-lidded and blasé, waiting to see what the ofay boy could do. The crowd around them had gone into slow motion, then coagulated into stillness like flies in amber, frozen as they were thrown—mouths open, drinks poised at lips, smoke clouds solidified out of nostrils and lips. Bix's hands trembled as he watched a bead of sweat dangle on the upper lip of a fine-boned cocoa-colored woman, her eyes open and glittering like one of those stuffed animals at the natural history museum.

The sounds in the room—laughter, breaking glass, catcalls, scraping chairs— all faded away into a strange, high-pitched buzz, like the sound of the rotary saw at the old man's coal yard, shearing off two-by-fours. For the first time in his life there was no music behind his eyes, in his skull—just this high-pitched, droning whine, metallic, mechanical. He listened in vain over that shrill squeal for the melody, something that had always been there for him to cling to, only now it was gone. The cornet in his hands caught the lights from over the stage and glared up at him like a mocking smile.

It happened in the span of perhaps a second, an eye blink between Louis finishing his solo and Bix raising the horn to his lips. Louis looked sideways at him, his wet grin glistening in the spotlight. The band thumped relentlessly behind him, but Bix wasn't hearing them—he felt the sound through the soles of his shoes. And in his hands was a brick, a block of wood.

It was gone just that quickly, as fast as the transition from Louis opening and closing his eyes. Bix raised the horn, blew. And sound came out, blessed sound, and he pushed it out into the smoke-stratified room and the noise of the crowd crested and broke over him like a tidal wave as the people began breathing again, moving again, tracheas closing around swallows of liquor, lungs inhaling joints, lovers' lips mingling saliva and salt, the bead of sweat dripping off the cocoa-colored woman's lip. And the sound was back, just that quickly.

He was so relieved and grateful that he stayed with the band all night until closing, seated back by the piano and drums, hunched over in his chair, blowing chorus after chorus of song after song. The crowd screamed, stomped, stood upon chairs and threw their heads back, howling at the mirrored ball on the ceiling like wolves under a metallic moon.

Then the doors finally closed and locked, and it was only him and Louis. Bix looked down at his shirt, which was plastered to his chest with sweat. He took it off and sat there in his undershirt, suspenders drooping at his hips, and blew some more. Only now it was the old stuff, the stuff he grew up with that Louis remembered, too—Royal Garden Blues, Sensation Rag, Tiger Rag. Their playing grew more introspective, contemplative, as they reached deeper into themselves to pull up sounds beyond the well-practiced and repeated phrases the crowds loved so well.

And then it was dawn and he slumped in the ladderback chair, arms dangling, legs splayed, sweating right down to his socks, embouchure shot and twitching from overuse. Louis sat across from him, teeth bared, eyes bloodshot, trumpet resting on a ham-sized knee.

"Yo a mess, boy," he grinned.

Bix looked around at the empty room as if coming out of a trance. "I need a drink," he said. Louis chuckled and handed him a thick white china mug redolent with the oily aroma of Chicago bourbon. He tried to get it to his lips, but his hand was shaking so hard he needed to hold the cup in both hands, like a beggar panhandling on a street corner.

The horn was on the floor at his feet, innocently mute, awaiting the sanctuary of the black velvet bag. Looking at it again made him shrivel inside as he relived the instant on the stage with the lights in his eyes when it had deserted him, when the animal had turned on him, the music had let him down, as if warning him of what could happen again, maybe next time not for a second, but forever.

He downed his drink, hissed fire through his teeth, and stood.

"Wheah you goin, boy? You come back home with me, we'll get Lil to cook us up a mess of eggs and sausage, and ya'll can sleep on the couch, what do ya say?"

Bix smiled a smile that felt wan and sickly. "I better get back to Indiana," he said. "We got a big show tomorrow."

"You mean today. Shit, it's almost seven in the morning. You ain't goin no-wheah."

"Nope. Gotta go."

The girl who had been sitting at his table was now sprawled across it, head on her arms, asleep. Bix reached around her to pull his jacket off the back of the chair and tugged his cornet bag out from under her arms. She never even opened her eyes.

Bix blinked in pain at the August sunlight glaring off the streetcar rails on 35th Street. Black people in neatly pressed clothing walked down the pavement on their way to work, some turning to stare at this wreck of a white boy crumpled in last night's clothes.

It took him ten minutes to get a taxi. But instead of going to Randolph and Michigan and catching the South Shore train back to Hudson Lake, he directed the driver to a downtown hotel. He checked into his room, bought four quarts of gin from the bellboy, and proceeded to get so drunk that he didn't wake up until two days later, when the hotel manager finally came hammering on the door.

Chapter 28

Al was coming. McGurn didn't find out until the last minute, but Al was coming to see the show, and to take a look around Hudson Lake, pleased with his new venue.

McGurn had Horvath do a final pass around the place to make sure everything was all set up. And it was—from the tables set with new paper party goods from a favored Chicago printing company that got a nice revenue from the deal, to the soda fountain up front, where Chicago liquid goods alternated with bottles of seltzer and syrups, provided by favored Chicago bottlers. So far, so good.

The crowds started arriving around seven—on the South Shore from Chicago and in flivvers of every type from the surrounding towns. The biggest crowds they'd seen around here since the Fourth, according to Horvath, who McGurn had slipped an extra sawbuck to for his troubles. He had to hand it to the guy—he'd done a great job with publicity, even on the South Bend radio station.

Everybody was in soup and fish, even Tony, who McGurn had stationed at the door in wait for Al's arrival. He tried to ignore the little rat's uneasiness; he was still convinced something was going to happen with Ray and the locals, even though there would be enough Chicago heat here tonight to put down any sort of insurrection that might spring up, unlikely as it seemed.

McGurn installed Joy at a table right in front, where she wouldn't fail to get the attention of that goofy little horn player. He'd picked out her dress himself, what there was of it. This was her night, too—hell, part of the reason he was here in the first place was because he'd met her that first day, when she'd given him the lowdown on Hudson Lake.

By the time eight o'clock rolled around, the place couldn't get any more packed. Eventually he knew he'd have to grease the local fire marshal to get around the codes, but by then he'd be able to buy this place outright and expand it, build out onto the beach, maybe even put an outdoor pavilion right next door. Yeah, this place was shaping up to be a fucking gold mine, just as he thought from the start.

ଡ଼ଔ

I sat there with a glass of spiked Orange Squeeze in my hand, my new gold and diamond bracelets clattering every time I brought it to my lips to take a drink. I smiled, just like Jack wanted, and made sure everyone who walked past could get a good, hard look down the front of my dress. And I waited to see Bickie one more time, knowing it would be the last time, because I was leaving for Chicago with Jack tomorrow after the last show.

ଡ଼ଔ

I won't go over there tonight, Harriet thought, leaning against the sink in the kitchen and half-listening to Mrs. Smith muttering behind her about how this was the worst-looking group yet. *I won't go over there for anything. I don't want to see him, or Joy, or that scary-looking fellow Joy had taken to running with, the fellow everyone was saying was a gangster from Chicago.*

As soon as she was done with her work tonight, she was going straight back to the Traubs to pack her bags. She had another three weeks to go here, but she'd worked out an arrangement with Mrs. Smith to be gone for a few days, ostensibly visiting Rudy in Indianapolis. She was going to Indianapolis, but not to see Rudy or her family. There was something she needed to know, something she had to be certain about. Then she'd come back, finish out the summer and leave for good, and never see Hudson Lake again.

ଡ଼ଔ

McGurn checked his watch again. "So what the hell are we waiting for again?" he asked.

Horvath mopped his brow with a sodden handkerchief and looked around the dance hall. "They're not all here. I mean, they're all here except Bix."

Bix. That little son of a bitch again. "Where the hell is he?"

Horvath shrugged, face twitching with nerves. "We don't know. He told Tram he was going to Chicago after the Friday night show to visit some of the fellows at the South Side clubs. He should have been back by now."

"Well, we already waited long enough. Let's just start the goddamn show without him."

"That's Tram's call," Horvath said. "I mean, I agree with you, I think we oughta start right away. But Tram might not...." Horvath started backing away, face gone pale, as McGurn advanced on him.

"Get the band on," he said. "People are sick of waiting."

ಶಿಂಞ

Ray was working the soda fountain, busily dispensing the legal stuff and making it known that other imbibements were available for those who wanted it. Tony had positioned himself at the front door, directly facing Ray, his face impassive. Ray grinned and saluted him; Tony just stood there, staring, chewing gum, not moving from the spot. First chance I get I'm gonna get that bastard outside and take him on, one on one, Ray thought. I don't give a goddamn who he works for.

ಶಿಂಞ

Cyrus Walker got the phone call letting him know the plan was on for tonight. Two dozen members of the Valley Klavern were going to drive out to Hudson Lake and burn a cross in front of the dance hall in an attempt to startle the patrons into good behavior and drum up some good publicity for the klavern.

But Cyrus had other things on his mind. Like where his son was.

Trent had come home from his job at the hardware store for dinner, but afterward sneaked out without a by-your-leave. Cyrus thought the last time he'd disciplined Trent things would start to change, but instead the boy had grown surlier than ever.

And when he'd finally come home, and Cyrus demanded to know where he was spending all his time, Trent had shouted that it was none of his goddamn business anymore, he wasn't a kid anymore but a man, and he'd go where he liked, see who he liked, and no old man of his was going to tell him what to do with his life anymore.

When Cyrus stood up, raising his hand to slap him across the face for his impertinence, Trent grabbed his arm in an iron grip and forced it down. And Cyrus suddenly realized that his son was at least three inches taller than he was. Then Trent went into his bedroom, came out with a suitcase, and left.

Cyrus telephoned headquarters and put out a call for the highway patrol to find Trent and bring him back home. And once he'd settled the issue with Trent, Cyrus would go take care of things at the Blue Lantern.

ಶಿಂಞ

"Ladies and gentlemen, welcome to the beautiful Blue Lantern Inn, the pride of northern Indiana. I'm Charlie Horvath, and I'm proud to present, direct from Detroit and St. Louis, the world-class Jean Goldkette Orchestra, under the direction of Mr. Frank Trumbauer. Tram, come on up and take a bow."

୫୦ଓଃ

Mitch Johnston had never seen so many citified types in his life. As he pulled his Ford into the graveled parking lot across from the Blue Lantern, a clutch of painted-up women walked past his car, laughing and blowing cigarette smoke. One of them turned around to look at him and nudged her friend, bursting into fresh laughter at him.

He reached under the seat of the Ford for the brown paper sack that held his neatly folded robes, and put it on the front seat. Then he put his hands on the steering wheel and waited until some of the other Hundred-Percenters showed up to teach these people a lesson.

୫୦ଓଃ

"Thank you, everyone, we're thrilled to see so many of you here tonight. I'm Frank Trumbauer, and I'm going to be the official judge of a special contest being hosted by WSBT, the radio station of the South Bend Tribune, broadcasting directly from the South Bend Tribune building in downtown South Bend. As you know, we've been the house band here at the Blue Lantern all summer. Now that summer's coming to an end, we wanted all of you who have come out and heard us to write us a letter in one hundred words or less why you think the Jean Goldkette Band is Number One. Yes, folks, this is just like a battle of the bands, only on paper! I'm the judge, and I can tell you I appreciate creativity and originality in the entries. The grand prize will be five hundred dollars in cash, and the four runners-up will get two hundred dollars each. The winners will be announced at the big WSBT-Blue Lantern Radio Frolic on Saturday, September Fourth. So sharpen your pencils, folks, and start thinking of reasons why you love this band!"

୫୦ଓଃ

"You got the cans of gasoline?"

Clyde Burgett, the auto dealer from Mishawaka, pulled up next to Mitch. He jerked a thumb toward his trunk.

"All we need. Got something for the cross?"

Mitch nodded and grinned. "Plenty of lumber in the trunk. Hope you didn't forget your robes."

"Nope, the missus pressed them right before I left."

They sat there a minute, not saying anything. Then the sound of music blasted out of the dance hall across the road, an up-tempo number that started Mitch tapping his feet on the Ford's floorboards before he remembered that the band was a bunch of nigger loving Jew rapists. He concentrated on trying to keep his feet still.

"I never did anything like this before," Clyde said. "Is it dangerous?"

"I was there for the South Bend riots," Mitch said, grinning with pride. "Nothing can happen to us when we got both God and the highway patrol on our side."

ᛒᛒᚷ

Mrs. Smith had gone upstairs to turn down beds for the night, finally leaving Harriet alone. She took off her apron and folded it neatly on a kitchen chair. The sound of the band came loud and clear from across the road, with one of her favorite songs, "Clementine from New Orleans." She'd sat and watched Bix play the solo a dozen times, delighted that every solo was different. She sank into a chair. She swore she wouldn't cry, but couldn't stop the tears that burned her eyes, cursing her weakness.

She'd wanted to marry him, to be with him forever. Even now, with Joy's revelations burned into her mind, she found herself thinking of all the other days and nights she'd spent listening to him play and rediscovering the wonder of each other's bodies over and over again, as if each time was the first time.

But there was no way to take back all the things that had happened since then. And she wouldn't go over there and see him. Not for anything. She lifted her head, waiting for Bix's solo, wondering how he'd change it this time. But instead, she heard the tame tones of Fred Farrar, using a mute and sounding not much different than Joe Dockstader.

Which meant Bix wasn't there.

ᛒᛒᚷ

"When's he coming?" McGurn pulled Horvath aside the minute the band started playing. "I heard people asking about him. We used his name on all the ads."

Horvath turned to the stage, where Tram was staring at him all through his playing. "I tell you, Mr. McGurn, I don't know. I tried calling some of the Chicago clubs he plays at, and nobody's seen him."

"Jesus Christ," McGurn muttered and walked back to the table where Joy was sitting and drinking. "I'll find out where the little son of a bitch is."

ᛒᛒᚷ

"Come here, Tony." The soda fountain cleared out right after the band started playing, and the runty little driver still stood there, staring at Ray.

He slouched away from the door and sauntered over to the fountain counter, saying nothing.

Ray leaned on the counter, putting his face right into Tony's. "You know, Tony, I'm beginning to think you don't like me very much."

Tony stared directly into his eyes without blinking, until Ray had to turn away, laughing to disguise his hatred of the man.

"Why, Tony? Why don't you like me? Your boss likes me. Hell, I'm just a good old Hoosier boy, don't mean no harm. What is it about me that bothers you so much?"

Tony didn't flinch. "You're a double-crossing son of a bitch, that's why. And Jack knows it, too."

Jack knows what?, Ray thought, laughing again. "Double crosser? Why do you think that?"

For the first time since he'd known him, Ray saw Tony smile. "Come on outside, Ray," he said. "I'll explain it to you."

†‡

Cyrus pulled up to the Blue Lantern in a county police car and got out, looking around and spotting Mitch Johnston first. Of course, the fool was all fired up and ready to go. As if burning a cross in front of the Blue Lantern was the most important thing anyone could do. A real life-and-death matter.

"We've got everything we need," Mitch called from across the parking lot, causing a necking couple in a closed coupe to break off from their activities and stare at him. "Gasoline, wood, you name it. Where you want it, Cyrus? How about right in front of the hotel?"

"Naw, in front of the dance hall," said Preston McCoy, the South Bend chiropractor. "Nobody will be able to miss it there."

"Cyrus, you all right?" Mitch came up to him and peered into Cyrus's face. "You look a little peaked."

"Go home, gentlemen," Cyrus said, head bowed. "This raid has been called off."

"Called off?" whined Mitch, sounding like a spoiled kid being told his birthday party was being cancelled. "Why?"

"Don't tell me the sheriff is giving you grief," Ronald Warner muttered. "He don't like this place any more than the rest of us."

Cyrus walked over to Mitch and laid a hand on his shoulder. "You know, I never asked you whether you had children, Mitch. Do you?"

Mitch blinked at him, surprised. "Why, yessir, got myself a couple of boys, eight and ten. Why, Cyrus?"

He patted Mitch's shoulder and moved away, back toward the car. "Maybe you ought to go spend some time with them, then."

ಬಂಛ

"How should I know where he is?" Joy said, grinning into McGurn's face. "I ain't seen him in ages." She drained her drink and held out her empty glass for a refill, waggling it under McGurn's nose.

"Don't give me that crap. I know you've been screwing the little bastard. And I don't give a shit. But you know where he is, and when I find out, I'm gonna find him and...."

"Why ask me? Ask that simp up at the hotel. She's the one spends every waking hour with him. Here, gimme a refill, will ya? Don't be stingy. Oh, look. There's Mary Pickford now."

McGurn looked up to see a plain-looking broad in a cotton housedress come walking across the floor of the ballroom, cutting through the dancing couples, her eyes riveted to the stage. She moved like a sleepwalker, and came to stand directly in front of the bandstand.

"Hey, sister," McGurn said, coming up next to her and touching her shoulder. "You a friend of Beiderbecke's?"

She turned to look at him, her face wet and swollen with tears. Then she looked over at Joy, shook her head, and turned around and walked out, just as slowly as she'd come in.

"What the hell kind of goofy shit is this!" McGurn muttered.

ಬಂಛ

"I had a son. My only son," Cyrus said, as the robed Klansmen stood around him, staring in disbelief. "His name was Trent. A boy seventeen years old. Well, he left home tonight. He just came back long enough to pack his things and go back to Evansville. You see, he went and got married a week ago. And there's not a damn thing I can do about it."

"Married who?" Clyde Burgett whispered to the chiropractor.

Cyrus turned and stared at them. "There's no use hiding it. Everyone'll know before long, anyway. That slut who got in trouble here last month. Crystal Hawkins."

ಬಂಛ

As they walked out the front door of the soda fountain, Ray and Tony looked up at the sound of a powerful car caroming into the parking lot, spraying gravel as it came. The car was low and black and powerful, with an engine that thrummed under its long hood like the guttural growling of a panther.

Doors opened, and four swarthy men packed into pinstriped suits got out. They stood there flanking the back passenger door. Out came a large, stocky man in a light gray suit; a diamond stickpin glinted in the folds of his dark silk tie. He wore matching gray spats and a fedora pulled low over his chubby face.

"Hey, howaya," he said and walked up to Ray, gripping his hand. "Name's Al. Nice little place ya got here. The music start yet?"

Ray's mouth popped open and he stammered something, but the man was gone, engulfed by the bulk of the four bodyguards flanking him on all sides.

"Jesus Christ," Ray breathed. "That's Capone, ain't it? It's Capone, ain't it, Tony, right?"

Tony sidled back to his position at the front door of the soda fountain. "Ray," he said, lighting a fresh cigarette, "you got good timing."

೮Ɱ೮ଓ

Al and his four bodyguards sat at the table right in front of the bandstand with Joy and McGurn. First McGurn gave him the grand tour, walking around with him on the promenade porch, pointing out the beach, the hotel, the cottages. Al nodded and smiled, periodically lighting a fresh cigar and shaking hands with all the help he encountered. When Mrs. Smith came out to the dance hall to see what all the commotion was, he made a show of taking off his hat and complimenting her on the pleasant little place she had there—an unexpected nicety that sent her scurrying back to the safety of the hotel's kitchen as fast as her fat legs would carry her.

Then Al and McGurn and the bodyguards came back to the table, ordered drinks and sat listening to the band. Joy was everything McGurn hoped she'd be—flirty and cute, chucking Al under the chin and pouring drinks for him from McGurn's hip flask. Al even asked her to dance, after slipping the bandleader a sawbuck to play the sweet stuff he liked best.

When he was through, he led Joy back to the table, pinched her cheek, and clapped McGurn on the back.

"Jack, I think you got somethin' good goin here," he said, pushing back his chair in preface to leaving, the bodyguards following his lead. "You go ahead and do what you gotta do to make this place work. I'll back you up." McGurn beamed and escorted Al and his entourage back outside.

Before he got back into the car, Al lit up another cigar and turned to McGurn. "What I wanna know is, where's that hot horn player everybody's talkin' about?"

And then the driver got into the long, black car and fired it up back out to Chicago.

McGurn stood out in front of the soda fountain and thought of the little son of a bitch and what he'd do when he finally laid hands on him.

಄ఴ

"We're gonna settle this right now, goddamn it." Ray took off his tuxedo jacket and hung it on a piling on the pier. Inside the dance hall, the Goldkette band was playing a fanfare to introduce the winners of the night's dance contest, another gimmick McGurn had introduced. There was a lot of loud clapping and cheering, loud enough to drown out Tony's response. Ray just saw his lips move.

"What? What'd you say, you fucking guinea?"

"Too many people around here. You wanna go one on one, let's go across the street. Back by the barn."

"Why, so you can get your wop paisanos to help you out?" Ray laughed. "Nothing doing. We settle it right here, once and for all. Hell, we can take it inside, you want to. Make it part of the entertainment."

Tony started walking back down the pier. "Back by the barn," he said, "if you got the balls."

"You got it, greaseball," muttered Ray, knowing that a quick stop at the phone booth in the soda fountain would have a half-dozen of the South Bend bootleggers here in fifteen minutes. On the way, he stopped in and went behind the counter, digging into a cardboard box of Horlick's malted milk mix for the gun he always kept there just in case.

He didn't remember his tuxedo jacket until later. And by then, it was too late to go back and get it.

಄ఴ

Mitch Johnston wasn't the kind of fellow who quit once he started to do something. Even when Cyrus and the rest of the Hundred Percenters got back into their cars and drove off, giving up on the idea of a Klan raid on the Blue Lantern, he hung behind, listening to the strains of the band, watching couples in the darkened autos, and thinking this place really needed to be burned to the ground, and the ground sown with salt, just like Sodom and Gomorrah.

He went around to the back of the hotel, away from the lights of the dance hallacross the road, and piled up an armful of the lumber he'd brought in his trunk. Then he took the gasoline can he'd lifted from the back seat of Clyde Burgett's flivver and poured the hot-smelling fluid over the pile of wood, standing back so as not to splash his Klan robes.

He was careful to get a torch going first, just like they did back in '24, when there was a big parade and celebration after the elections that put all the Klan-backed candidates into office. He'd just turned around to get the big wooden cross he'd nailed together when he noticed the small contained fire he'd started was beginning to creep away and expand, laying down a thick layer of smoke.

And that the bottom hem of his Klan robe was starting to smolder.

ॐ

When reports of a fire at the hotel filtered into the dance hall, people started screaming and running for the exits. Charlie Horvath got on stage and tried to calm everyone down, telling them everything was under control, but once people got a whiff of smoke and gasoline the dance hall emptied out in minutes.

Some stood on the darkened shore of the lake and watched orange flames shooting into the sky behind the hotel; others got into cars and pulled away down the dark country roads. A few of the more intrepid ones helped Buddy Smith and Harriet haul water from the kitchen to douse the flames. When water didn't work, they used dirt and blankets, and eventually managed to tamp it down. Long before the only fire truck in New Carlisle came screaming down Chicago Road, Mitch Johnston's fire was little more than a smoking wet mass of blackened lumber piled between the back door of the hotel and the little yellow cottage behind it. He'd never even gotten the cross lit.

In less than an hour, everything was over and done with. The band was back playing, McGurn was walking around surveying the grounds, Tony was back at the entrance to the soda fountain. But more than half the crowd had left for other venues or home, and they didn't come back. Something had changed about the Blue Lantern, they said later, something was different, flatter, duller, not as much fun as before.

Nobody ever figured out who had tried to set the fire, although Mitch Johnston turned up a few days later, walking with a limp and looking embarrassed.

And early the next morning after the dance hall was closed and everyone gone, Tony pulled McGurn's Lincoln around to the shore, opened the trunk, heaved a tight-wrapped, weighted bundle over his shoulder, struggled with it to the end of the pier, and rolled it off the planking into Hudson Lake, where it sank to the bottom without a trace.

Chapter 29

"I'll only be gone for a couple of days," Harriet said, touching Buddy's arm, the one that had been broken. "You can't get rid of me that easily."

"It's all because of him," Buddy muttered, scowling, looking at the charred pile of wood where the fire had been. "He screwed everything up. I hate that son of a bitch."

Harriet sighed and took a sip of her coffee. She wasn't about to go into details with anyone, least of all Buddy. "Come on, Buddy. I'll help you get the yard cleaned up, and then we'll have breakfast. How about some French toast? My sisters always said I make the best French toast."

He looked at her. "I really used to like him, you know. He was just so different from everybody else. He didn't treat me like some punk kid. But now—well, I just don't trust him anymore."

Harriet stood and stretched, trying to keep her voice calm and impersonal. "I noticed another policeman came around asking if anyone saw who started the fire. Think they'll ever catch whoever did it?"

"And I really don't like the way he treats you. I saw you with him plenty of times. I saw how you look at him. And he acts like it was nothing. Maybe I should just go over there and call him out, once and for all."

She sat next to him again and put her arm through his. "Buddy—please don't let's talk about this anymore."

Buddy looked down and placed his hand over hers. He slid a glance at her, as if to ascertain the appropriateness of the gesture and when she smiled, patted her hand firmly. "He's not like us, Harriet. No matter how much we kid ourselves that he is. I mean, just look at him. Can you imagine him living here in New Carlisle? Playing at the dance halls on weekends like Joe Dockstader or Verne Ricketts, and the rest of the time working down at the Studebaker plant?" He grinned as Harriet laughed at the thought of Bix turning into a Hoosier.

He was right, of course. She could never picture Bix being someone like her father, a farmer whose dirt-creased hands were slow and patient, whether he was wrapping a sprained ankle on Harriet or helping a mare to foal. Her mother had been too busy with the babies to bother with Harriet; it was her father who splinted her sprains and applied bandages when she fell out of trees or skinned her knees.

The last time she'd seen those hands they'd been clean for once, nails and all, folded across the chest of his best churchgoing suit, and she'd been kneeling in front of his casket. She always thought he should have done something more with those hands than digging dirt.

"I know you think I'm just a punk kid," Buddy said. "But I really care about you. I think you're wonderful." He stared at the ground and squeezed her hand.

Bix's hands were nothing like her father's, she thought. They were restless, always moving, on cornet valves or a keyboard or on a table, drumming to some melody only he could hear. Buddy was right; Bix could never be like them. And it would be wrong to try and make those hands do anything else except what they were created to do. Even though he said he wanted to marry her, Harriet knew that marrying Bix would be like cutting off his hands, trapping him in a life he was totally unsuited for. So no matter how she felt, she knew what had to happen. She'd leave Hudson Lake and never see Bix again because it would hurt too much, knowing she could never really have him. And she'd go back to school and become a doctor, just as she always knew she'd do.

Harriet looked at Buddy—for the first time, really looked at him—and for an instant she saw behind the spotty complexion and sulky attitude a trace of the man he would become. A very decent man, in fact. Perhaps a man very much like her father.

"Buddy Smith, whoever gets you is going to be one very lucky girl," Harriet said. "Thanks for being so kind. For being my friend." She leaned over and kissed him on the cheek. He got up and walked away fast, and she could tell from the redness at the back of his neck that he was blushing.

"Well, well, if it ain't Harriet and Buddy-boy. Got yourself a new boyfriend, honey?"

Harriet looked up to see Joy come sauntering up the path from the beach, cigarette in hand, clutching a bathrobe around herself. Buddy stopped, trapped between the two women and looking for a way to get around Joy. She snapped the cigarette away and reached into her pocket.

"Now, don't go runnin' away, kiddo. I got something needs doing." She took some folded bills and thrust them toward Buddy. "I got two suitcases and a trunk up in my room you can bring downstairs. This oughta cover it. I'm getting out of this dump."

Buddy glanced from Joy to Harriet, his eyes feral. Harriet nodded and Buddy turned back to the hotel, walking past Joy and ignoring the bills she held out to him.

"Hey!" she shouted. "You think you're too good to take my money now?"

Buddy looked back at her and shook his head. "No charge, ma'am. I don't need money for taking your bags."

Joy's face went red. "Why, you little punk, you been eyeballin' me for the last three months, and now you're gonna treat me like I'm your grandma? Ma'am! That's a hot one. I wasn't no ma'am that time you were peekin' at me in the bathhouse. Ha, didn't think I saw you, huh? Does your mother know how you been abusin' yourself, right out in public?"

Harriet cringed. "Go on, Buddy," she said. "I'll wait for you here." She watched as Buddy ran into the kitchen, slamming the screen door behind him.

Joy walked further down the gravel path and stood a few feet from where Harriet sat on the back steps.

"Same old Harriet," she said, sounding tired. "Always the good girl doing the right thing. It must be nice, waking up sober every morning and knowing just what you're gonna do all day. Boring, maybe, but nice."

"I'm sorry to see you're leaving," Harriet said, the words sticking like glue to the roof of her mouth. "I'll be leaving myself in a couple of days."

"Well, goody goody gumdrops," Joy grinned, reaching into her robe to scratch an arm. "Goin' with Bix?"

"You know better than that," Harriet whispered, suddenly unable to meet Joy's eyes.

"Yeah, you're right. A good girl's gotta do the right thing. And fellas like Bix are good enough for some laughs, but not much else, right?"

Oh God, if you only knew, Harriet thought, a hard pearl of anger beginning to expand in her chest. If only it was that easy. "Look, Joy, we were friends once. I'd like to think we could be friends again. There's no reason for us to part with any hard feelings...."

"Oh yeah, I know, kid. I know." Joy pulled out a crumpled pack of Camels, shook it, then crushed it between her hands and threw it to the ground. "Empty, goddamn it. No, there ain't any hard feelings. Fact is, there ain't any feelings at all. We got nothing in common, never did. Hell, if you seen me on the street somewhere, you'd look the other way and pretend you never knew me, kid! I know that." She put out a hand for Harriet to shake. "So, good luck with your college, and your boyfriend, and your bein' a doctor. Who knows, maybe someday I'll come to you sick and you'll fix me up and say to your nurse, 'Hey, I used to know that jane.'" She turned to walk away, but Harriet pulled her back by the hand.

"Joy, can you ever forgive me for—you know, for loving him?" Her eyes sought Joy's, hoping to see a hint of the warmth and soft-heartedness she'd known so well. Instead, Joy's blue-green eyes chinked in a laugh as she pulled her hand away.

"Point is, kid, can you ever forgive yourself?" And then she banged through the kitchen door and was gone.

Chapter 30

Joy

Before I left Hudson Lake for good, I was bound and determined to find my red satin slipper.

Jack warned me to have my stuff packed and ready to go when Tony came to get me with the Lincoln later that day. And now all my stuff was packed in the shiny new luggage, all except the red satin slipper that I knew was somewhere in the little yellow cottage.

Jack didn't say nothing last night before he left, but I could tell he was mad. It was supposed to be the busiest weekend of the season, he spent a fortune on advertising to make sure that it was. But then the crowds just got thinner and thinner. I heard it, too, even before the fire—people talking about how the band wasn't up to snuff, how they were heading out to Playland Park or the Riverside Resort or somewhere else.

Bix finally showed up late on Sunday afternoon. He looked terrible—paler than I ever saw him, even in the middle of a Chicago winter. He looked nervous, and his hair was a mess, and his tux was all wrinkled, like he'd slept in it. He wasn't playing so hot, either.

I'd waited for weeks for him to say something to me, hoping he'd try and stop me from doing what I was doing. He'd had his chance that night on the porch of the Blue Lantern, when he warned me about Jack. But he never said nothing else, and so I knew he didn't care about me anymore, that he had Harriet and he didn't give a damn if I went with Jack or not.

I hadn't been to the cottage in weeks. The weeds were higher now, but otherwise the place looked the same—flies buzzing around the bottles and cans on the front porch and the Buick covered with dust, a big spider web stretched between the side view mirror and the hood. There was a hole in the screen door that wasn't there before, looked like somebody put their foot through it.

I knocked, but nobody answered, so I knocked again. There were no sounds from inside. The screen door was open so I went in.

There were bottles and glasses all over the piano, shoes and clothes on the floor. None of them were mine. It was as quiet as a tomb.

I turned the corner from the front room and stood in the doorway of the darkened bedroom.

God knows I didn't want to see him again. But there he was in the bed, one foot sticking out of a mess of yellowed sheets, with a pillow over his head. I could hear him snoring from across the room.

I saw the slipper right away under the bed, along with dust balls, old newspapers and empty bottles. All I had to do was lean over, put my hand under the bed and pick it up. But instead I leaned over, put my hand out and pulled the pillow off his face.

He slept like somebody just hit him over the head with a two by four. I could smell the booze sweating out of his body from where I stood. I knew nothing would wake him up when he was sleeping off a drunk. I could scream, shake him, beat a drum. He'd just keep sleeping. So all I had to do was get my slipper and leave.

But instead I stood there looking at him and thinking about how it had been when he showed up here that first afternoon, when we kissed by the lake and then came back here.

The cottage had been clean then; the boys hadn't even unpacked their suitcases yet. Their instrument cases were lined up by the door, and the bed was made up with a scratchy green Army blanket and clean sheets that smelled like bleach and sunshine.

We sat on the edge of the bed, just touching a little, both of us nervous. I remembered him lifting up my skirt, pulling down my bloomers, and stopping when he saw the scar there. Then he ran his fingertips along the scar and looked up at me from between my legs, like he wanted to ask me something, and before I could start crying again he stopped me with his tongue, changing the tears to only the sound of me breathing, harder and harder, helping me to run away, and then a different kind of crying. And then both of us on the bed, breathing hard together, running away.

But all the running had only brought me back here, and that first day may as well have been part of another life. Was, in fact.

So I bent over and picked up the red satin slipper and carried it back to Room 4 at the Hotel Hudson and went into the dresser drawer where I'd hidden Jack's guns. I felt off-balance; the slipper in my left hand was so light I forgot it was there, but the gun in my right hand was heavy, weighing it down at my side like a giant's fist.

I didn't remember walking back up the path to the little yellow cottage, creaking up the steps, opening the screen door. But the next thing I knew I was back at the bed like time hadn't passed at all, like I'd never gone back to the hotel and gotten the gun.

He hadn't moved. I reached down to touch him one more time, but my hands were full so I dropped the slipper and put the nose of the gun up under his left ear. He twitched, but kept snoring.

I wanted to look closer, into his ear like I could look into his mind, so I knelt up on the bed, bedsprings singing their familiar song, and straddled him, thighs tight against his ribcage, just the way he always said he liked it. The pulse beating behind my knees mingled with the sludgy tempo of his heart knocking around in his chest. I had both hands on the gun now, and pushed the muzzle up against the little rounded bump behind his ear, that cute, crooked little ear.

I knew how the gun worked, knew it was loaded, saw Jack loading it himself. Just click off the safety—like that—and it would fire. And after I did, I'd lay down next to him, put it into my mouth, click it again, and do the same thing. Get it right this time. Finish what I'd started to do to him, my other baby, my real baby. What I'd tried to do, what Vern had caught me trying to do. The real reason they took my baby away. The real reason I left, after I found out Vern was going to have me taken away, too.

Because I tried to kill him, my Michael. After the lady from the American Eugenics Society told me what his life would be like, and that the best place for him wasn't at home with me, but in an institution. I'd taken him into the barn and carried him upstairs to the hayloft and had the rope around his neck when Vern came in and grabbed Michael away from me and slapped me, over and over, calling me words I'd never heard him say before, words I didn't even think he knew. And right after that Michael went away forever, and in a way, so did I.

Now I looked down at Bix sleeping underneath me, and thought of Michael, saw his face under Bix's. I didn't think about what I was doing; it was something I couldn't control, like how my voice rose out of my throat to wind a harmony around whatever melody he was playing. From far away in the corner near the ceiling, I watched myself on the bed, wondering why Joy was doing that? Didn't she love Bix? Why would she want to hurt him?

And then he opened his eyes. He said, "What the hell," and brushed away the gun. It thumped to the floor and scuttled under the bed, harmless as a mouse. He dug the heels of his hands into his eyes, opened them again, wider, and looked at me. "You all right?" he asked. He put his hands on my hips. "You're crying."

I poked my tongue out of my mouth and tasted a tear that had slithered down my cheek. Then I touched his face and felt like I was coming to, my arms and legs shaking like there was a hunk of ice in the middle of my guts.

I sank down on his chest and he put his arms around me, rubbing my back, pulling the sheets over me.

"I could kill you," I shuddered into his ear, the same one the gun had just pressed behind.

"I know," he said. "I'm sorry, baby. I'm really sorry."

And then the screen door banged open. Buddy Smith was standing there, saying there was a woman here from Montana asking for somebody named Dolly Schoenhof, wondering if it was me.

So I leaned down to kiss Bickie and went out to meet her. I knew who it was. I'd been waiting for her for a long time.

She stood on the porch of the little yellow cottage, big old pocketbook held over her stomach like a shield. Under the brim of the cloche her face was pinched and tight, like a flower bud that had withered on the stem before it ever bloomed. The only part of her that moved were her hands on the strap of the pocketbook.

"Millie," I said. "Long time no see."

Her face got even tighter, her pale lips clenched into a bloodless slit. "We've been looking for you since you left. Did you think he'd just let you go like that?"

"What's wrong? He need help on the ranch? Why don't he hire a cook?"

The woman shifted her feet nervously, but stood her ground. "He still loves you, Dolly. I don't know why. He sent me to bring you home."

"And why couldn't he come and bring me back himself?"

She didn't answer, and the way she had her cloche pulled down low, I couldn't tell anything from her eyes, either.

I laughed, and it felt like my old laugh, the one I used to laugh back home in Montana before I ever even thought of marrying Vern, the old laugh that used to echo out over Hudson Lake. "That's what I thought."

And then there was a low, powerful whirring, coming closer. Down Chicago Road poured the black, shining length of Jack's Lincoln, with Tony behind the wheel. Millie and Buddy stood there listening and looking, and the screen door of the hotel kitchen opened and Mrs. Smith and Harriet came out and stood on the back porch to watch.

I took Buddy's arm and leaned up to give him a kiss. "There's my ride, sweetie. You wanna go get my suitcases and tell Tony to put 'em in the trunk?" Buddy walked off, touching the red lipstick imprint I left on his cheek like it was a burn from a red-hot poker.

"I'm going now, Millie," I said, reaching out and patting the woman on the arm. "Tell Vern I'll settle up with him about the money."

"What about your son?" the woman said. "Don't you care about him?"

"He's dead, remember? That's the way all of you wanted it."

"You know he isn't. You know where he is. And...."

"He's dead. And you can tell Vern I'm dead, too." I looked up at the Lincoln, where Tony was closing the trunk on my belongings. It was a nice day for a good, long ride.

I felt everyone watching me as I walked down to the Lincoln. Tony held the door open for me and I got in and pulled on my hat. I rolled down the window and waved goodbye to everyone as the car drove down Chicago Road. I left my hand stuck out the window, waving, for a long time, until the car made the turn and disappeared, until there was nothing for them to see of me except the dust in the road.

Chapter 31

Jean Goldkette got off the train and stood looking at Hudson Lake. This time of day it was quiet, and even though Frank Trumbauer knew he was coming, he didn't know why.

Goldkette fit a cigarette into his amber holder and walked toward the Blue Lantern. He wondered if the musicians would be glad to leave here, and imagined they would. After all, a place could be too bucolic, he thought, too peaceful. You could only swim so much before you got waterlogged.

Trumbauer came out of his cottage with a towel around his neck, lanky in a saggy black bathing suit. He looked up and did a movie-comic double take at the sight of his boss.

"Jean? I didn't expect you so soon."

Goldkette smiled and clapped him on a sunburned shoulder. "Pack your bags," he said. "We're going on tour."

ഇൻൽ

The boys sat sprawled in the empty dance hall as Tram laid out the plan.

"We'll hook up with the rest of the orchestra, take a couple weeks in Detroit to tighten up the act, and then we'll hit the road. Traveling by bus, with Charlie handling everything. First Chicago, then Massachusetts."

"Woo hoo!" Pee Wee hooted. "And end up in Noo Yawk!"

"Makes sense to me," Itzy said. "We've had all summer to rehearse. We've never sounded better."

"Where we playing?" Ryker asked.

"The Music Box in Boston, and a couple of the smaller towns in Massachusetts. And then New York."

"Where?"

"Roseland."

The musicians murmured, throwing in a few impressed whistles.

"Roseland! Jeez, Tram, this is the real stuff, no kidding!"

"Lotta hot women in Noo Yawk, boys!"

"Hell, it'll be great to be moving around again—after going to seed out here all summer."

Bix flopped onto the stage and stared up at the crooked-moon backdrop, his hands behind his head, as dreamily as if he was under a real moonlit sky. "I'm ready," he said softly, thinking of throwing instruments into a vehicle and just hitting the road, remembering the feeling of wheels moving beneath him, just like when the Wolverines gigged around the Midwest, carting their equipment around in Dick Voynow's jalopy. Free and easy.

Only this would be the big leagues—world-class ballrooms, a big, comfortable bus, and some of the best jazzmen in the business. Guys he'd played up against long enough to know exactly what they'd do and when, a knowledge that made it easy and fun to work with them. And good friends now, too, all of them—Itzy and his nightly piano serenades, Pee Wee, that bottle baby and his unpredictable temper, laconic Dan, easygoing, patient Fuzzy, and Tram—always the big brother, the Dutch uncle to them all.

"I'll be goddamned glad to get out of that stinkin' cottage," Pee Wee groaned and everybody laughed.

Bix thought of the lone red satin slipper under the bed and gazed at the painted moon. "Me too," he said. *As soon as I say my goodbyes.*

ಬಂ

"So you boys are leaving." Martha topped off the jelly jar with a fresh dose of corn mash as Bix polished off the crusts of his sandwich.

"It's the big time, Martha," he said, grabbing her around the waist and kissing her withered cheek. "Boston, New York—the Roseland! Ever heard of it?"

"Sure. Fletcher Henderson plays there," she said, grinning at the stunned look on his face. "Why so surprised, son? That's one hot band. But maybe you fellows can teach them a trick or two."

"We'll miss you, Bixie," Mary said, stroking his hair and putting a piece of peach cobbler in front of him. "Things just won't be the same around here without you, will they, Sister?"

"Oh, you haven't seen the last of me. We'll be back, maybe even next summer. Somebody's gotta keep Joe Dockstader on his toes. And I'll write you girls from everywhere we go. Hell, before I'm done, you'll have postcards from around the world!"

Martha walked with him to the front porch, her hand on his arm. "We'll miss you, boy," she said. She stood on tiptoe and whispered into his ear. "And what about the girl? That nice Harriet?"

He flushed and stared at his feet, saying nothing.

"Bix, don't forget what I told you about that wild boy I knew when I was young," Martha said, her smile sad.

"Oh, Jeez, Martha, please don't worry about me," he said, crushing her old bones together in a final hug. "Hell, what's gonna happen? I'm young, I'm healthy, I got everything going for me. I got all the time in the world for that stuff."

"But sometimes time runs out faster than we think it will. Don't leave without saying goodbye to her."

ଅଓ

He tricked Harriet into meeting him, having Buddy tell her Mrs. Smith needed her to bring some empty bottles down from the soda fountain. Then after she and Buddy got there, he came out of the boathouse with a set of oars and threw them into the rowboat that was tied to the end of the pier.

"I even remembered the oars this time," he said. "Come on, let's go out on the lake."

She glared at Buddy. "Why did you do this to me?"

Buddy stared at his feet, then gazed at Harriet, his eyes sad. "You can at least talk to the guy, Harriet," he said. "That's all he wants now."

"What did he do, give you money? Buy you a drink? That's pretty much all he's good for."

Buddy backed away, and then ran off the pier.

Bix gestured at the boat. "Look, I know you don't want to talk to me. Or see me, or anything else. But we're leaving in a couple of days, and I just wanted a chance to say goodbye."

She finally relented and got into the boat, refusing to take his hand and let him help her in. Over in the dance hall the Indianans were playing. The sound of the music drifting over the lake sounded hollow and lost, like ghost music. Harriet stared down at her hands entwined in her lap, shivering with apprehension.

He waited until they were in the middle of the lake, with no other boats or swimmers around. Then he stopped rowing and sat looking at her. She felt his eyes, but refused to look up. Finally he spoke.

"What did Joy tell you?"

"Everything."

"About Ruth?"

"Yes."

"Is that why you went away?"

"That's none of your business."

He bit his lip, staring into the black water of the lake. "What else did she tell you about?"

She turned her face away from him and picked at the lace on her dress. "Your family. Your drinking. Your failing school."

"You knew all that. There must be something else."

She finally turned her fury on him. "Besides the fact that you disappeared for two days without a trace?"

"I was in Chicago playing at the Sunset, that's all. And afterward I guess I...."

"Yes, you went somewhere and got drunk. Like you always do."

He was silent, lips pursed. "You said you loved me. That day in the cemetery."

"Before I found out what you're really like. How could I love somebody who just wants to drink and play music? Is that all you think there is to life? Well, I have plans, Bix. I have dreams. And I'm not going to let you or anyone else make me forget about them."

"I never asked you to." He tried to put his hands on her shoulders and she finally let him, covering her face with her hands.

Then she looked up at him, reached out and grabbed his hands, her mood suddenly shifting from anger to a fearful need to know. She dug her fingernails into the palms of his hands, feeling him flinch.

"What did you do to that little girl back in Davenport?"

His face went white. Wordlessly he took her hands and placed them back into her lap. Then he picked up the oars and started rowing toward the pier.

"I knew you wouldn't be able to give me one of your nice, easy answers to that," she went on. "A five-year-old girl. What kind of a sick, twisted—and you touched me with those hands. And I let you. I *wanted* you to. My God!" She shuddered, staring into the water.

"You never even asked me if it was true," he said. He sounded sad. "Neither did he."

The Indianans must have been taking a break, because the music had stopped. In the silence all she could hear was her own heart hammering in her chest, and the plash of the oars in the water. She finally looked up and watched his face as he rowed.

"Neither did who?" she asked.

"My father."

"*Was* it true?"

He stopped rowing and stared long and hard into her eyes, until she finally had to look away. Then he started rowing again, speaking softly over the sound of the oars moving the water.

"After everything that happened that year, he didn't think he needed to ask, either. He knew I was no good. He always knew, but that year I proved it. I flunked every subject in junior year. I got caught drinking. And then there was the music. After awhile, I couldn't help it. I just wanted to be where the music was, just wanted to play all the time. Didn't care about anything else. Every time we talked, it ended up in an argument. Some were pretty bad. I wanted to run away, but my brother talked me out of it."

He swallowed and wiped his forearm against his face. "I spent as much time away from the house as I could, just to keep from antagonizing him. There was a park on the other side of town. And that's where I met her. The girl. Lillian."

Harriet stared, felt her eyes straining in their sockets.

"She came to the park almost every day with her kid sister. She was seventeen, and the kid sister was about four or five, I guess. Me and Lillian would keep an eye on the kid while she played. One thing led to another and—well, we got pretty friendly out behind the field house a couple of times."

"And?"

"And then the kid started showing up at the park by herself. I asked about Lillian, and found out the kid saw us fooling around and told her father. And the next day when I got home from school, there were two cops waiting for me with an arrest warrant."

"On what charge?"

"Lewd and lascivious act with a minor. The old man probably knew he couldn't make it stick with a girl who was almost eighteen, so he'd try it with the kid sister. And I guess it worked. My father believed it, at any rate."

"What happened?"

"They arrested me. 'Nothing you do surprises me anymore.' That's what he said. There was a grand jury hearing and the kid's old man told them a bunch of crazy stuff about what I tried to do to her. He ended up dropping the case, but it didn't matter. To my father, I was just as guilty as if they'd tried and convicted me. I still am."

They were almost back at the pier. Harriet felt drained, as if her internal organs had been scooped out and replaced with sawdust.

"Anyhow, after school ended it just seemed like a good idea to get the hell out of Davenport, so I got a gig on one of the riverboats. And in the fall he sent me to Lake Forest Academy. Anything to keep me out of sight."

She watched him and it was like watching a stranger. Just another musician in the band who made them clap and whistle and dance when he played, but who after he'd packed up his instrument and got ready to leave, became just another nondescript person who would disappear into the crowd.

"I went to see Rudy when I was away," she said calmly. "We're going to get married after all. Right after Labor Day."

He didn't say anything, just kept rowing. They reached the pier and he tethered the boat to the pilings. This time she let him help her out, the touch of his hand as impersonal as the handshake of a stranger.

They stood on the pier and for a second Harriet remembered another evening when they'd stood here together, that evening they'd gone fishing on the lake. It seemed like a million years ago. She stood on tiptoe and kissed him on the cheek.

"Goodbye, Bix," she said softly. "I hope you find something besides music that makes you happy."

"I thought I had."

She felt her stomach twist inside her, thinking how easy it would be to believe him, to put her arms around his neck and kiss him, to let her feelings for him out of the cage she'd forced them into. She wanted to touch him so badly she had to clench her hands into fists at her side to keep from grabbing him. She felt her face painfully using every muscle to hold a friendly smile in place, her throat ache to keep her voice calm and kind. And even with the official confirmation of what her body had known for weeks, she managed to walk away from him without looking back.

80CB

"Goodbye, Hudson Lake," Tram said from across the aisle as the South Shore car pulled out of the station.

"Good riddance, you mean," Pee Wee muttered, slouched in his seat, hat pulled low over his eyes, which were bloodshot from drinking at last night's farewell party.

Bix sat and gazed out the window, looking for the last time at the hotel surrounded by its cloak of overgrown trees, and the little yellow cottage behind it, the Buick immobile as ever. Just as the train started accelerating, he caught a glimpse of someone running alongside. Buddy Smith, sweat crescents under the arms of his shirt, waving, holding aloft the cornet mouthpiece. Bix grinned and gave him a salute and Buddy waved back, keeping pace with the train until it speeded up and he stood at the end of the platform, still waving.

He'd miss Buddy. He was a good kid, after all. In a way, he'd even miss Mrs. Smith, and the Hawkins sisters, and everyone else from Hudson Lake. Bix always missed pieces of his life he left behind, like Ruth and the Arcadia ballroom and St. Louis. In a week or two, Hudson Lake would be nothing but a three-month summer gig he played in 1926, the place and the people who he knew here a compact, self-contained memory, like a glass globe that whirled snowflakes when you shook it. Maybe he'd be back some day—more likely, he wouldn't. No commitments, no strings, no regrets.

But somehow it had been different this time, having Joy here, and Harriet. The leaving didn't feel as easy as it usually did. He thought of Martha's words, about how sometimes time ran out when you least expected.

Goodbye, Bix. I hope you find something besides music that makes you happy. And a red satin slipper left under a bed.

The dance hall flew by, open to the afternoon breezes, Joe Dockstader's band pumping out an insipid version of "Sweet Sue" which trailed faintly behind the train. And then there was the lake, a smear of blue surrounded by trees, sun glinting off its pocked surface like a scattering of silver coins. Bix turned and looked and stood up in his seat, hands pressed against the window, watching until the last blue flashes of the lake disappeared into the Indiana countryside.

Chapter 32

Joy

After I left Hudson Lake that August, Jack set me up in a nice little flat on Sheridan Road out by the curve along the lake, with all modern furniture and a spiffy view. He bought me clothes and jewelry and a car, and hired me to sing at the Green Mill. Not that I had to; he gave me all the money I needed. But he always said I had a good voice.

I didn't see a lot of him—he was busy with his job. And there were times when he did come around that I didn't want him there. He could be rough and mean, especially when he'd been drinking, and a couple of times I couldn't show my face at the Green Mill until the swelling went down.

Then he started coming around less and less, and stopped paying the rent on the flat, and I didn't have much choice but to move back to a rooming house, like in the days when I first came to Chicago. After awhile I didn't have anything left except the clothes he bought me. I hocked most of the jewelry, all but the diamond rope necklace that reminded me of the day I left Montana. I'd never sell that.

I managed to find a job at a café on the North Side, waiting tables and singing sometimes when they let me, like back when I first met Bickie.

And Bickie? Well, he ended up in the gravy, making three hundred bucks a week with the big Paul Whiteman Orchestra, making records and even playing on the radio and at Carnegie Hall. But every time he came through town, he'd call me—from a speak or a train station or wherever he was—and we'd meet up for coffee or drinks or a sandwich.

He was still the same sweet-natured Bickie, still listened to everything I had to say like the rube that he was. A couple of times when I was down on my luck he'd slip me some money, waving me off when I told him I'd pay him back. "This is the money I owe you, remember?" he'd say, and the memory of that spring of 1925 when he was broke would come up between us like a sad little ghost.

There was the other memory, too—of that afternoon in the little yellow cottage on Hudson Lake, when I wanted both of us dead. But Bickie never mentioned it, and neither did I. Although he probably didn't remember, I did, and I was ashamed of acting so crazy. After all, if I'd died in Montana that first time, when I really wanted to, I would have never met Bickie at all.

The last time I saw him was at the Chicago Theater when the Whiteman band came through town, and I went to see him backstage after the show.

He'd changed a lot by then. He had a potbelly from drinking and those little-boy features were hid now in the puffy lines of his face, and he had a silly little moustache that he said was good for his embouchure, but to me just looked like he was trying to imitate Paul Whiteman. And he had what musicians called a café tan, fish-belly pale, like he never went outside in the daylight anymore. But when he smiled I could see it was the same old Bickie, and that he was glad to see me, after all.

He took me over to the Three Deuces, a basement joint down the street from the theater on State Street where the musicians always went, and I listened to him play until daybreak. It was like old times. I told him he could come back to my place, or I'd come to his hotel if he wanted me. But he was drinking so much that by the end of the night his friend Bill Challis had to practically carry him out and put him into a cab.

The next afternoon he called me from the train station; I could hear the noise of the crowds and the sound of conductors calling out destinations in the background.

"It's killing me," he said, or that's what it sounded like.

"What? Bickie? I can hardly hear you. Are you all right?"

"I'm so tired, Joy. Now we're supposed to be going to Hollywood to make a movie. I don't want to go."

"Stay here in Chicago, then. Everybody knows you here, you can get plenty of work." And we can be together, I thought. I knew it was stupid, but I had to try.

"No, I can't. Pops is depending on me." I heard him cough, a loose, sickly sound, and then a deep inhalation. He laughed. "Joy? Remember Hudson Lake?"

My hand tightened on the phone. "How can I forget it?" I whispered, knowing he wouldn't be able to hear me over the noise on his end of the line.

"You never let me down," he said. "You were the only one who didn't."

"Bix, please stay," I said, the words tumbling out without my being able to stop them. "I'm worried about you."

He laughed again, sounding carefree, like he was about to get back on the Bobs roller coaster for the umpteenth time and was looking forward to the first big drop. "I'll be fine. You know me. Gotta go, they're hollering last boarding call. Take care of yourself, huh? I'll see you next time I'm in town."

I knew I'd never see him again.

Chapter 33

February 1929
Cleveland/Chicago/New York City

He had to get back to the band.

Bix pulled on his overcoat and clattered down the iron steps of the hotel fire escape, slapping his pockets to make sure he had money, train ticket, cigarettes, and a pint.

It was cold, Christ, it was cold, and he felt his lungs seize up as he panted down the steps. He started coughing again and had to stop, rubbing his chest, wishing away the pain that bit into him with every breath.

He'd grab a taxi to the train station and sleep on the way into Chicago, where he'd transfer again to Grand Central. So when he hit New York he'd be ready to go see Pops. Then he'd explain everything, about why he ditched the male nurse Pops had hired to keep an eye on him here in Cleveland, the guy who was supposed to make sure he got on the train back to Davenport. But he didn't need to go back to Davenport, he wasn't that sick. He felt better now. He'd make Pops understand how important it was for him to stay with the band. They needed him; he couldn't let everybody down, leaving his chair empty just when they were getting started on another tour.

Besides, there wasn't anywhere else for him to go.

ଔଓ

It was snowing hard by the time the train pulled into Grand Central Station. He found a speak a block away, a hole-in-the-wall filled with taxi drivers between shifts and guys with ink-blackened skin from the printing district just down the street.

He'd bought another pint on the layover in Chicago and drank it on the train. After a week on the wagon, the gin had hit him like a sledgehammer. At first he'd been sick, running to the men's room at the end of the sleeping car and puking into the chipped porcelain washbowl, embarrassed as the other passengers washing their hands and adjusting their clothes in the mirrors turned to stare at him.

But now, as he ordered a shot at the bar, he felt himself coming back to normal. He was still shaking, still cold, sweating and clammy under his layers of clothes, and his chest hurt every time he took a breath. But he felt better now. Like he was going to make it. Like just another shot would put him back on his feet and he'd be able to do a show, or hit a rehearsal or recording session and not miss a beat, just like before.

Bix glanced down the bar and signaled the bartender for another. Looking around, he pulled the cornet in its black velvet bag out from under his coat and put it on the bar. That way, he couldn't forget it in case he had to hurry out. Too many times he'd left it places, the fellows laughing and teasing him about it. The bartender poured, and Bix drank, feeling the burn of the alcohol easing loose the knots in his lungs. This goddamn cold—if it weren't for this goddamn cold he couldn't shake, none of this ever would have happened.

He'd been sick with a fever from this goddamn cold, that was all. He wasn't crazy, like they'd made it sound. He didn't remember busting up the furniture in his hotel room. They told him about it later, after he was in the hospital, before they released him to send him home. But he felt better now, really. Ready to get back to work.

Somebody laughed and he turned around to look at the tables behind him. Three guys in snow-dusted overcoats were pouring shots from a bottle and laughing at something. At first he thought he knew them, maybe from a session, but no—they were strangers. He shot back the gin and gestured at the bartender for another.

The third shot set him up like a new man. He looked in the mirror behind the bar. Christ, he needed a shave. He'd go to the hotel on 44th Street first and clean up before he went to see Pops. That and get something to eat, maybe, and a little coffee, that was the ticket. He glanced in the mirror again and noticed a guy at the end of the bar, long nose, hat pulled low over his eyes, staring at him. Something familiar about him, too, but he couldn't place it.

There was another burst of laugher from behind him, and this time when he turned around, he caught them looking at him. Just like a lot of the Whiteman guys did behind his back, pulling stupid jokes on him—brake shoes in his valise, water in his hip flask, and laughing, always laughing. He pushed away from the bar and walked past their table on the way to the can, feeling their eyes on him the whole time

He walked up to their table. "So what's funny?" he asked.

One of the men, a jowly guy looked like a goddamn mick, smiled happily into his face. "I don't know what the hell you're talking about, pal."

Bix lunged over the table at him and grabbed him by the tie. "Hey, Paddy, you're the one laughing. So something must be funny, either that or you're fucking crazy, so which is it?"

"Better leave now!" the bartender yelled, coming out from behind the bar and pushing Bix toward the door.

"Yeah, yeah, I'm going. I've been thrown out of better places that this shithole, anyway. You can all go fuck yourselves," he said, and swaggered down the hallway toward the can.

He stood in front of the urinal, just finishing up, and buttoned his fly. Then he heard the door open behind him and footsteps sliding on tile.

"Your name Beiderbecke?"

He turned around. The runty guy from the end of the bar.

"Who wants to know?"

"I been looking for you for a long time. This is from Jack." Out of the corner of his eye, Bix caught a glimpse of a glitter in the sickly overhead light of the toilet, the light sliding off a knife blade, and then there was a fire, searing right above his groin. He stared down in amazement at the nickel-sized drops of his own blood oozing from between his fingers and splattering the dirty black-and-white tiled floor. He dropped to his knees, to his face. Then the polished two-toned shoes were on him, kicking him in the ribs, the groin, while he tried to cover up as best he could.

From his vantage point on the floor, he watched as the man's shoes headed for the door and left. And then he focused all his attention on the black and white tiles, alternating like the keys on a piano, wondering whether he'd be able to inch his way along the floor to the door, the amniotic stink of the urinals in his nostrils, dragging himself along by fingertips, thinking of the cornet he left on the bar, thinking how hard it was snowing out there, thinking of his cornet and another snowy night, the night in Chicago he'd met Joy at the Friar's Club, the cold, and dirty snow melting at his feet, and once he got to the door, how would he get out?

He reached it at last and managed to pull himself up on the doorframe with one hand, holding his guts in with the other, blinking in distant surprise at the long smear of blood on the floor behind him, trailing from the urinal to the door, and his hand, which looked like he'd dipped it into red paint.

He managed to stagger out to the sidewalk and hail a Yellow cab, and slumped into the back seat, pressing a wad of paper towels from the toilet against his abdomen, under his overcoat. Outside the cab window the snowy gray streets swirled by, the same streets he'd walked with whatever musicians he was with, searching for booze and music and places to play it, an ocean of sound that seemed as if it would never end.

But after awhile, the sounds started to blur, and so did the cities—Cleveland, St. Louis, Chicago, New York, all the ballrooms and dance halls and big movie theaters and speaks blending into a single generic City, gray and monolithic, with a body of water if you were lucky, or maybe the green expanse of a park here and there to remind you that trees and grass still existed somewhere.

Bix got out at the old familiar hotel on 44th and paid the driver, remembered to take his cornet, still clutching his gut. The pain had shrunk from the immediate searing pain to a dull, constant throb, so he was able to walk slowly past the desk man into the elevator cage. The operator gave him a knowing grin, smelling the gin, thinking he was loaded, as usual.

He lurched through the darkness of the room and into the can, dropping his cornet and his overcoat on the way, pulling off his jacket, peeling away the soggy red paper towels, the blood-wet shirt sticking to his belly, opening his trousers, Jesus Christ, it was bad. Really bad. Right above his groin, a gaping red mouth that just kept bleeding, as much as he wiped the blood away, it just kept coming. He ran cold water into the sink and found some washrags, soaked them, wiped and wiped until the water in the sink went pink, then red.

The floor was soon littered with bloody washrags so he took a bath towel and held it against himself, pressing hard. His head was humming, not the way it usually did with music and tempos, but with a weird, high-pitched telephonic buzz, the same noise he'd heard that night at the Sunset when the music let him down and he knew for the first time that all this was for keeps.

His stomach quaked, lurched, and clutching the towel, he leaned over into the sink and vomited bile and blood, choking on the corrosive feel of it. The corners of the room seemed to shrink into darkness, and the light over the mirror grew very bright. He closed his eyes, both arms over his abdomen, and let the light burn behind his eyelids, until his head was filled with a warm yellow glow, a strangely familiar color.

And then he remembered the lemon yellow of the sky over the beach at that little lake in Indiana. What was it called again? Hudson Lake.

He dropped to the floor, draped limp against the bathtub. Yeah, Hudson Lake. If he closed his eyes tight enough, he could be back there. And it would be summer again, and the weather was warm and breezy every day. He'd lie on the hot sand baking the cold out of his bones and his lungs and watch Pee Wee and the guys swimming in the water, and the dance hall where they played every night was right there, cool and dark and inviting during the day, so when he got too hot he could go in there and sit down at the piano and work on his song. And Joy was there in the little yellow cottage across the road, sleeping until he came to wake her up, sliding down into her arms, touching her, listening to the noises she made that he liked so much.

And at night there was a place to play, everybody having fun, nobody worried about complicated charts or recording dates or strings of weeks and months where all you saw was the inside of a train and the inside of a ballroom. Just *this* little ballroom, safe and snug and familiar as home, with its crooked yellow moon backdrop and the row of windows along the sides that let in the sweet night breezes. And when he was tired there was a bed, and when it rained, oh, when it rained ...

Even the rain was warm. Warm that day, warm and whispering outside in the trees and at the window of that farmhouse, and Harriet there with him, sweet and warm, naked and wrapped around him until he fell asleep.

Maybe he should have married her and taken her on the road with him, like Tram and Mitzi. Or no, maybe Joy. Joy would have loved it.

And whenever he wanted to, really wanted to, he could have gotten on the South Shore train, back to Chicago, and taken the train back home again, back to Davenport, where if he really wanted to, he could have lived the rest of his life.

Working with Dad and Burnie at the coal yard. Marrying a girl like Vera, the girl he'd loved as a kid at Davenport High School, or Ruthie, or Harriet. Not having to worry about getting her pregnant, *wanting* to get her pregnant, watching her grow round and glowing, pressing his fingertips against her belly and feeling the life kicking around inside, kissing her there where she was so big and bulging...

And then the babies, lots of them, the house on Grand Avenue filled with them, Mother and Sis with a kid on each lap, everybody laughing, like the old days when he was a kid with his cousins at Oma's big house on Seventh Avenue...

And on weekends, there'd be Esten and Fritz and Lee and the other guys coming around, instruments all loaded up in somebody's jalopy, and they'd go to the Elks Hall, and Danceland, just like when they were kids, playing for the hell of it, just because they loved it.

And it would work, too, he'd be happy, until—oh God, until all of that faded away like the memory of a movie after you walked into the blinding daylight. Until the babies started crying, the wife started nagging, the flat theatrical backdrop of everyday life became too much and the music in his brain started getting louder and more insistent, and everything else started shrinking and fading away, like it always did. Until there was nothing anymore but him and the horn and the piano and the music, all he needed, ever needed, really. Until the music drove everything and everybody else away.

But for a minute in time, that summer of 1926 on Hudson Lake, he had himself believing it could have been different, that he could have had the music and everything else, too. That he could have had it all. Just like in the movies.

His lips moved to the lyrics of a half-remembered song, something that captured all of that, the sweetness and the promise of that summer, even though it hadn't mattered to him then. He lifted a hand, almost like he could reach back and touch it somehow, feeling warm lake water on his fingertips. His fingers closed on nothing.

And when he opened his eyes he was in a bathroom at the 44th Street hotel, lying naked in a poppy field of towels blooming with his own blood, and the darkened corners of the room crept out and blended until the whole world was black and cold.

Chapter 34

August 1931

It took him another two years to die.

It happened in August, a month that always made Bix feel blue, a time of year when leaves were still green and the weather still hot, but summer was ending and you knew it.

He was alone and his heart gave out, from the heat and the pain in his lungs and delirium tremens from a last-ditch attempt at drying out. The man across the hall came running over when he heard Bix screaming about Mexicans with knives lying under the bed, waiting for him to lie down. Then he pitched forward into the man's arms. By the time the man had eased his body to the bed and returned with the nurse who lived on the floor, it was already too late. The nurse felt for a pulse that wasn't there and closed Bix's staring brown eyes with her thumbs.

His mother and brother came to take him home to Davenport. The two of them sat huddled together, stunned and stiff-faced, in the passenger car of the train; Bix rode alone in the back. Along the way they passed through all the cities and towns where he'd played and drank, from his days with the Wolverines in 1924 up to the private train car commandeered by the Paul Whiteman Orchestra in 1929 for the big trip to Hollywood. But this time there would be no one-night stands, no stops in any of those towns, no visits to familiar speaks and dance halls and movie palaces to play and drink with friends he'd made along the way. This time he was just passing through.

Now that he was home, they were going to keep him there. On a bright Tuesday morning they anchored him down in Oakville Cemetery, under a gray granite slab that matched all the other Beiderbecke headstones.

At last he was one of them.

ဆာၤ

Harriet Braun was giving shots to a line of kids at Hull House in Chicago when she saw the picture in a newspaper lying with a stack of magazines on a nearby table. It was an unsmiling studio portrait of him wearing a tuxedo and an effete little moustache, eyes luminous. Although she hadn't seen him since August 1926, she recognized him right away. She gestured to a nurse to watch the kids as she swept the newspaper off the table and ran into the courtyard, reading what she already knew.

Leaning into the brick wall, she felt it bite into her cheeks, and let the tears tremble through her. She put up her arms, holding the wall, remembering everything in the instant it took for her to take another shuddering breath.

When she got home that night, she dug through a box in the closet and found some souvenirs from the summer of 1926 at Hudson Lake. A faded red ribbon of dance tickets. A clipping from the South Bend Tribune about the band: "These exceptional artists have won the hearts of all who have heard them, and have secured a permanent foothold in the esteem of every dancing group in this section of the musical world." A Japanese paper fan. And the letter, still sealed, that he'd slipped under the Traubs' door that rainy morning. She turned the envelope over in her hands.

She wondered if she should open it after all this time. Maybe it was better not to know what it said. Just like he'd never known how her unfailing practicality had ultimately failed her.

If she'd been practical, she would have gone back home to Indianapolis and accepted Rudy's proposal. And then she would have gone to the South Bend doctor her cousin Myra had told her about and given him the money she'd made over the summer to pay for an abortion.

But her body, that same illogical body that had so willingly opened itself to him in the first place, wouldn't let her tamper with the tremendous force their coupling had set into motion. It was as impossible for her to stop as a tidal wave.

She couldn't go home; her mother and sisters would never accept or understand her irrationality. She couldn't go back to Rudy; she saw him one last time to tell him it was over, and then never saw him again. So there was nothing to do but seek out Joy, the woman who had once called her little sister, to try and get some help, to find a safe haven to stay while she waited for Bix's baby to be born.

She remembered walking from the L to Joy's flat on Sheridan Road, carrying her suitcase, the quintessential girl in trouble. At first Joy had laughed, the mean, brittle sound of it cutting like jagged shards of glass. But after they'd sat over coffee in a kitchen that had never seen a home-cooked meal, Joy had hugged her and cried and patted Harriet's stomach and said she'd do anything to help Bickie's baby. She owed him that much.

So Harriet told her family she'd found work in Chicago and would be going back to school next year. She stayed with Joy in the apartment McGurn paid for, earning her keep the way she always had, by cleaning and cooking and taking care of her.

Fall and winter passed. Harriet's body, which she once thought she knew so well, ripened and swelled into an alien life form—breasts ballooning, abdomen distended and tight as a drumhead, a seed pod ready to pop. Toward the end, when it was hard to move around, she let Joy spoil and pamper her, and sometimes, when both of them felt lonely for him, sleep with her. As they lay together, Joy's hands touching her the way Bix had touched her, she'd marvel at how those two contrasting vessels—Bix's hard, flat torso and Joy's lush hollows and curves—could both contain people who loved her.

Sometimes they argued. Joy thought Harriet should write to Bix and tell him about the baby. Harriet refused. She knew forcing him to do what the world thought of as the right thing would make him try and do something he was incapable of doing. Ultimately, Joy agreed it was true.

And then in May, Harriet went to the Chicago Lying-In Hospital and gave birth to an eight-pound, three-ounce boy with a squashed, red face, a mass of auburn hair, and long-fingered hands he perpetually suckled.

Joy came to see her and the baby, carrying an armload of roses for Harriet and a stuffed doggie for the kid. She laughed, and cried, and held the baby on her lap, on her shoulder, eyes glassy with tears even when she was laughing. She sang to him, every song she knew, songs more appropriate for a nightclub than for soothing a newborn.

Gray eyes squinting, he studied her face and listened intently as she stood by the window, holding him up to see the stream of traffic on the streets below, and the wind-tossed trees with their braces of new green leaves.

Harriet cuddled and nursed the baby for a week, then turned him over to a Catholic orphanage where he already had parents waiting to take him home.

She stayed with Joy for three more months afterward, working as an assistant in a Cook County Hospital laboratory, labeling blood samples and typing charts, putting money aside. And in the fall, she went back to college.

It had been just over a year neatly incisioned from her life, as surgically as if lifted away with a scalpel. And when she got back to school, her resolve to become a doctor was no longer elastic enough to stretch and accommodate a different-sized dream. It had calcified into a goal that shimmered, miragelike, always a year or two in the future. She had thought of and worked toward nothing else.

Until today, when the sight of his face made her remember—the afternoon in the attic under the waves of rain, the nights in the little cemetery, the brightly lit musicians on the bandstand with him standing to take a solo, looking right at her, his eyes twinkling. And always, that first twilight on Hudson Lake, his white hand held up and beckoning to her like a distant, fading star.

She looked down at the unopened envelope and picked open the sealed flap, sliding it out, reading it for the first time.

July 27, 1926

Dear Harriett (sp?) –

Well I suppose your not speaking to me like everyone else around here after what happened on the Fourth and all the other stuff. So I just thot I'd write a note to set the record straight.

First, I never told that crazy girl to come up here with all that moonshine. She is nuts, and I tried telling her to go back home way before her aunts showed up. They're nice old girls and I had to work hard to smoothe things over.

As far as Joy is concerned, I've been trying to get her to tell me what's wrong for weeks now. Whatever she thinks I did to that girl (which I didn't, by the way), she was blue way before all of this.

Finally, I never said anything to your boy friend that would have given him the idea that you and me were an item, but he took me aside anyhow and warned me to stay away from you. I wanted to punch his lights out but refrained from doing so because of you.

Anyhow, I just wanted you to know all this because the truth is, I really do miss our conversations.

Your fishing buddy,

Bix

ഽᏝᏟᎶ

Joy

Somebody in the hotel was always playing the radio. All day long, sweet stuff that was heavy on strings and nasally tenor vocals, stuff you didn't want to listen to very long. And at night the music from the club downstairs would filter into my room while I was doing what I needed to do. The stuff from the club was a little better, more hot than sweet, because the owner didn't want to pay a lot of fiddle players; all he could afford these days was a five-man group, heavy on the horns, and the boys were glad to get the work.

He let me sing in exchange for the use of the room upstairs, where I was able to take my customers and get it over with as fast as I could, while cigarettes burned in an ashtray on the nightstand and the sound of the radio upstairs banged into the sound of the band from the club downstairs.

I thought about how different music was now as the guy got dressed, then leaned over and slapped my bare rump goodbye, the bastard. I put my arms behind my head, looking at the watermarks on the ceiling. Yeah, music was different, heavier on the drums. You never heard a tuba for percussion anymore, or a banjo.

The band was on break, and the radio upstairs was coming in loud and clear with ads for soap flakes and cigarettes and gum. And then I heard it, a sound I hadn't heard in years, clear and sweet and riding over the sound of Tram's C-melody sax and into my ears. It was Bickie.

I closed my eyes and let the sound of his cornet seep into me, through my ears and my skin, penetrating right down to my bones. And for a while, listening to that long-ago recording of "Singin' the Blues," I forgot about how much my back hurt these days, and the hard little lump I'd been feeling deep in my left breast, and how the face that looked out at me in the mirror every day looked less and less like the Joy he would have known. For a couple of minutes, he was alive again. And that made me smile, lying alone on the saggy mattress that was drifting through time and somehow, so slow it seemed like it was standing still, heading back to a shore where he was waiting for me.

Epilogue

August 1939

Their fluttering black veils incongruous amidst the green of trees and lake, the nuns from St. Vincent's Orphanage herded their wards away from Bluebird Beach and toward the platform for the South Shore train back into Chicago.

Buddy Smith watched from the kitchen window, thinking how his mother would have complained about having to put up all those rooms to accommodate the weekend party of orphans, even though the nuns were good for it and paid in cash. He closed the big black ledger and stacked it on top of the hotel register, the one that went back thirty years, names and addresses and dates fading into the oblivion of blue ink and yellowing paper.

"Look at those little devils," said Alvie Best with a chuckle, pointing to the clutch of orphans. "All shapes, colors and sizes. Where d'ya suppose they all come from?"

Buddy shrugged and pulled a heavy clump of keys from his jacket pocket. "I got to talking to one of the sisters. Lots of families broken up because of hard times. Fathers leave or die, mothers can't afford to keep the family together. The only place left for them is the orphanage."

Alvie grunted. "Yep, times is tough. God knows I don't have to tell you that." His voice softened. "You sorry about having to sell the place, Buddy?"

The key ring felt heavy in the palm of Buddy's hand. They were all there—the master key to every room in the hotel, the bath house, the boat house, and the dance hall. Every boyhood memory he had was tied up in those keys and the doors they opened and locked. He hefted the keys, as if to remember, then laid them on top of the hotel register. "No," he said softly. "It's time."

"Your father did a wonderful job with this place. Your mother, too, rest her soul. Sorry things been so tough for you the last couple years. What with your ma takin' ill, and you havin' to come back here to try and make a go of it. And then your Kathy. What a shame. You know, my aunt died in childbirth, but at least the baby lived...."

"I'm gonna go make sure the dance hall is locked up," Buddy said, his hand going back to the keys. "I'll be right back. Then we can sign the paperwork."

The Blue Lantern stood across Chicago Road, the heat waves rising from the pavement making its façade shiver in the heat. Buddy walked toward the cool tree-shaded porch of the dance hall, listening to his feet on the pavement and to the chatter of the children waiting for the train to take them away. He pushed the key into the lock, opened the door, and immediately smelled the ghost of the soda fountain, of ice cream sundaes long consumed, of bootleg gin evaporated into nothingness. Then through the French doors into the dance hall, where the sound of his footsteps echoed against the floors and walls and ceiling.

And another sound, of tentative fingers on the piano.

His heart froze in his chest. *My God, I know this place is haunted, but ghosts aren't real, and they sure can't play the piano!*

The boy looked up, guilt in his eyes. Buddy's heart started beating again. It was only a kid. One of the orphans, looked to be around ten or twelve years old. He scrambled to his feet and stared at Buddy with big, dark eyes.

"What the hell are you doing here?" Buddy said, trying to sound stern. "Aren't you supposed to be waiting for the train? You want to be left here all alone? Go on, get out of here. The nuns will be looking for you."

The boy pushed back a hank of darkish hair and looked down at his feet as if he was ashamed. But he didn't move away from the piano. One hand rested possessively on the yellowed ivory keys.

Buddy walked up the steps to the stage and looked at the boy, who now jammed his hands into his pockets and stood there, head hanging, as if prepared for the inevitable scolding.

"So you're a musician, huh?" Buddy said, grinning.

The boy finally met his eyes and grinned back. "Yeah. They got a piano at the orphanage, but it's always out of tune."

"I used to play music, too, a long time ago," Buddy said. He looked up at the faded crooked-moon backdrop, then out at the empty, gleaming sea of the dance floor. "You wouldn't know it now, but the biggest bands in the country played on this stage. Guy Lombardo. Ben Selvin. Benny Goodman. Lots of them." He looked around, remembering. Then he looked back at the kid. "Well, what are you waiting for? Go ahead."

"You mean play?"

"Sure. Give me your best shot." Buddy crossed his arms over his chest and waited.

Tentatively at first, then gaining in confidence, the boy's fingers ranged over the old piano's keys, pulling out sounds that Buddy hadn't heard in years. He stood mesmerized, listening as the boy played tune after tune, familiar songs played in a way he'd never heard before. There was a precocity about the playing that went from exuberant brassiness to hushed contemplation, all in the turn of a moment.

But when he was done and the piano was quiet, the boy was just a boy again, with dirty hands, lank hair, face a scramble of freckles. He looked up at Buddy, his face an odd blend of truculence and a yearning for approbation—a look that Buddy somehow *knew*, that he remembered seeing on someone else's face a long time ago. Or maybe on a face he was destined never to see in this life.

Without thinking, he reached out and put a hand on the boy's head, feeling him flinch at the contact. Silence held for an instant, a heartbeat of time in which volumes could be silently spoken, seas emptied, universes hatched and grown and imploded. "That was wonderful," Buddy said softly. "You really are a musician. I'd be proud if I was your father."

Buddy thought he felt the boy sigh from deep inside himself, as if he'd been waiting an eternity to hear those words. But then he was ducking out from under Buddy's hand, gathering up a baseball and catcher's mitt from under the piano and heading for the French doors. And then he paused, his form silhouetted against the harsh August sunlight.

"Next time bring your horn, if you haven't lost your lip," the boy said. "I'll be back." Then he slammed out the door and was gone.

And now that he knew where to find him, and that he'd never lose him again, Buddy knew that's just what he'd do. "I will, son," Buddy murmured. "See you soon."

Author Bio

Laura Mazzuca Toops is a Chicago-area writer and teacher with three books in print: "A Native's Guide to Chicago's Western Suburbs" (Lake Claremont Press), "The Latham Loop," and "Slapstick" (Amber Quill Press). She is a 21st century anachronism who doesn't belong in this time or place. A collector of vintage clothing, 78 rpm records and memories, she teeters on the edge of sanity by balancing her mundane present-day life against the vague memories of the fun times she had back in 1927 in New York, Chicago and another body.

Don't miss any of these other
exciting historical novels

➤ Apache Lance, Franciscan Cross
    (1-933353-44-9, $18.50 US)

    ➤ Harry's Agatha
    (1-933353-23-6, $16.95 US)

    ➤ Mary's Child
    (1-933353-11-2, $18.50 US)

➤ The Storks of La Caridad
    (1-931201-21-x, $18.50 US)

Twilight Times Books
Kingsport, Tennessee

"**Hudson Lake** is a vivid, poignant, sexy tale of the Jazz Age, built around one of America's greatest and most intriguing musicians. Laura Mazzuca Toops knows her music, and her history."
Reviewed by Kevin Baker, author of "Dreamland."

"Captures the intoxicating mix of energy and danger that defined the early days of jazz."
Reviewed by Bill Ott for *Booklist.*

In the summer of 1926, jazz lovers from all over the Midwest go where the weather is hot and the music hotter—the Blue Lantern Inn on Hudson Lake, a rural Indiana dance hall where the season's resident jazz band features a young cornet player named Bix Beiderbecke.

Meticulously researched, "Hudson Lake" creates a snapshot of the Jazz Age, following the brilliant, but doomed, Bix through the speakeasies and music halls of Prohibition Era Chicago and Indiana.

Seen through the eyes of the two women vying for Bix's affections, the haze of bootleg liquor parts to reveal a world where Louis Armstrong and Al Capone haunt the nightlife. Where a nod to the soda jerk gets you an altogether different drink. Where jazz brings the Chicago Mob out to the country and on a collision course with an angry mob of locals who don't much care for the amoral ways of city folk, alcohol and musicians.

What people are saying about Twilight Times Books:

Apache Lance, Franciscan Cross ~ 2006 *WILLA Award Finalist*
"This is a tale I wouldn't hesitate to recommend. It offers a look at several conflicts that would have occurred during this period between cultures and the individuals from those cultures. Talented author, Florence Byham Weinberg has created a wonderfully lifelike cast of characters with definite personalities who will pull you into their world and make you believe it could have happened exactly like this."
Reviewed by Anne K. Edwards for *In the Library Reviews.*

"**[The Storks of La Caridad]** works on two levels. First, it is a rollicking mystery full of plot twists based on real events, interesting characters modeled after historical figures and more than its share of red herrings, mostly invented by Weinberg. Second, it's a scholarly re-creation of 18th century Spain, from the dress to the architecture to the food, thoroughly researched and seamlessly written. And let's just say that Weinberg knows her Inquisition and her colonial Catholicism."
Reviewed by Steve Bennett, Book Editor for the *San Antonio Express-News.*

Order Form

If the books are not available from your local bookstore or favorite online bookstore, send this coupon and a check or money order for the retail price plus $3.50 s&h to Twilight Times Books, Dept. BP107 POB 3340 Kingsport TN 37664. Delivery may take up to three weeks.

Name: _____

Address: _____

_____

Email: _____

I have enclosed a check or money order in the amount of

$_____

for _____ .